LAST WILL AND PUZZLEMENT

A RUBY FINCH MYSTERY

Enjoy! *Melissa Nordhoff*

MELISSA NORDHOFF

Publisher Page
an imprint of Headline Books
Terra Alta, WV

Last Will and Puzzlement
A Ruby Finch Mystery

by Melissa Nordhoff

To order additional copies of this book or for book publishing information, or to contact the author:

Headline Books
P.O. Box 52
Terra Alta, WV 26764
www.HeadlineBooks.com
mybook@headlinebooks.com

Publisher Page is an imprint of Headline Books

ISBN 13: 9781958914175

Library of Congress Control Number: 2023939030

PRINTED IN THE UNITED STATES OF AMERICA

Dedicated to my grandmother, Helen Finch, whose colorful tales and fiery spirit inspired this story.

JUNE 2000

RUBY

My grandmother, Evie Collier, is waiting on the front stoop of my cottage in a cardboard box marked Priority Mail. Bear-hugging the box against my chest, I carry her inside. After slicing through the packing tape, I fold back the flaps. A second box, wrapped in bubble wrap, is nestled inside. I open that box and find her ashes—divided and sealed into six Ziploc baggies—scattered amongst packing peanuts. I swallow my dismay and my tears at the unceremonious treatment of my beloved grandmother's remains. This is, after all, what she wanted.

When we learned of her plans, my twin brother, Roddy, and I begged Gigi (our name for her) to have a "normal" funeral, but our pleas were no match for her frugality or eccentricity. Using Ask Jeeves, she searched for cheap cremations and, with a fifteen-minute phone call, had her no-frills $895 cremation planned. Crème de la Cremations (I kid you not) picked up her body ten days ago.

Not sure of the appropriate place to store Gigi's ashes, I clear out my vintage white enamel bread bin, line up the baggies in a tidy row, and close the lid. Miss Bennet (Jane, not Elizabeth), my cheery, rosy-pink tea kettle, waits patiently on the stove. After flipping on the burner, I rifle through my basket full of herbal tea bags until I find a chamomile-lavender blend. I pop it in my favorite polka-dot mug and stare at the bread bin. Something's missing. Plucking a cheery daisy from the vase on my kitchen table, I lay it across the top of the bin. Better.

I pick up the phone and dial the familiar number. Seconds later, when I realize what I've done, my stomach clenches, and I drop the phone like a hot potato. Every evening, I'd unwind with a cup of tea and a phone chat with Gigi. Sadly, I don't need the phone tonight; Gigi's in the bread bin.

Miss Bennet whistles, and I pour the steaming water over the tea bag. I slip off my ballet flats and black beret and sit cross-legged in the chair.

"The party was a hit," I say to the enamel bin.

It feels wrong. Too cold and impersonal. I get up, pull one of the baggies from the bread bin, and set it on the table in front of the chair across from me.

"Kaycee—that's the birthday girl—loved the grape-squashing barrel so much her feet were stained by the end of the day. The artist's studio was a hit, too. The kids actually created some impressive paintings."

I dunk the tea bag to release the flavor and thank my lucky stars that I own my own business—Make A Splash! Event Planning. Most of the time, I have as much fun as the guests.

"Kaycee's mom's best friend was super impressed with the whole Italian adventure vibe and has hired me to plan her family's reunion."

Normally, this is when Gigi would congratulate me or impress me with some obscure fact about wine-making or Renaissance paintings. I stare at the bag of grayish-brown ashes with disgust. This isn't working. As I tuck her back into the bread bin, I'm almost overcome with longing. I yearn for one more conversation, one more laugh, one more adventure.

My doorbell rings, saving me from my descent into sadness. I hurry to the front door, close one eye, and look through the peephole. John Davenport, Gigi's longtime lawyer, waits on my stoop.

"Hi, Mr. Davenport," I say, opening the door.

He's sharply dressed in a pinstripe suit and crisp white shirt. The V of his Windsor knotted tie lies perfectly centered between his collar points. He gives my paint-spattered artist's smock and black leggings the once-over.

"Work clothes," I explain and smooth my unruly strawberry blonde curls.

"Ruby, I'm glad you are home. May I come in?"

He's carrying a package about the size of a hat box. It's wrapped in plain brown paper tied with twine.

"Of course." I extend my arm to welcome him inside. "Shall we sit at the table?"

"Indeed," he agrees and tilts his head with a slight bow.

He sets the package on the green and white checked tablecloth (a hand-me-down from Gigi) and sits erect in one of my ladder-back chairs. I rescued a set of four from Goodwill and painted them cheery lilac.

"First, let me offer my condolences to you and your brother. I've known Evie for seventy years and will miss her greatly. She was one-of-a-kind."

A vision of Gigi in her favorite outfit—leopard print leggings and a purple sequined shirt—flashes into my mind, and I smile. "Thank you."

"Down to business," Mr. Davenport says as he lays his hand on top of the box. "I am tasked with executing Evie's last wishes. I am assuming you have received her ashes?"

"She was on my front stoop when I got home from work. She didn't tell us where to spread her, though. Is it up to Roddy and me?"

"No, but let's not get ahead of ourselves. First things first: Open the package."

After untying the twine and ripping off the brown paper, I discover a large teakwood box embellished with carved lotus flowers and inlaid with Gigi's initials—E.F.C. Two keyholes are on the side of the box. I try to lift the hinged lid, but it's locked. I glance questioningly at Mr. Davenport.

"To open the box, the two keys must be inserted and turned simultaneously."

Mr. Davenport pulls a small jewelry box from the breast pocket of his jacket and hands it to me. Inside, a delicate filigree chain with a tiny gold key shines up at me.

"I have already delivered the key to your brother. You need to complete her funerary wishes together."

"Is that what's in the box? Does it tell us what to do with her ashes?"

"According to Evie's precise instructions, that is all I may say at this time."

Mysterious and characteristically Gigi!

***

I call Roddy two seconds after Mr. Davenport leaves, and we plan to meet to open the box. After changing into my favorite True Religion jeans—which I got at a consignment boutique for twenty bucks—a sunflower-printed peasant blouse, and my Kelly-green canvas slip-ons, I'm out the door.

Ephrata (If you want to pass for a local, make sure you put the emphasis on the first syllable. And, for crying out loud, don't say Lan-CAST-er County, it's LANK-isster.) Anyway, Ephrata Borough is small, so it takes me less than five minutes to get to our favorite tavern, The Lincoln House. I claim our usual table. Roddy strides through the door less than five minutes later. As he walks past the original wooden bar, a pretty brunette tries to catch his eye. She throws him a flirty smile, appreciating his emerald green eyes and chiseled face. As I expected, he ignores her. His divorce from Clara eleven months ago is still too fresh.

I stand up to give him a hug and a peck on his freckled cheek. His blond, five-o'clock shadow prickles my lips.

"Hey, Sis. How was your party?"

"Really good! One of the guests was so impressed she hired me for her event."

"Good word-of-mouth. You can't ask for more than that."

As I slide back into the half-round barrel seat, Kelsey, our usual server, arrives at our table. "Hi, guys. What can I get you?"

We order Grasshoppers in honor of Gigi. The sweet minty cocktail was her favorite in the last two decades of her life. She claimed it soothed her stomach.

The Lincoln House's wavy glass windows, weathered tin ceiling, and dim lighting add an appropriate air of intrigue to our meeting.

Roddy pats the top of the wooden box. "Pretty cloak-and-dagger. Don't you think?"

I laugh. "Typical Gigi. She made grocery shopping an adventure. Why should her send-off be anything less?"

Kelsey brings the drinks. Roddy and I clink glasses. "To Gigi!"

Roddy sips his cocktail. Bits of the creamy green concoction cling to the stubble around his upper lip. "Do you remember the superheroes caper?"

"You mean the one to save the village surrounded by evil forces?" I flash back to that particularly fun excursion.

He licks his lip, clearing the remnants of his drink, and nods. "Yep, that's the one."

I smile and feel the memories—excitement, contentment, and pure joy. "How could I forget? The three of us stormed the grocery store armed with our list of needed supplies."

"And dressed in our capes. I desperately wanted Gigi's gold one," Roddy says, laughing.

"Not me. I loved my red one. Wore it to school for a week." I twirl the cocktail straw and watch the whipped cream melt into the green liquid. "I miss her so much."

Roddy nods. "It's hard to believe she's gone." His green eyes mist.

I sniff and swallow. "Yeah. Somehow, I thought she'd beat it." I dab my eyes—identical to my brother's in shape and color—with the corner of my cocktail napkin.

Less than a year ago, Gigi received the diagnosis—stage 4 pancreatic cancer.

"No lachrymosity," Roddy admonishes.

We chuckle at the inside joke. Lachrymosity was on the list of Gigi's favored words. She claimed to deem words as favored based on how they rolled on her tongue. ("I like the mouthfeel when I say it," she declared.) But we knew it was her inventive way of elevating our vocabulary. As kids (okay, I'll admit it—as adults, too), whenever we correctly used one of Gigi's favored words in conversation, we'd get points. Once we earned fifty points, we'd get a special treat: an ice cream sundae, a new book, a caramel latte from Starbucks, or movie tickets.

After blowing my nose and taking a deep breath, I tap the teakwood box. "Well?"

"Here's to finding out what we're in for," Roddy says, raising his glass.

He scoots his barrel seat beside me. We remove the chains from our necks and each slide a key into a lock.

"One, two, three..." Roddy says, and we turn the keys.

The lock clicks, and we lift the lid. We laugh so hard at the first things we see I almost pee my pants: two deerstalker caps, two magnifying glasses, and two pipes.

"Should we put them on?" I ask, lifting them out of the box.

"Why not?" He situates the Sherlock Holmes hat on his head and tucks the pipe in the corner of his mouth.

A few patrons stare. Kelsey returns and asks if we'd like another round.

"Brilliant," Roddy says out the side of his mouth with a pitiful British accent.

I tip my hat from side to side. "They're from Evie," I explain to Kelsey.

"Figures." Kelsey smiles. "I miss her already. I was so sorry to learn she passed."

Twenty years ago, after our grandfather (Pop, aka Pete) died, Gigi became a regular at The Lincoln House. Promptly at five o'clock every day, she'd saunter in, her ever-present heels clicking on the wooden floors, and slide into "her" stool at the corner of the bar. "Gives me the best view," she'd say. Her spiky white hairstyle ends tipped in purple, green, or blue to match her outfit, and her bright red lipstick belied her age. Even in her last years, no one would've ever guessed she was in her eighties.

"Yeah," Roddy agrees. "She was one-of-a-kind."

Kelsey squeezes both our hands. "Hey. This next round's on me. For Evie."

"Thanks," we say, battling back tears.

Roddy clears his throat and lays the pipe on the table. "Onward!" He lifts out the top envelope marked *Open First.*

The envelope contains a letter and instructions. Roddy reads the letter to me.

> My dearest loveys,
> So, I'm on to my next adventure. My life has been full and wonderful, and raising you was my greatest thrill. My only regret is not having more adventures with you, but I have left one more for you. You'll feel my spirit as you discover the secrets I couldn't share.
> My eternal love,
> Gigi

Gigi raised us since the day we were born. Roderick Finch, our father, was shot in Vietnam when we were barely peanuts in our mother's womb. Ella, our mother and Gigi's daughter, died in childbirth. Determined to make up for our tragic beginning, Gigi gave us a daily dose of fun delivered with abundant love. Pop was left to set boundaries. A free spirit himself, his rules lacked consistency and bite.

"What secrets?" I wonder out loud. "Gigi was an open book."

"Apparently not," Roddy says, taking a gulp of his Grasshopper.

With the faintest whiff of apprehension, I unfold the instructions and read them to Roddy.

1. Costume is optional, but it would make your quest a lot more fun!
2. Solve the enclosed puzzle to determine the first location.
3. Every location you'll visit is special to me. Spread a bag of my ashes at each spot to commemorate its importance in my life.
4. After spreading my ashes, determine the significance of the locale.
5. When you've uncovered what you think you need to learn, contact John Davenport and explain the importance of the site. If you're correct, he'll give you the clues necessary to find the next location.
6. When all locales have been visited and you understand my legacy, John will read my will, and you can claim your inheritance. If you still want to.

"If we still want to? Cryptic," I say.

"Gigi was always good at upping the drama. Onto the puzzle?" Roddy opens the envelope marked: *Find the first location*. He unfolds the paper and smooths it out.

FAVORED WORDS:

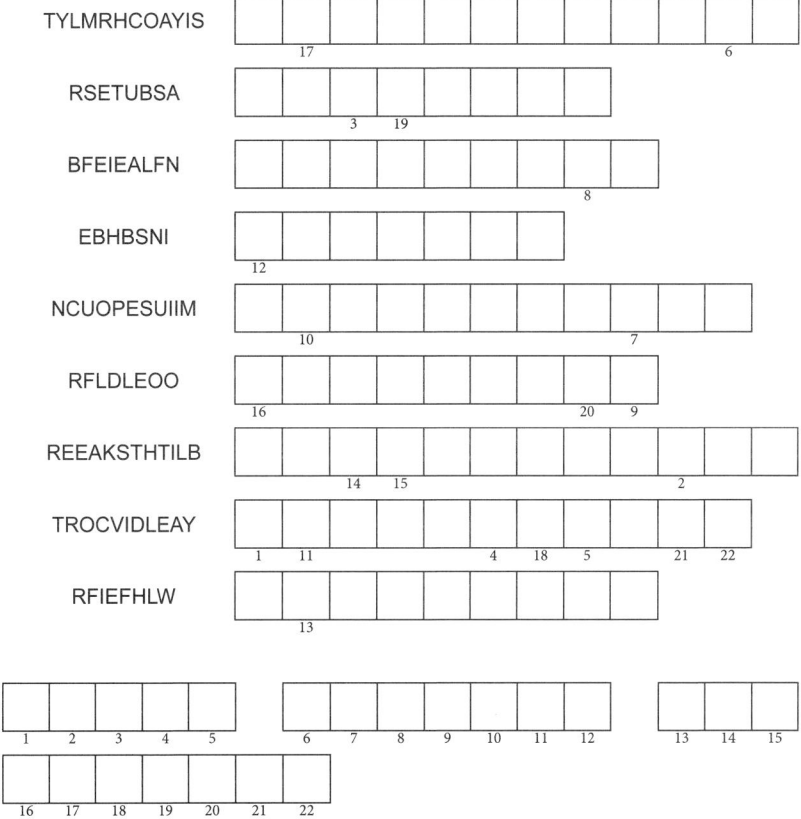

It's a word jumble—Gigi's favorite type of challenge. She had the daily newspaper delivered just for the puzzles.

"Ugh," I grunt. I hate word jumbles. "I was hoping for a cryptogram or crossword."

Convinced that learning to think logically was vital to success, Gigi made us complete at least one puzzle every day before dinner.

"Do you still solve a puzzle a day?" I ask.

He chuckles. "I do. Habit."

"Me too." I smile.

"Well, this one can count for today!"

JULY 1976

EVIE

Evie and Pete rocked on the bricked front porch of their Spanish Mission-style house. They bought it four years ago after they sold the store. In a neighborhood of split-levels and ranchers, its architecture stuck out like a sore thumb—exactly why Evie chose it. After forty years of stifling herself, she was glad to be back in the borough of Ephrata. No longer concerned with the judgment of customers, Evie could be Evie.

In 1932, she and Pete bought a big old farmhouse in Vogansville—a tiny country village that had more cows than people—and converted its detached garage into a general store. Knowing she needed to be accepted to gain customers, Evie toned down her flamboyant style. Plain, floral dresses, an apron, and sensible shoes were her uniform. She even learned to speak Pennsylvania Dutch to better communicate with her Amish and Mennonite neighbors. From an outsider's perspective, their life was ordinary. Just how they had wanted it to appear.

Every so often, as Pete and Evie sipped their cocktails, they'd catch a blur of purple fabric as Ruby ran by or a green streak when Roddy zoomed past on his bike. The twins were in a mad dash to complete the scavenger hunt Evie had created for them. Evie's scavenger hunts were never simple. The twins needed to use creativity, logic, and critical thinking skills to win. Today's hunt started after breakfast and was still going strong after dinner.

A squirrel Evie named Flash ate an almond on the porch, a mere two feet from her bright red toenails. Instead of being a run-of-the-mill cat lady, Evie was the crazy squirrel lady, taming a scurry of them with Pavlovian conditioning. The wind chimes tinkled, and Flash scampered up the ash tree. After the high humidity of the past week, the slightly chilly breeze was a welcome relief.

"Refill?" she asked Pete.

"Yes, and a sweater, please."

Evie's white platform sandals tapped on the tiles as she made her way to the rustic wooden bar cart in the dining room. She fixed herself and Pete a Tom Collins. A cherry floated on top and an orange slice balanced on the rim of her Baccarat crystal highball glasses. She didn't splurge often—it wasn't wise to be flashy—but when she did, it was for only the best. Slipping a rainbow-colored crocheted poncho over her short sleeve blouse, she rolled her eyes as she draped Pete's old-man cardigan over her arm. *He used to be so dapper.* Drinks in hand, she returned to the porch.

The wind blew what little gray hair Pete had left into a messy side swoop. His belly hung over the white belt Evie bought him. After handing him his Tom Collins, she arranged his hair back into place and gave him his sweater. He gazed at her with adoration, and she melted. When she looked into his baby blues, the years dropped away, and she saw the raffish man she fell head over heels in love with.

"You're still a looker." Pete pulled Evie in for a smooch.

"YUCK!" Roddy yelled, spotting their kiss from the yard.

Ruby stuck out her tongue.

"You'll understand when you're grown-ups," Evie assured the ten-year-olds.

As the kids dashed around the side of the house, Evie noticed a man loitering across the street. She trotted down the brick steps onto the walkway for a better look. He jammed his hands in his jean pockets and hurried down a side street, only giving her a glimpse of red hair. Prickles of dread crawled up her neck, and she pulled the poncho tight around her. *It could've been Donald.* For months after he darkened her doorstep five years ago, she imagined she saw him around every corner.

"Evie, what are you doing down there? Come finish your drink," Pete yelled from the porch.

She stepped off the walkway into the yard and bent down to pluck a cottony dandelion from the yard. "I'm pulling weeds."

Roddy and Ruby careened around the corner of the house into the front yard and ran circles around Evie. After another quick scan across the street, she held the flower up to the twins.

"Make a wish."

The children blew the white seed pods into the summer breeze.

"You make one," Roddy said to Evie, snapping another puff from the grass.

Evie pursed her bright red lips and blew. *May I never see the likes of Donald Fraser again.*

She ruffled their hair. "Have you finished the hunt?" she asked, guiding them onto the porch.

"All except this one." Ruby held up her paper and pointed to number four on the list of thirty. *Construct a comestible chapeau.* "I think chapeau is French for 'hat,' but I don't know what comestible means."

Roddy chimed in. "And I'm done except for writing a haiku poem. I can't remember if it has fifteen or seventeen syllables."

"Well," Evie said, relaxing back into her rocking chair. "Why are you standing here? Sounds like you need a dictionary and an encyclopedia."

The kids raced towards the house's library—Evie's favorite room. Her curiosity was insatiable, and she devoured books. The floor-to-ceiling bookshelves were filled with every kind of tome imaginable. Because Roddy and Ruby loved climbing the rolling ladder, Evie kept the World Book Encyclopedias and the dictionary on the top shelves.

"Those two are whip-smart," Pete said, marveling at his grandkids.

Evie agreed wholeheartedly, and that's why, even though the twins were enrolled in the Gifted Program at school, she continually challenged them.

"They sure are. You know, I've been thinking," she said.

"Dear Lord, give me strength," Pete said, only half-joking. "When you get to thinking—watch out."

She ignored his jab. "Maybe we should send them to private school."

"You know how I feel about taking from our nest egg. You never know when one of us will break a hip and need home health care."

She suppressed her eye roll. *Now he's even thinking like an old man.*

"Pete, you know we have enough, but if you don't want to dip into our coffers, we could come out of retirement and have the tuition in no time."

Pete pushed down on the arms of the chair to stand, his seventy-year-old knees cracking on the way up. He moved in front of Evie's rocker with his hands on his hips.

"Evie Collier, you promised! I'm too damn old for those kinds of shenanigans."

"Well, I'm not," she snapped.

"Evie...," he warned.

"Harrumph." Exasperated, she waved him away. "Fine. A promise is a promise. Public school will do." She took a sip of her Tom Collins and glared at Pete. "But just you remember," she said, wagging her finger. "I'm not too old for anything, and I damn well never will be!"

JUNE 2000

RUBY

We order a second round of Grasshoppers, two pens, and a stack of cocktail napkins and get busy solving the puzzle.

"First one's easy. I used the word tonight." He writes *lachrymosity* into the squares on the puzzle.

I scribble letters on my napkin, trying to solve the second word: *subreast, straubes, abstures, abstruse.*

"Got it," I yell. "Abstruse."

"Oh, how obscure," Roddy jokes.

I roll my eyes at his lame pun.

Once we've unscrambled each word—*ineffable, nebbish, impecunious, folderol, blatherskite, valedictory, and whiffler—*we plug the numbered letters into the proper spot and find our location: *visit Tollman Hat Factory.*

"I never remember Gigi mentioning a hat factory," Roddy says.

"Me either," I say, taking the last sip of my drink.

Roddy's stomach gurgles. "I'm starved. Want to order dinner?"

I shake my head. "Nope. Tight on money this week. How about I make dinner?"

Roddy laughs. I basically have a two-meal repertoire: eggs and spaghetti.

"Spaghetti it is," he says.

Roddy has the cooking chops. He considered culinary school, but his practical nature won out over his dream, and he became a high school accounting teacher.

Once home, I pull one of the two pans I own out of my freshly painted mint green cabinets and start heating the water. I finished the remodel three weeks ago. Gigi helped me pick out the colors and gave me pointers on how to prep the cabinets. Sanding and scraping off the old paint was a messy nightmare, but I love the new cheery vibe. I'm glad Gigi got to see the finished version.

"Where's the telephone book?" he asks as I gather the boxed pasta and Ragu sauce from the cupboards.

"In the hall closet. Under the mail bin."

Tight on space, I converted my hall coat closet into a makeshift office. A hinged board pulls down to serve as a desktop that extends past the door jamb. A folding chair is tucked on the right side of the board, and my printer is on an overturned crate on the left. Three shelves are mounted to the back wall, the lowest of which holds my monitor and computer tower.

"Got it," Roddy yells from the hall.

Bringing the directory into my tiny kitchen, he stands at the Formica counter and flips through the Yellow Pages. After throwing the pasta into the boiling water, I chop a head of iceberg lettuce and some carrots for salad.

Reaching the T's, he says, "Here it is. Tollman Hat Factory. It's in Adamstown."

"Great," I say. "Not too far. Call to see when they're open."

Roddy grabs my cordless phone out of the charging base and dials. He covers the mouthpiece. "Answering machine." He listens for a few minutes and hangs up. "They close at five. Monday through Saturday, ten to five."

"Perfect. Let's go tomorrow. Unless you already have plans."

"Get real," he says. "Tomorrow's good."

Since his divorce, Roddy's social life has been little to none. Not only did Roddy lose his best friend when he caught him cheating with Clara, but he also lost his house, his dog, and his dignity. Rather than fight her, he washed his hands of the whole mess. I wish I could fix it, but I guess he just needs time to heal.

I dump the sauce into my second pan and strain the noodles.

"Great. We'll take Sally. Let's get an early start. I'll pick you up at ten," I suggest.

Roddy thinks it's ridiculous that I name things. After I bought my adorable yellow convertible bug, Sally, I drove her straight from the car dealership to introduce her to Roddy.

He rolls his eyes at me. "The car is Sally, the dogwood tree is Delilah, and your house is Pearl. Get a dog; maybe then you'll stop naming things."

I shrug. "We'll see. So ten, okay?"

"Suits me," he agrees.

Roddy grabs the bowls of lettuce and sets them on the green checked tablecloth. I plate the spaghetti and join him at the table. He twirls his fork, collecting a mouthful of noodles.

"You know what. I was thinking..."

"God help me," Roddy interrupts. "When you get to thinking—watch out."

I punch his arm playfully. "Why don't you just crash here tonight? We could look through all the old photo albums. Kind of like a private memorial to Gigi. Whaddya think?"

"Hmmm. Reminiscing. Gigi would approve."

***

Awakened by me clanging around in the kitchen, Roddy stumbles out of the spare bedroom.

"Shower. Tylenol," he groans.

Last night's wine-fueled reminiscing has made his morning difficult. Luckily I had the good sense to stop at two glasses.

"Crapulent?" I tease.

"Hmph! My least favorite of Gigi's favored words," he growls.

"Because you've suffered from it too often." I use a lighthearted tone, but since his divorce, I have worried about how much he drinks.

He sticks his tongue out at me.

I hand him two Tylenol. He turns on the kitchen faucet and uses his cupped hand to get enough water to swallow the pills.

"Coffee before shower?" I ask.

He grunts a yes, and I pour us each a cup. "So, what are we looking for?"

He shrugs. "Who knows? Maybe Gigi met Pop at the factory. Or maybe Gigi owned it. Maybe she was a silent partner. That could be our inheritance."

I laugh. "Unlikely."

Although we never lacked anything, Gigi and Pop made sure we understood the value of a dollar. Other than a rare extravagance, Gigi shopped at secondhand stores for everything: clothing, housewares, tools, bikes. "Waste not, want not," she'd say. Made sense. After all, she'd grown up during the Depression.

"I guess we'll know what we're looking for when we find it," Roddy decides.

After taking the last sip of my now lukewarm coffee, I open the bread bin and retrieve one Ziploc bag of ashes, and set it on the counter. I wrinkle my nose. "It seems so undignified to dump Gigi out of a plastic baggie."

Roddy grimaces. "It really does."

I twist my curls while I think. "I know," I say, clapping my hands. "I have the perfect thing."

I run to my powder room and root through cupboards and drawers. A few minutes later, I find it.

"Ta-da!" I return to the kitchen, waving a silver sequined pouch in the air. "Snazzy, right? Gigi would approve. And look." I unzip it. "It's coated on the inside. The ashes won't stick. Good?"

"Brilliant."

***

June's morning sun warms my cheeks, and my long hair swirls in the wind. Roddy pulls on a hoodie and leans back against the headrest, watching the puffy clouds float in the blue sky. With the top down, the drive is chilly. Sally (with a little help from me) makes her jaunty way to the Tollman Hat Factory.

I park in a visitor's lot between the factory and a small stream. The brick building looms over the trickling water, blocking the morning sun.

I frown. "I don't want to spread Gigi here. It's so industrial."

"Maybe it won't seem so bad after we find out what this place meant to Gigi," Roddy suggests.

"I hope you're right."

When we push through the double doors of the factory, we're accosted by the odor of wet wool. The factory is one enormous open room. Machines whir, hiss, and pound in a mechanical rhythm. A grizzled man, wearing a gray fedora banded with teal blue, sits behind an antique wooden desk.

"Can I help you?" he asks.

"Yes." Roddy dives into the cover story we cooked up on the way over. "I am researching manufacturing in America. As the oldest hat factory in existence, we were wondering if we might be able to schedule a tour and get some background information."

"What kinda information are you lookin' for?"

I chime in. "We haven't narrowed down our angle as of yet. We were hoping to visit, absorb and see where the history leads us."

He looks at his watch. "I got ten minutes before my break. I'll give you the five-cent tour."

"I'm Ruby," I say, extending my hand. "We really appreciate this."

"Call me Buster," he says, offering me a weak handshake. "Follow me, but don't touch nothing."

Buster stops in front of a machine moving fluffy white wool into another machine. Small fibers float in the air and tickle my nose.

He starts his spiel. "Most of the machines we're usin' are the originals from 1868. This here machine feeds the clean wool into a carding machine." He waves us forward. "Then the rollers comb the wool thin, and it gets wrapped around this piece." He points to a long rod covered in a web of wool.

"It looks like quilting cotton," I remark.

"Yep." Buster moves to the next spot. "Here's where the cut the rough hat shape and then press it under these machines to harden it."

"Harden it?" Roddy asks.

"It's called hardening, but it ain't actually hard. Better word would be toughen it up."

At the next machine, water is squished into the wool, and the wet animal smell intensifies.

The smell is pungent, and I fan my nose. "Wow, it smells like a sheep in the rain."

"Pretty much is." Buster looks at his watch. "We got to speed this up. Almost break time." He quickens his pace. We barely have time to look at the machine before Buster's onto the next one. "So here they hammer the wool, then it goes into the dye tub, then it goes on these machines to block and shape the crown and brim."

Buster points across the room to a long line of sewing machines. "That's where they add sweat bands and trim. We good?"

"I, uh," I stutter, surprised the tour is over.

"Well," Roddy says, "We really appreciate the tour. Do you have any history on the owners or the employees or how the factory weathered the Depression or...?"

Buster interrupts with an inconvenienced sigh. "Well, why didn't you say so in the first place? The hat store's got a history exhibit about the factory. That's probably what you want."

"Sounds like exactly what we want," I agree. "Where is the store?"

Buster waves his arm towards the end of the building. "Go back out to the parking lot and follow the stream past the factory. You'll come to an old stone carriage house. That's the store."

As soon as we walk past the factory, the landscape opens up. Where the brick monstrosity no longer shadows the bank, little patches of buttercups bloom. I jump when a big old bullfrog plops into the water.

"Did you see that?" I giggle.

"I did," Roddy says.

Fifty yards more and maple trees line the banks, their branches dipping gracefully towards the trickling stream. Birds chirp merrily in the branches. The stone façade of the carriage house peeks out between the leaves. The scene is beautiful and serene.

"This is where we'll spread Gigi's ashes," I say.

"She'd like this."

Arriving at the store, we walk around the carriage house to the street side. Worn wooden doors flank a set of double glass doors. Old gas lanterns are affixed to the stone wall. A strap of sleigh bells jingles when we open the front doors. Rows and rows of hats are displayed on floating plank wood shelves. I run my fingers along the crisp brim of a boiled wool Trilby. An antique wagon, stacked full of more hats, takes center stage of the store.

"Welcome to Tollman's. May I help you?" a college-age woman says from behind a massive brick and wood counter.

I walk to the counter. "Yes. Buster at the factory said you have a museum display. Could we see it?" Even though I'm speaking, the young lady's eyes are trained on Roddy. I'm used to it. Women always swoon for Roddy's rugged features and wavy blond hair.

"Of course," the woman says cheerily. "Follow me." She leads us through rows of felted hats, straw hats, and leather hats to a small side room. "Take your time. Photos are allowed. And when you're finished, feel free to try on some hats."

"Thanks," Roddy says.

She brushes his arm with her fingertips as she walks back to the counter. "Let me know if I can help you with anything else."

I roll my eyes.

"What?" he says, genuinely confused. Roddy's oblivious to his effect on women.

"Please. Don't you get sick of adoration?"

He waves his hand, dismissing her words. "She was just being friendly. Let's focus on why we're here."

The little room is jam-packed with memorabilia. Framed black and white photos cover the walls. Benches topped with hat stands sporting every shape, style, and color of vintage hat line the perimeter of the room. Three glass cases full of ledgers, time cards, employee rosters, and the like fill the center space.

"Wow," I say, taking it all in. "We could be here for hours."

"Yeah," Roddy agrees, looking overwhelmed. "You start on the walls, and I'll take the glass cases. Fair?"

"Sure."

I notice the photos are arranged chronologically, starting with a tintype of George Tollman on opening day in 1868, and continuing to a 1985 celebratory shot when the company became employee owned.

I want to narrow my search. "If Gigi or Pop worked here, what year do you think it would've been?"

"Hmm." Roddy strokes his chin. "Thirties or forties, I'd guess."

I move along the wall until I find a group shot dated 1930. I scan the black and white faces looking for Gigi or Pop amongst the crowd. Nothing. There are a few more shots dated 1930. One has a toothy fellow grinning from ear to ear. It's captioned *Joe Johnson, promoted to floor manager.* I move further along the wall to 1931.

Bingo! "Here she is," I shout.

We study the photo of our young grandmother. Gigi is one of ten ladies sitting in a row behind a bevy of new sewing machines. Toothy Joe has his arms draped around Gigi and a dark-haired, doe-eyed young woman. His hands rest just above the women's breasts.

I touch my fingertip to her grandmother's face. "She looks so young."

Roddy closes one eye to do the calculations in his head. "She would've been seventeen in this photo."

"That's the boss." I point to Joe. "Seems a little too friendly, if you know what I mean."

"Different times," Roddy says.

"Same feelings," I counter, piqued by his insensitivity.

I quit my advertising sales job four years ago because of rampant sexual harassment by male clients. When I finally worked up enough nerve to tell my boss—also a woman—what was happening, she told me to suck it up. I quit on the spot and am a million times happier. But harassment is still a sore subject with me.

Roddy tilts his head and taps it against mine. "Sorry. Wasn't thinking."

"Not unusual," I tease.

"Back to it," Roddy says, returning to stare into the cases full of memories.

I scan five more years' worth of photos, but Gigi is in none of them. "Maybe she didn't work here long because I don't see her in any other shots."

"Maybe," Roddy says as he homes in on items from the thirties. "Damn, this whole place almost burnt down in August of 1931. Take a look at this article in the *Lancaster Journal*."

I skim the yellowed paper dated August 5, 1931. "Arson suspected? Wow. You don't think...I mean Gigi's instructions made it sound like we might not like what we learn about her... could the fire have been payback for a handsy boss? That's crazy right?"

Roddy shrugs. "It sounds crazy, but I don't know what to expect. What could we learn that would make us not want our inheritance? I suppose it could be as bad as arson. I suppose it could be worse."

I pale at the thought of my beloved Gigi being a criminal. "Let's not jump to conclusions. The clerk said we could take photos. I'll grab my digital camera from the car and bring Gigi's ashes too. Okay?"

Roddy nods. "I'll keep looking."

Thirty seconds after I return, Roddy finds two pink pieces of paper. Dated July 8, 1931, each paper has *BUGGER OFF!* scrawled across it. The pink slips were given to: Elizabeth Fry and Evelyn Fisher.

"Crap, Ruby," Roddy says glumly. "Gigi was fired. And not long before the fire."

My mouth falls open, and I rush over to look for myself. "She was fired? A month before the fire? Oh man, it looks bad."

"It does," Roddy agrees. "But, innocent until proven guilty. All we know for sure is Gigi worked here in 1931 and got fired a month before."

"True." I nod. "I'm sure it's just a coincidence. Maybe the woman who was given a pink slip the same day..."

"Elizabeth," Roddy adds.

"Yeah, Elizabeth. Maybe she's significant to Gigi's life."

"Like an accomplice?" he asks.

I shake my head with vigor, shedding my misgivings. "No. Like a dear friend who changed Gigi's life in some special way."

He takes hold of my hand and squeezes it. "My eternal optimist. I'm glad you're wearing your rose-colored glasses."

"I'll snap photos of everything that has anything to do with Gigi, and then we can spread her ashes." I click away, documenting what we found. "Done. Are you ready?"

Roddy nods, and we walk back into the hat store.

"Did you find what you needed?" the clerk asks Roddy.

"Yep, thanks."

"Come visit again soon," she calls in a hopeful voice as we head outside.

Behind the store, a gentle breeze flutters the maple leaves. A few large rocks jut from the bank into the stream. The crystal-clear water gurgles and twirls as it flows around them. We sit side by side on the flattest boulder. Roddy drops a stick into the current and watches it float downstream.

He inhales. "Shall we do it?"

I nod and unzip the sequined pouch. A few tears trickle down my cheeks as I prepare to let go of a part of Gigi. We each take hold of a corner and tilt the pouch upside down. Gigi's ashes pour into the babbling water. Some lift and swirl in the air like a plume of smoke before being swept into the waters. When the pouch is empty, we sit quietly on the rock holding hands, and watch our Gigi float away.

1931

EVIE

Wanting to make a good first impression, Evie smoothed down her checked flour-sack dress and fluffed her honey-blonde pageboy before walking through the front doors of the hat factory. The clangs and whirs of the equipment, accompanied by the trill of the sewing machines, melded into an industrial symphony.

Evie was relieved to have nabbed the sewing job. With her daddy out of work, money was tight. Her momma took in as much laundry as she could. Her back was humped and her hands were raw from hours of scrubbing, but she didn't even earn enough to keep Evie's daddy in hooch. Evie's fifteen-dollar weekly payday would put food on their table.

A dark-haired girl about Evie's age entered the factory right behind her. "Are you new too?" she asked, tucking a stray pin curl back in place.

"Uh-huh. First day."

"Me too! I'm Elizabeth Fry, but everyone calls me Bess."

Bess smiled, and her round, dark-chocolate eyes crinkled at the corners. She clasped her hands in front of her in delight. "Oh, I just know we're going to be bosom friends."

Evie laughed out loud at her declaration. A stern woman with gray hair pulled into a tight bun stormed over to them, glaring.

"Girls!" she reprimanded. "This is a place of business. Stay quiet until Mr. Johnson takes you to your stations."

As soon as she turned her back, Bess stuck out her tongue, and Evie choked on a laugh. The woman whipped her head around, and Evie and Bess stood ramrod straight and silent. As the woman walked away, Bess grabbed hold of Evie's hand and squeezed. They held hands until Mr. Johnson arrived.

"Well, whadda we got here?" Mr. Johnson said with a smile too big for his face. "Ain't you two a pair of lookers?"

Much as she would've liked to knock those oversized choppers out of his mouth, Evie batted her eyes. Jobs were too scarce to risk making the boss mad.

Bess swiveled her shoulders from side to side. "We're your new girls."

Mr. Johnson wrapped an arm around each girl. "Come on, kittens; I'll show you to your stations."

As they moved into the bowels of the factory, the earthy smell of wet wool intensified. Mr. Johnson guided them to a row of sewing machines and pointed to side-by-side machines.

"These are your stations. You girls will be sewing bindings. Glory here will show you how to do it. Won't you, doll?" He winks at a busty blonde.

"Sure, Joey, I'd be glad to," Glory cooed as she hand-stitched a satin lining inside a white cloche hat.

Mr. Johnson squeezed her shoulder "Atta girl." He turned to Evie and Bess. "I'll check on you two after lunch."

Without a word, Glory sat in front of Evie's machine and grabbed a derby from the wooden rack. She positioned the brim of the hat between the edges of the brown grosgrain ribbon and under the presser foot. Cradling the crown with her left hand and guiding the brim and ribbon with her right, she pushed the foot control, and thirty seconds later, the binding was attached. After trimming the ribbon, she flipped the edges under and completed the binding with a few more stitches.

"All yours," she said, moving out of Evie's station.

"Glory, thanks ever so much for your exhaustive guidance," Evie said, dripping with sarcasm as she slid into the chair in front of her machine.

Glory rolled her eyes, flounced to her station, and continued her work.

Bess bit her top lip to keep from laughing. "Easy peasy."

They each grabbed a derby and some grosgrain and got to work. The binding on Evie's first hat was a puckered mess.

"Rip it out and start again," Glory said helpfully.

Bess's first attempt was no better, leaving a tangled jumble of thread on the feed dog and a seized bobbin.

"Oh, for Pete's sake," Glory huffed. "You've got a thread jam."

"I definitely prefer strawberry," Bess quipped.

Glory was not amused.

After several more tries, Evie and Bess had each successfully added the binding to one derby.

Evie wiped the palms of her hands together. "Whew, I think that's enough for one day."

Bess laughed. "Only nine more hours to go."

Twenty hats in, the task required less concentration, and the girls were able to chew the fat as they worked. Evie learned they only lived two miles apart and were both born in May. Like Evie, Bess also lost her older sibling to the Spanish flu and had a boozehound for a dad. Neither Evie nor Bess had a special fella, but they were keen on finding one. They both loved to cut a rug and were game to sneak into a speakeasy. They agreed Mr. Johnson was a crumb, and they'd do their very best to steer clear of him. By the end of their ten-hour shift, Evie had a best friend.

JUNE 2000

RUBY

In my pith helmet and khaki safari vest, I lead ten similarly dressed nine-year-old boys, three doting moms, two bored dads, and a partridge in a...(just kidding), and one baby-faced uncle down the mile-long wooded trail of Swatara State Park to the fossil pit. I've equipped each member of my expedition crew with a backpack containing a chisel, rock hammer, assorted picks and brushes, safety goggles, plastic baggies, and a chart identifying the types of fossils we're likely to find.

Birthday boy Brad dreams of being a paleontologist, and his mom and dad hired me to give him and his guests a "real" experience. After a little digging (pun intended), I discovered a site guaranteed to offer up trilobites and crinoids galore.

I stop in front of giant piles of sedimentary rocks and swing my backpack off my shoulders onto the ground. "Okay, team, this is it."

"It's ginormous!" Brad jumps up and down.

The kids are talking over each other. "Can we climb to the top?" "Can we go? Can we go?" "I'm gonna find dinosaur bones!"

"Listen up." I raise my hand in the air. "Safety first. To be on the piles, you must have your safety goggles on. Grown-ups too!" I throw a stern glance, and the moms and dads and the kids giggle. "Understood?"

They all nod and slide the goggles onto their excited faces.

"Also, spread out and give each other plenty of room. And watch where you're swinging your hammers. Got it?"

Impatient nods.

"Miss Ruby?" Brad calls.

"Yes?"

"How old are the fossils we're going to find?"

Details are the difference between good and great. Since my business's success depends on referrals, my events must be great.

"About 375 million years old from the Paleozoic Era. Back then, this was a shallow ocean," I answer.

"So, these are all marine animals?" He points to the chart of fossils.

Smart kid. "That's right, Brad. Good reasoning."

He puffs up his chest and smiles.

"Okay, gang, are you ready?" The boys lean forward, ready to run. "On your mark. Get set. Dig!"

Ten sets of feet run up the piles of rocks, whooping and hollering as they go. The parents climb much more slowly. Brad's uncle walks over to me. Even though he's my age, he's still out of breath from the relatively easy hike. He's wearing the safety goggles over his John-Lennon-style glasses.

Biting back a chuckle, I point at the goggles. "You only have to wear them when you're on the pile."

"What?" He strikes a pose. "And miss out on the chance to look this good?"

I laugh. "It's true. Not many men could pull it off. But you? You elevate the look."

"I really do." He wipes the glistening sweat from his bald head and slips the goggles into his pocket. "I'm Uncle Marty, by the way."

"Hi, Uncle Marty. I'm Miss Ruby."

After drying his sweaty hand on his khaki Bermuda shorts, he offers it for a shake. His hands are smooth, like a baby's bottom, and his skin (as Gigi would say) is British White.

"You did your homework, planning this shindig," he says. "How did you even find this place?"

"Research."

"Apparently a lot of it. Paleozoic Era? I'm impressed."

"More specifically, the Middle Devonian Period of the Paleozoic Era," I say, showing off my knowledge.

His cheeks dimple when he smiles. "Beauty and brains."

The flush starts in my belly and works its way up. I change the subject before it reaches my face. "So, Uncle Marty. What do you do?"

"I'm a newshound. For *Lancaster Intelligencer Journal.*"

My thoughts zip to the article about the arson at the hat factory. "It used to be called the *Lancaster Journal*, right?"

"Yep. One of the oldest papers in the U.S. Started in 1794. You know publishing history too? A Jackie of all trades."

"Actually, I'm delving into a new project and could use some information. Do copies of your papers from the thirties still exist?"

"On microfilm. We have every edition ever printed."

"UNCLE MARTY!" Brad yells from the top of the rock pile. "I found a brachiopod! Come see!"

Marty slips on his goggles and grabs his backpack of tools. "So, Miss Ruby, why did the paleontologist go to the doctor?"

"I don't know. Why?"

"He discovered a dino sore."

I groan at his cornball joke. His periwinkle blue eyes dance with fun. He starts towards his nephew but turns back to me. Pulling a crumpled business card out of his wallet, he says, "Call me, and we can set up a time for you to look through the microfilms."

"Thanks. I will, but no more bad jokes," I say, winking.

"I don't make promises I can't keep."

***

I open one eye at the jangle of the ringing phone. I'm tangled in the sheets and don't have the energy to move. Last night, after eating some takeout I found stuffed in the back of my fridge, heartburn kicked in, and I barely slept a wink. The answering machine picks up, and I listen as the caller leaves a message.

"Hi Ruby, this is Janet Davis. I work with Marty, and he spent all morning raving about what a creative, awesome event you organized for his nephew's birthday. I'd like to talk with you about planning an anniversary party. Give me a call at your earliest convenience. 717-555-2323."

It was sweet of Marty to talk me up. My work week is light, so I was going to call him to see if I could look at the archives. Maybe I'll offer to treat him to lunch for his referral.

I crawl out of bed and pad to the kitchen to offer a cheery good morning to Mr. Coffee (I would've called him Wilbur, but he already had a name). His on button shines at me like a giant smile. By the time I pee and wash my face, the tempting smell of freshly brewed coffee has moseyed through the house, and my mouth is watering.

Before I settle in with my morning cup of sunshine, I step onto the front porch and bend down to grab the daily paper. The fetid scent of skunk assaults my senses and a wave of nausea hits me. (I'm overly sensitive to pungent smells and noise.) I sway as I stand up and reach my hand out to the porch post to steady myself. A white-haired man with a grizzled beard jogs halfway up my brick walkway.

"Are you okay?" he calls from ten feet away.

He's a stranger, yet I feel like I recognize him. I inhale a slow breath, and the queasiness passes. "I am. Thanks."

Concern darkens his jade-green eyes, and he rubs his chin. The morning sun highlights hints of faded red in his hair and beard. He opens his mouth to speak but simply nods and walks back to the truck parked in front of my house. He turns and gives me one last look before stepping into the beat-up black Ford.

MAY 1972

EVIE

Evie mixed two more gin Rickeys and handed one to her lifelong friend.

Bess patted the empty side of the mattress. "Sit with me."

Evie slipped off her clogs and crawled onto Bess's bed, tucking one of the Otomi embroidered throw pillows—picked up during an Acapulco vacation—behind her back. The bright-colored turban wrapped around Bess's bald head accentuated the sallowness of her skin. Following her double mastectomy, she endured three rounds of chemo and radiation, and still, cancer ravaged her frail body. There was nothing left to do, so Evie and Bess drank cocktails and reminisced.

Bess's husband, George, shuffled into the room with a too-bright smile pasted on his weary face. Drooping shoulders revealed the weight of his sadness. "How about hors d'oeuvres for my two best gals?" He set a tray with a pecan-crusted cheese log and crackers in the middle of the bed.

Bess laid the palm of her hand on the side of his face. "Thanks, love."

He kissed her forehead. "You bet. I'll leave you hens to it."

Evie spread cheese on a cracker and offered it to her friend.

Bess waved it away and took a sip of her cocktail. "I'll stick with this."

"You've got yourself a good man," Evie said, munching on the cracker.

Bess chuckled. "Sure do. Do you remember the first night we met? At the drum?"

Evie thought back to the thrumming, carefree nights at the local speakeasy. "I swear George started stashing dough for the wedding ring the minute he laid eyes on you!"

"You mean laid eyes on my bubs. I don't think he saw my face during our whole first jitterbug." Bess rubbed her flat chest wistfully. "I miss them."

"They *were* glorious. Let's toast to them." Evie raised her glass.

"Cheers." Bess laughed and clinked glasses with Evie. "They got me in a lot of trouble, though. Remember Joe Johnson?"

"Unfortunately, yes."

"What a creep!" Bess shivered at the memory. "When he cornered me in the hallway after our shift, I was sure he wasn't going to stop at a grope."

Evie's anger flared as she remembered finding Joe pressing her best friend against the wall. "That's why I kicked him where it hurt."

"Earned us our pink slips," Bess smiled proudly.

"He got his." Evie shrugged. "He thought he was dealing with some fresh-off-the-farm peaches. Guess we showed him."

"We surely did!"

They clinked glasses and drank in the sweetness of their shared history. Evie crawled out of bed to freshen their cocktails. She added a little extra sparkling water to hers and a little extra gin to Bess's.

"And what about the night we got stuck in the trunk of George's Chevy Fleetline?" Evie recalled as she climbed back onto the bed beside Bess.

Bess linked her arm through Evie's. "Oh yeah! At the drive-in. We always did like the thrill of getting away with something."

"We can be glad we had the bottle of booze with us."

"Yeah, but as tight as the space was, we spilled more than we got in our mouths."

Evie laughed. "Probably a good thing. We would've been drunk as skunks by the time the fellas got us out."

Herds of memories stampeded through Evie's mind. She snuggled closer to her cherished friend. They sat, sipping their gin Rickeys, in companionable silence.

Half a cocktail later, Evie noticed a single tear sliding down Bess's cheek.

"I've had a good life. A rich, full life. I only wish I could see baby Gail grow up."

Evie didn't offer the usual platitude—you'll be watching her from heaven. If there was a heaven, Evie wasn't sure she or Bess would get there after all they'd done.

She took hold of Bess's hand and squeezed. "She'll be an inimitable young woman."

Bess laughed. "Oh-ho. I'm glad my granddaughter is favored-word-worthy."

"More than worthy. As are you, my dear, inimitable friend."

The women hugged tightly, their love for each other palpable.

George knocked on the doorframe to announce his presence. "Time for your morphine, Bess."

Evie and Bess pulled apart.

"I'd chop off my left boob...oh, that's right, I already did. I'd chop off my left leg for some grass," Bess announced.

Evie spit her drink across the bedspread in laughter. George rolled his eyes.

"What? I'm not dead yet," Bess said. "And, as for you, George Royer Finley, it's not like you haven't sampled your fair share of Mary Jane. Half our product went up in smoke."

Evie recalled Bess and George dabbling in the marijuana trade. Local farmers were recruited to plant and harvest the crop, and Bess and George sold it—some through Evie and Pete's store. At first, Pete was hesitant to sell it, but having gotten away with much worse, it didn't take a lot of persuasion. One book in the Vogansville General Store's lending library was extremely popular—Steinbeck's *Tortilla Flat*. Evie hollowed out her copy and stuffed it full of goof-butts—twenty cents apiece, five of which the store kept. When it became painfully obvious that George liked their product way too much, he and Bess gave it up for less tempting things.

Exasperated, George ran his hands through his still-dark hair. "Good God, woman. That was close to forty years ago. Let it be."

Bess would when she took her last breath—six days later.

JUNE 2000

RUBY

I slide a few quarters into the parking meter and walk two blocks to the *Intelligencer Journal* building. Cars beep their annoyance at the slow pace of morning traffic. Business-suit-wearing people stride down the sidewalk, hurrying to get to work. According to the clock mounted on the façade of the five-story building, I arrive at 9:25. Five minutes to spare before my meeting with Marty.

After corralling a few stray curls back into my ponytail, I swipe on cherry lip balm and straighten my sundress. I wanted Roddy to join me, but he took on a few side jobs during his summer break from teaching. Today he is painting a front porch.

I grab the massive brass handle and swing open the glass door. A blast of cold air hits me as I enter, and I shiver in my sleeveless outfit. A sweatered receptionist greets me.

"Good morning. How may I help you?"

"I have an appointment with Marty Metzger."

"Have a seat." She gestured to a row of mustard vinyl-covered chairs. "I'll let him know you're here."

A few minutes later, Marty arrives. A giant smile has kidnapped his chubby baby face.

"Ruby! Great to see you." He notices the goosebumps covering my bare arms. "I should've warned you. They keep it

Siberian-cold in here. We'll swing by my office before heading to the archives. I'm sure I have a spare jacket."

"Sounds good," I say with a shiver. "I'd hate to give you the cold shoulder."

He chuckles. "Clever."

My insides warm despite the freezing temperature. "Thanks."

We take a left into a giant space filled with rows of employees boxed on three sides by chin-height fuzzy walls.

"Here we are." He points to a cubicle. "My office."

Dozens of family photos are tacked on the fuzzy gray dividers. I point to an older version of Marty, hugging a stunning white-haired woman. "Your parents?"

"Righto," Marty says. "And, of course, Brad, Becky, and Bart," he adds, pointing to shots of his nephew, sister, and brother-in-law.

Piles of paper form a horseshoe around the edges of his desk. A ruled yellow tablet and three sharpened pencils sit neatly in the center of the ordered chaos. He notices my gaze.

"I'm old school. I like to hear and feel the scratch of a pencil on paper. Gingers up my creativity."

"My grandma, Gigi, was the same way. She wrote so much she had a permanent lump on the side of her middle finger where the pencil rubbed."

"What did she write?"

"Bedtime stories, puzzles, research, to-do lists, letters, poems, lullabies, lunchbox notes. She always has—had—paper and pencil at the ready."

"She passed recently?"

He noticed my slip. "Yes. Actually, that's what my research project is about. Gigi's final puzzle."

He cocks his head and waits for me to explain.

"My twin brother, Roddy, and I have to solve one last puzzle to claim our inheritance."

"Your Gigi sounds nifty."

His quirky vocabulary is growing on me. Reminds me of Gigi's use of favored words.

"Incomparable." I caress the spot on my middle finger to rub in the memory.

Marty ducks under his desk and drags out a bin filled with dirty Tupperware, crusty forks, a few empty cups, a pair of sneakers, some hats and gloves, and a crumpled suit jacket.

"My dirty little secret," he says, embarrassed by his untidiness.

I raise a finger to my closed lips. "I'll never tell."

He shakes out the jacket. A few crumbs fall to the floor. He holds it up, and I slide my arms into the sleeves. The jacket hangs almost to my knees, and the sleeves are inches too long.

"Fetching," he teases.

"You rock safety goggles. I rock oversized menswear."

"Indeed you do." His dimples deepen. "To the bowels of the building," he says, extending his arm towards a hallway.

We pass dozens of cubicles, weave through tables full of advertising clip art, take a right at a row of computers, and head down the stairs into the basement.

"What dates do you need?" he asks.

"Let me start with August 5, 1931, and I'll work forward from there."

He pulls a metal box full of reels from a shelf and plucks one out. "This should contain all of August 1931. If you need to read further, each reel is labeled with a month." He demonstrates how to click the reel into place on the machine and to flip from page to page. "Got it?"

I nod. "All set."

"Do you remember how to find my desk if you need me?"

"I do."

"Alrighty then. Crack on," he says, heading out with a jaunty wave.

Marty's the living embodiment of Sally—cheerful, sunny, and makes me smile.

"Marty?"

He stops and turns to face me. "Yeah?"

"I forgot to thank you for your glowing recommendation. Janet hired me to plan her parents' anniversary party. Seventies themed to commemorate the year they married."

"Groovy." His fingers form a peace sign.

I like a man who isn't afraid to look silly.

"Can I treat you to lunch? To thank you for this," I wave my hand over the microfilm reader, "and, for Janet."

"Absolutely! I packed three-day-old spaghetti, so my intestinal tract thanks you."

"Does noon suit you? Two hours should give me plenty of time to find what I need."

"And two hours will give me time to scribble my next assignment. Noon it is."

He tips his imaginary hat and heads to his desk. I dive into 1931.

I scroll the film until August fifth's headline stops me. *FIRE RAVAGES TOLLMAN HAT FACTORY.* It's the same front page Roddy and I saw in the factory museum, but the story is continued on page five. I forward the film to read the rest of the article.

> The after-hours blaze trapped two employees—Miss Glory Mahoney, seamstress, and floor manager, Mr. Joseph Johnson.
>
> Firemen rescued the pair, who suffered third-degree burns. The on-duty nurse at Reading Hospital indicated they would make a full recovery.
>
> One fireman told this reporter that arson was suspected. Fire Marshal Gerald Lober noted only that the investigation continues and a ruling would be issued shortly.

I bite my lower lip. If Roddy and my conclusion is correct, and Gigi was angry about being fired, knowing that Joe Johnson was inside when the fire started casts more suspicion her way. I pull a notebook out of my oversized straw purse and take some notes before moving on to August 6.

I carefully read through the August 6th and 7th issues, but they reveal nothing of interest. However, an under-the-fold headline on August 8th's front page grabs my attention: *FIRE RULED ARSON.*

> The Tollman Hat Factory fire has been ruled arson, according to a statement from Fire Marshal Gerald Lober.
>
> Lober plans to question several persons of interest in the coming weeks. The scene should be released by Friday.
>
> Albert Anderson, a representative of the family-owned business, thanked the fire department for its massive effort to save the factory.
>
> "The Tollman family is eager to rebuild and get our people back to work," he said.

Icy dread slinks up my spine, and I wrap Marty's jacket tight around me. Nausea bubbles in my belly. I'd be devastated if Gigi had set the fire. I root around in the bottom of my bag until I find a ginger candy. (Along with ibuprofen, it's one of my purse staples.) As I suck on the lozenge, I rest my forehead in my hands and concentrate on my breathing. After a few minutes, the queasiness passes, and I resume my research.

I scroll through two weeks' worth of headlines (*Lindys Fly North On Treacherous Hop, King of Philadelphia's Bootleggers, Max "Boo Boo" Hoff Eludes Indictment, Gandhi Withdraws From 2nd Round Table Conference In London, Babe Ruth Hits 600th Career Home Run*) until I hit August 22nd. *Arsonist Arrested* screams the headline. I brace myself for what follows.

Jacob Dillworth, a former Tollman Hat Factory machinist, was arrested yesterday for setting the fire that seriously injured two employees.

Thank God it wasn't Gigi! I massage the worry from my eyebrows. Her "secrets" have me more frazzled than I realized. Stress creeps back in. What if we find out she's done something truly horrible? How will I reconcile the new truth with my old memories?

"Almost ready?"

I didn't hear him coming and jump at Marty's voice.

"Sorry," he says. "Didn't mean to startle you."

"Lost in memories."

"You look sad. Did you find something disturbing?"

I rally a smile. "No, actually, good news. And yes, I'm ready as soon as I rewind the film."

I quickly flip through the 1931 issues of the paper until all the film is on the reel. I pull it off the microfilm reader and tuck it back in the box between July and September. Marty returns it to its proper place on the shelf. I grab my purse. We leave his borrowed jacket on his office chair and head out of the sub-zero building into the summer sunshine.

Marty's round glasses darken in response to the bright sunlight. I slip on my purple-tinted aviator shades.

"So, you know the city. Where to?" I ask.

"Do you like seafood?"

"Love it!"

"Then Kegel's it is. It's about half a mile away. Are we walking or driving?"

I twirl and look up at the puffy white clouds floating in the blue sky. "Definitely walking."

We stroll down King Street, window shopping as we go. I point to a Modernist painting of a cow head spanning the entire front window of an art gallery.

"Moo-ving," I quip.

He chuckles and counters with a joke. "Know why cows have hooves instead of feet?"

"No. Why?"

"They lactose."

I groan. "I thought we agreed on no bad jokes."

He shakes his head, "Oh no. I told you I couldn't make that promise."

As we pass a spice and herb shop, a jumble of curry, cinnamon, and rosemary drift onto the sidewalk from its open door. We walk a little farther, and I stop to check out an adorable flowered romper showcased in the display window of a high-end boutique. The price tag reads $120.

"Whew, out of my budget."

"Out of their mind," Marty says.

As we pass the bronze statue of a man reading a paper at the entrance to Steinman Park, I ask, "Was journalism always your calling?"

"Yep. Woodward and Bernstein were my Batman and Robin."

"So you're living your dream."

He rubs his chin. "Well, no Pulitzer yet, but I did blow an Amish crime ring wide open."

I throw my hand across my chest and lean back, feigning astonishment. "Do tell."

"Yep." He shrugs his shoulders and turns his palms up. "I know it's hard to believe, but I uncovered two local Amish farmers stealing rare heirloom seeds from their neighbors. They were selling them out-of-state to the highest bidder."

"Shocking." I cover my mouth with my hand.

"Horrifying." He throws his palm against his forehead.

"Scandalous." I giggle. "You were robbed. That story should have won you national acclaim."

"Indeed, it should have," he agrees, laughing. He inhales a deep breath and sighs contentedly. "So, what about you? Was party planning always your raison d'être?"

"No. But being my own boss was. Speaking of work." A lava lamp shines from a shop window. "That would work brilliantly for Janet's party. Mind if I pop in the store and buy it?"

"Of course not. I'll browse the platform shoe section while I wait," he jokes.

The shop is a hodgepodge of decades: disco balls displayed beside a banana leaf print, a frilly floral side chair, topped by a throw pillow with graphic red lips. I give the store a quick once over, checking for anything else I could use. When my stomach growls in protest, I wrap up my browsing and buy the lamp and an ABBA record. As we exit, my gut flips when I spot the same white-haired man I found parked in front of my house leaning against a stone building a few doors down. When he realizes I've spotted him, he dodges between two parked cars and jaywalks across the street.

"Damn fool!" a driver yells, nearly hitting him.

"That guy has a death wish," Marty says.

Stunned at seeing him again, I blurt, "That guy was at my house a few days ago."

Marty furrows his brows. "He was? Do you know him?"

"No. I don't." Worry itches my neck, and I swat it away. "I'm sure it's just a weird coincidence," I assert and really hope it's true.

Marty puckers his brows and shakes his head. "I'm not so sure I'd just brush it off. He could be following you."

Fear's bony hands dig into my shoulders. I shake my head forcefully, trying to loosen its grip. "I'm certain it's just a coincidence."

"Maybe." Marty shrugs. "But do me a favor, and stay vigilant. If you see him again, especially at your house, I think you should call the police."

The police? Marty's overreacting. Kindly-looking old men

are not stalkers.

"I'm sure it's nothing sinister," I say. "Maybe he's connected to Gigi's puzzles."

"In what way?"

I shrug. "Maybe he's some sort of referee, making sure we follow her instructions. Or maybe a lifeline if we get in a jam figuring something out. Yes! I'm sure that's it! If he's following me, he must be Gigi's helper."

Now that I have a logical explanation, my anxiety eases.

Marty frowns. "Are you convincing me or yourself?"

I wave off his skepticism. "You don't know my grandmother. When Gigi is involved, all things are possible."

1931

EVIE

Evie peeked around the corner of the back of the Tollman Hat Factory. Joe Johnson's prize possession—his emerald green Model A—was parked in the far corner of the lot. She waved Bess over and whispered, "The coast is clear."

Luckily the few windows in the back of the factory were covered in grime, making it nearly impossible to see in or out. The women ducked behind the other cars in the lot as they weaved their way to the Model A. When Bess pulled the black shoe polish from her purse, Evie paused.

"What?" Bess asked, sensing her uncertainty. "He deserves it."

The image of Joe Johnson pressing against her best friend, hand gripping her bottom, and Bess's terrified eyes blotted out any hesitation. Evie scooped out a rag full of the thick black stain and wiped the cheery yellow wheel spokes until they were a dull brown. Bess polished the gleaming green hood. With hours until the work day ended, the women hoped the shoe polish would leave a permanent stain.

This was the first time Evie and Bess had seen each other since being fired three weeks earlier. Evie had landed a position with the Caldwells, a well-to-do family in Lancaster. She cleaned their five-bedroom Colonial, laundered their clothing, cooked meals, ran errands—really anything the missus required. It paid less than Tollman, and the hours were longer, but at least she had a job.

Bess had gotten lucky too. Her cousin was getting married and giving up her bookkeeping position at the Ephrata National Bank. Knowing Bess had studied bookkeeping, business arithmetic, and typing in high school, her cousin recommended her for the job. She started a week after throwing her pink slip in Joe Johnson's arrogant face.

After blackening Joe's car, they hopped on the trolley bound for Ephrata.

"It's devastating how rarely we see each other," Bess pouted. "But I have something for you."

"You do?"

Bess handed Evie a tiny pouch made from a beautiful handkerchief. A sprig of lavender was hand-stitched on the corner, and it was tied with a white hair ribbon. "Open it."

Evie untied the bow and discovered a delicate gold chain with a heart locket. BF was etched on the back.

"It's beautiful but too expensive. I can't take it."

"It was mine, so it didn't cost a thing. See." She traced the initials. "Bess Fry. Open the locket."

Evie carefully pulled the heart apart. A tiny blue forget-me-not was pressed into the heart-shaped cavity.

"So you don't forget me." Bess leaned across the trolley seat to hug Evie.

"Like I ever could." Evie held her best friend tightly. Feeling tears threaten, Evie pulled away and clapped her hands. "I have a swell idea. Let's go to the speakeasy on Saturday night. Whaddya think?

"Aces!"

***

Evie could hardly wait to meet Bess at the drum. She was desperate for some lightheartedness to punctuate the drudgery of her days. Occasionally she imagined herself lady of the house, pretending her hardest chore was which of the fine dresses to don for an evening at the theater. The escapes were short-lived; the burn of reality was always as close as her own raw hands.

"Evelyn, take Mr. Caldwell's watch to be cleaned and oiled," Mrs. Caldwell said, handing Evie a gold and diamond Hamilton pocket watch.

"Yes, ma'am. Where shall I take it?"

"Bowman Watch Company. On the corner of Duke and Chestnut. Make sure you give it to George, John, or Charles Bowman. It's valuable, and I don't want just any scrub touching it."

Evie carefully wrapped the watch in Bess's hand-stitched handkerchief and tucked it in her worn leather pocketbook. By the time she walked to the watch shop, the humid summer air had frizzed her hair. She smoothed her golden locks as best she could before opening the shop door. A buzzer announced her entry. The shop was stuffy. Already heated from her walk, droplets of sweat trickled down her back. A spot-free glass showcase displayed dozens of pocket watches, rings, and brooches. Evie stepped up to the case waiting for a clerk to appear. When she laid her hand on the case, the heat from her palm steamed the glass. She searched for a call bell but found none. As she paced around the tiny shop, her impatience grew. Mrs. Caldwell would not approve of the errand taking all afternoon. She held the door open so the buzzer would continue to blare.

"Coming! Coming!" a baritone called from the back.

Evie's heart fluttered when the young man sailed through the door. Chestnut waves of hair, styled longer on top and short on the sides, topped a classic Roman face—broad forehead, strong nose, and square jaw. And his eyes—an intense blue, crackling with intelligence and a hint of roguery. He was the most handsome man Evie had ever seen.

"How can I help you, Miss?" He wiped his hands on his apron.

"Are you George, John, or Charles Bowman?" Evie hid her nerves behind haughtiness.

Evie was sure the man saw right through her put-on airs.

"None of the above. I'm Pete. Pete Collier. Pleasure to meet you," he said with a cheeky wink.

Evie hung her head as she dug the watch out of her pocketbook so Pete wouldn't see her blush. Something about his confidence made her feel like a tongue-tied schoolgirl. "I need to give this to George, John, or Charles Bowman. To be oiled and cleaned."

Pete held out his hand. "I can take care of that. I'm one of Mr. John's students."

"No, no," Evie said, equally afraid of brushing his manly hand with hers as she was of angering Mrs. Caldwell. "Mrs. Caldwell specifically said I should give it to George, John, or Charles Bowman."

"Well," Pete said, leaning his elbows on the glass case, "That's gonna be tough. George doesn't see customers—or students, for that matter. Mr. Charles is home with a summer cold, and Mr. John is in the middle of teaching a watch-making class. He sent me to help you, so let me help you."

Dots of sweat rimmed her upper lip. She fanned her face with her hand, dizzy from the heat.

"You're a bit green around the edges." Pete came out from behind the counter and guided her outside. "Let's get you some fresh air."

The sticky August air offered little relief. Pete led Evie around the building, through a wrought-iron gate, and into a tree-lined courtyard. The shade dropped the temperature by ten degrees.

"Have a seat." Pete directed her to a garden bench. "I'll bring you a cold drink."

Evie sat on the ornate iron garden bench under a willow tree. The slight breeze cooled her face, and her dizziness subsided. *What a fool I've made of myself.* A few minutes later, Pete returned with two RC Colas.

"May I join you?" He pointed to the empty side of the bench.

"Of course," she said, accepting the cold soda. Evie savored the first sip of the sweet cola. She hadn't splurged on this kind of treat in a long time. "Thank you, Mr. Collier. I feel much better."

"Please, I'm just a regular Joe. Call me Pete."

His indigo eyes dazzled Evie. *Not even within the same hemisphere as regular.*

Breaking his gaze, she unwrapped the watch and dabbed her face with the handkerchief. "I really do need to give this directly to one of the Bowmans. Can you help me?"

When Pete raked his fingers through his thick, shiny hair, Evie imagined it was her fingers entwined in his locks. A loose wave swooped across his forehead.

He raised his eyebrows and shrugged his palms open. "Miss...I'm sorry, I don't know your name."

"Evelyn Fisher," Evie replied, dropping her eyes to his powerful jaw and full lips.

"Miss Fisher, the best I can do is give you my word; I'll hand it directly to Mr. John. Whaddya say?"

His lips look pillowy soft. I bet he's a good kisser.

"Miss Fisher?"

She reluctantly dragged her gaze from his lips. "Call me Evie," Evie inhaled and squared her shoulders. *Okay, Evelyn Fisher, you only get what you have the courage to take.* "I say that will be fine—on one condition."

His eyes sparked with amusement. "A condition, you say. And what might that be?"

"Meet me at the drum in Ephrata this Saturday. I'm in need of a dance partner."

JUNE 2000

RUBY

Roddy's already hard at work when I pull into Mirabella's (my name for Gigi's house) stamped concrete driveway. He's kneeling in front of mounds of yellow impatiens spilling over the border rocks, softening the edges of the walkway. Pop planted a bumper crop of the vibrant flowers as a teasing nod to Gigi's tendency for impatience. A neon blue garden tub is half full of weeds. Even though the anemic morning sun has barely warmed the air, Roddy's hair is plastered to his sweaty forehead.

"Gloves are on the porch," he yells when I'm within earshot. "And will you bring me my bottle of water?"

I walk under one of the three arches and onto the bricked front porch. I haven't been to Mirabella since Gigi died. Swallowing the lump in my throat and wiping away tears, I grab the garden gloves and Roddy's plastic bottle of water.

"Where's the reusable I gave you?" I ask, weaving through the flower bed to hand him the water. "I can't believe you're still using disposable plastic bottles. You know the plastic garbage patch already covers over 600,000 square miles of ocean."

He holds his hands up in surrender, "It's too early for a scolding. At least wait until after lunch."

"Sorry," I say sheepishly. "I'll get off my soapbox."

"Great, because it's gonna be hard to pull weeds from up there," he jokes.

I slip on the gloves and kneel beside Roddy. Until we solve Gigi's last puzzle, we're in limbo as far as what will happen with the house. I hope he inherits it. His one-bedroom on the third floor of the Royer's Pharmacy building is the Eeyore of apartments. The dingy gray walls, fogged windows, worn, stained carpets, and gloomy lighting sucks all happiness from you as soon as you walk through the door.

"I ordered a scoop of mulch to be delivered this week," he says as he digs out a dandelion. "I have only one side job lined up, so I'll have time to spread it."

When Pop died, Roddy inherited Mirabella's lawn care. Though not particularly squeamish, Gigi had the keenest disrelish (her words) for dirt under her fingernails. Being only fourteen, I jumped on Gigi's bandwagon—not because I minded dirt, but because it was a great way to get out of chores. Now, I pitch in occasionally.

"I'll pay for the mulch since you're donating the labor," I offer.

"Deal." He wipes the sweat from his forehead, leaving a smear of mud behind. "So fill me in on what you found at the newspaper office. You said it was good news."

"Yep. The Tollman fire was arson, but Gigi wasn't involved. A guy named Jacob Dillworth was arrested for the crime."

"That is good news. I wouldn't know what to think if it had been Gigi."

"I know, right? I gotta admit, I'm kind of scared to uncover her secrets. What if it *is* something horrible? I don't want to tarnish my memories."

He stands up and rubs his muddy, gloved hand over the top of my head. "I know. If it's not rosy, you don't want to see it."

I stand and brush the grass and dirt from my knees. "What's wrong with a positive attitude?" I snap.

"Nothing, until it colors the truth."

Annoyed, I grab the tub full of weeds and storm to the backyard. Hmph! At least I'm not some Gloomy Gus who grumps away his life. As soon as the thought pops into my mind, I feel bad. Roddy wasn't cynical until Clara gutted him. I dump the weeds onto the compost pile behind the shed and return to the front yard.

Roddy's pruning the azalea bush. I stuff the trimmings into a compostable bag.

"Look, Ruby, don't be mad. All I'm saying is you can't shove this away because it might not be nice. It's Gigi's last wishes. We have to do this."

***

The sun gets higher and hotter, and we break for lunch. Roddy pulls out a teal stool from the arched recess of the enormous kitchen island. Gigi used colorful, handmade Talavera tiles to top the island and serve as the backsplash between the warm white upper and lower kitchen cabinets. Antique coffee tins from nine brands of coffee are lined up between the top of the cabinets and the ceiling: De Soto, Luzianne, Bailey's Supreme, Mother's Joy, Savarin, Elna, Pickwick, White House, and Avalon.

Other than a few bottles of RC Cola (Gigi's favorite) and an unopened jar of pickles, the refrigerator is bare. Roddy had already cleaned out the perishables. I grab a can of tuna and some crackers from the pantry.

"Lunch." I hold up my find.

As we munch, we discuss the Tollman Hat Factory and its significance to Gigi.

Roddy stacks a forkful of tuna onto a cracker. "Maybe it has to do with the skills she learned working at the factory."

"Sewing? That's no secret. We knew she could sew."

"Yeah, but maybe she used her skills to commit a crime."

"The Case of the Uneven Hem—A Crime Against Fashion," I say dramatically.

He throws a cracker at me. "You're an ass."

"Okay, okay. I'll bite. How could she sew for crime?"

"Maybe she sewed stolen diamonds inside the lining of a jacket and took them across the border. Or maybe she transported government documents."

He looks so earnest; I bite my lip to keep from laughing. "I suppose she could've been a smuggler or spy. Or maybe the importance is more straightforward, like a person. What about the woman who got fired the same day she did?"

"Elizabeth Fry?"

"Yes, Elizabeth..." A snippet of a memory gives me pause. "Roddy, think back to our first day of kindergarten."

"Okay?"

"There was a woman with Pop and Gigi. She had big brown eyes and dark hair. Remember? She was taking pictures of the four of us."

"Kind of." He furrows his eyebrows. "She was Gigi's friend. Right? I have vague memories of her playing hopscotch with us at the house."

"Yeah, yeah!" I wag my finger excitedly. "I remember that too. I think that might have been Elizabeth Fry."

"What makes you think that?"

"The photo of Gigi in the row of women. With the boss hanging over them. I thought the woman beside Gigi looked familiar."

"Hmm. I don't remember thinking that when I saw it," Roddy says.

"When I get home, I'll print it out and show you. Plus, there's the locket. Do you remember the heart locket Gigi wore?"

"Yeah."

"One night, when I was twelve or thirteen, I found Gigi crying in her bed. She was holding the locket and rubbing the heart between her fingers. When I asked her what was wrong, she said she was missing her best friend."

"And?" he says impatiently.

"And I asked Gigi where her friend was. She told me she had died, and the locket was all she had to remember her by."

"Okay, but why do you think the locket belonged to Elizabeth Fry?"

"I'll show you. Be right back."

I run upstairs to Gigi's room and fling open the door. Nothing's been touched. Her sheets are rumpled, and her slippers wait on the floor by her bedside. *Tuesdays With Morrie* lies open and face down on her bedside table, ready for her to resume reading. The jasmine-vanilla scent of Shalimar swirls around me like her ghost. The grief, triggered by the smell, knocks the wind out of me, and I collapse onto the floor. Roddy must hear the thump because seconds later he's cradling me in his arms.

Tears stream down my cheeks. I'm ashamed of myself. Gigi lived a long, wonderful life. We were blessed to have her raise us well into adulthood. I need to buck up and be grateful for the time we had together.

"Sorry," I say. "Her perfume. I wasn't ready."

"No need for sorry," he says, kissing my forehead. "You're allowed to cry. You're allowed to have bad days. You don't have to be perpetually sunny."

I wipe my tears on my sleeve. "I'm okay, really."

I stand and walk over to Gigi's free-standing jewelry box. It sits under two rows of artfully displayed vintage hats. Everything from fascinators and berets to turbans and cloches. As a young child, I loved trying them on while Gigi applied her makeup. More tears threaten to spill, and I blink them away.

"Come over here," I say. "I want to show you the locket."

I open the lid. Pop's gold and diamond Hamilton pocket watch is lying beside his wedding ring.

Roddy picks up the watch. "Pop loved this watch."

"He did." Pop's ghost joins us in the room.

Roddy holds the watch by the chain and swings it back and forth in front of my face. "You are getting very sleepy."

We laugh at the memory. That's what Pop did every night before Gigi herded us to bed. Roddy replaces the watch in the box, and I close the lid and open the top drawer. Gigi's Art Deco platinum engagement ring sparkles between the foam pads, her wedding band wedged beside it. I pull out the engagement ring and try it on. The huge diamond covers most of the bottom part of my ring finger.

"Pop must've saved up for years to buy her this," I say.

"I'd say. It's got to be at least a carat."

Tears press at the back of my eyes, and I quickly slide the ring back into the drawer. "It's got to be in this one." I slide open the bottom drawer.

Gigi's gold heart locket is nestled in the foam padding. I lift up the delicate chain, and the heart sways at the end of it. "See." I show Roddy the locket. "Look at the initials."

"BF," he says.

"I thought it meant Best Friend, but now I think it stands for Beth Fry." I gently open the heart and find a faded forget-me-not inside.

"You might be right. I don't know how this gets us any closer to discovering Gigi's secrets, but let's call Mr. Davenport and see if that's what we needed to learn."

We head back to the kitchen and look up his number in the phone book. His secretary picks up on the first ring.

"Hi. This is Ruby Finch. Evie Collier's granddaughter. May I speak to Mr. Davenport?"

"One moment, please."

A few seconds later, Mr. Davenport comes on the line. "Hello, Ruby. I suspect you and your brother have deduced the significance of the first location."

"We have. Roddy's here with me."

"Hi, Mr. Davenport," Roddy yells.

I hold the phone receiver between our ears enabling Roddy to hear the conversation too.

"Hello back," he says politely. "So, if you'd be so kind, tell me the first location."

"Tollman Hat Factory," we say in unison.

"Well done. And the significance?"

Roddy motions for me to speak. "We believe our grandmother met her best friend, Elizabeth Fry, at the factory."

"Bravo. You are correct. May I assume you spread the first portion of Evie's ashes?"

Roddy answers. "We did. In the stream behind the store."

"Excellent. I am now able to provide you with puzzle number two."

"Can you email it to me now? We'd love to get started."

He chuckles. "Evie would approve of your enthusiasm. What's your email address?"

"MakeASplashEvents@aol.com."

"It will be sent momentarily. Good luck."

"Success!" I raise my hand for a high five.

Roddy slaps my hand. "Ready for round two?"

"Let's do it."

We enter Gigi's beloved library. The books filling the floor-to-ceiling shelves are old friends, and their woody smell is comforting. Roddy boots up the computer, and I browse the titles. Classics mingle with the latest thrillers. Harlequin romances are tucked between presidential biographies. Gigi read anything and everything and encouraged us to do the same.

The bottom shelves hold our memories: portfolios stuffed with drawings from our childhood art classes, scrapbooks showcasing certificates from awards we won and milestones we achieved, dozens of photo albums, yearbooks, and thirty-nine leather-bound ledgers (one for each year Pop and Gigi owned the store).

"Okay," Roddy says. "We're all set. Log in to your email."

I enter my password and find Mr. Davenport's email in my inbox. I double-click, and the next puzzle pops up along with the instructions: *Solve to find your next location.*

A	B	C	D	E	F	G	H	I	J	K	L	M	N	O	P	Q	R	S	T	U	V	W	X	Y	Z
X					K			N																	

```
          A                              I       A
 _  _  _  _  _     _  _  _  _  _  _  _  _     _  _  _  _  _  _
 B  B  T  O  X  Z  P  D  A  J  Z  N  A  X  I  U  A  J  Y  Y  I

                   F                    A
 _  _  _  _  _  _  _  _  _  _  _  _  _  _  _  _  _  _  _  _  _  _
 A  Y  R  Z  D  R  Y  K  Q  E  W  D  X  Z  Q  A  J  D  U  P  Z  E  P

       A        A
 _  _  _  _  _  _  _  _  _
 I  X  Z  A  X  U  P  D  R
```

1965

EVIE

"Mom, I can't do it. I just can't." Ella flung herself across the floral bedspread topping her twin bed and burst into tears. "I want to marry for love, not because I have to."

Evie tidied the desktop and hung some strewn clothes to give her temper time to cool before responding. "Ella," she said to the back of her child. "At this point, you need to marry for stability. For you and your unborn child."

Ella covered her head with her arms and sobbed into the comforter. "It's not fair to Roddy, and I'm too young."

Evie sat on the bed beside Ella and stroked her toffee blonde hair. "Roddy adores you. How many times did he propose?"

"A lot." Ella sniffled and pushed up to sitting.

"And he was thrilled when you finally accepted," Evie said, grasping her daughter's hand.

Ella's head dropped, and her shoulders slumped. "It'll be too hard."

Impatient with her whining, Evie stood and put her hands on her hips. "Ella Ann Collier, stop this pity party at once. Yes, you are young. Yes, marriage is hard, and raising a child is harder, but life is a series of tests. Without challenges, you'll never realize what you can become. Now, dry your tears and put on this wedding dress so I can alter it. You're going to be a beautiful, blushing bride and Roderick Finch, a doting groom."

Ella grudgingly slipped into the three-quarter-length sleeved empire-waist wedding gown. A crystal-embellished sash separated the fitted lace bodice from the full silk skirt. Pete passed Ella's bedroom as Evie fiddled with the pillbox hat and veil.

"Be still, my heart," he said, smiling with pride. "You are beautiful."

"Thank you, Daddy," Ella said with little enthusiasm.

"Why so mopey?" he asked.

Evie shot Ella a warning glance.

Ella sighed. "Growing up is bittersweet. I'll miss living here with you...and Mom."

Pete kissed each of Ella's cheeks. "We'll miss you too, but the door is always open. Roddy's a fine young man. You two will have a wonderful life. Just like your mother and me." He threw Evie a wink.

"Scoot," Evie said, nudging Pete out of the room. "We have a dress to fit."

Evie closed the door behind him. Once certain Pete was out of earshot, she took hold of Ella's upper arms and stared her straight in the eyes. "You will *not* mention any of this to your father. It would devastate him. Trust my plan. It's the best solution for all concerned."

Evie's sheer force of will made it impossible for Ella to disobey.

JUNE 2000

RUBY

I hear the rumble of Hank—Roddy's gas-guzzling red Jeep Cherokee—in front of my house. He's early for our excursion. We solved the cryptogram and are headed to the second location of Gigi's puzzle—Bowman Technical School, Corner of Duke & Chestnut, Lancaster. I wash down a blueberry muffin with a glass of milk, pull my curls into a ponytail, grab a light jacket, and almost head out my front door. Shoot! Forgot Gigi. I retrieve the sparkly pouch from my bedroom end table and pull another baggie full of ashes from my bread box. I dump her remains (as lovingly as you can dump) into the pouch. Tucking Gigi into my straw purse, I walk out the door.

Roddy jogs up the four steps and onto my boxwood-lined walkway. "Let's take the Jeep."

"And spew toxic emissions from your cracked muffler into the air? No thanks."

He scowls and heads towards Sally. I unlock the doors, put the top down, and pop a fresh daisy into the bud vase. He rolls his eyes.

"What's with the crankiness?" I ask.

"You mean besides dealing with your judginess?"

I stick out my tongue and start the engine.

"I saw Clara last night."

This is huge. He's been avoiding Clara like the plague.

"Why? Where?"

"I bumped into her at the grocery store."

"And?"

"And what?" he snaps.

This conversation is like picking my way through land mines. I take a moment to consider my words as I back out of my driveway onto the quiet street.

"And what?" he growls. "Spit it out."

I inhale and release my breath slowly. "From your...distress, I guess I thought you actually had a sit-down with her."

"Why the hell would I do that? I have nothing to say to her."

At a stoplight, I turn to face him. "Because of this," I say gently.

"Because of what?" he grits out through clenched teeth.

"Clara's effect on you. You get really wound up by a chance meeting. I mean, it's been almost a year. Maybe if you two cleared the air..."

When he caught Clara in flagrante delicto, anger, shame, and pain stole his words. He didn't confront her; he just threw his house key on the bed and walked out the front door. They've never talked about what happened. They simply dissolved their marriage.

Roddy stares straight ahead. The light turns green, and I turn onto Route 272. When I have the top down, I avoid the highway. I try to enjoy the mellow morning sun warming my cheeks, but Roddy's silent stewing is unsettling.

Fifteen minutes later, with his head hanging, he mutters, "You can't understand."

I feel the dig, but I suppose he's right. I've never had a long-term relationship. Maybe I'm too picky, but inevitably—a few months in—my fella's cute little quirks have become intolerable annoyances, and we stop dating.

"You're right," I admit. "I'm sorry to be judgy. There's no timetable for grief."

He gives my arm a brotherly punch signaling all is forgiven and changes the subject. "So, Bowman Technical School. Any guesses on what we'll find?"

I shrug. "Not a clue. I'm swamped with planning a huge anniversary party. I haven't had time to do any research about the school."

"Guess we'll find out soon enough."

From 272, I enter downtown on Duke Street. "Keep an eye out for Chestnut," I tell Roddy.

"There it is," he says.

I take a left and find a parking spot a block away from our destination, in front of Musser Park. Children's feet lift high as they soar upward on rows of swings. Their laughter carries happiness across the park, and Roddy and I smile. We raise Sally's top. Before locking the doors, I tuck my camera into my purse beside Gigi and grab a tablet and pen.

"Ready?" I ask.

"You bet."

We stroll the city sidewalk until we reach a three-story brick building on the corner of Duke and Chestnut. Two concrete steps lead to a four-panel white front door sporting a beautiful eucalyptus wreath. Yellow zinnias and vinca vines cascade from white window boxes. Other than a white-faced clock mounted on the left side of the building, it looks like a house, not a school.

"Is this it?" Roddy asks.

I shrug. Spotting a brass plaque under the clock, I take a closer look.

BOWMAN TECHNICAL SCHOOL

1877-1992

At this location: 1912-1979

"It was here," I say, pointing to the plaque. "But it moved in 79."

"Great. Now what?"

Before I answer, a hunched gray-haired man with a cane opens the front door. He startles when he sees us staring at the plaque.

"Can I help you?" His voice is hoarse like he's a three-pack-a-day smoker.

"Umm," I say. "My name is Ruby, and this is my brother Roddy. We're delving into our grandmother's history, and the Bowman Technical School had some significance to her."

"Not too many youngsters are interested in their elders' history. Good for you."

Being too close to middle age for comfort, I'm delighted he's called us youngsters.

"Can you tell us anything about the school?" I ask.

"Not really. My daughter bought the place in 1998. By then, it had been converted to offices. She did a complete overhaul, including getting rid of the giant front display windows. She only finished the project at the beginning of this year." He responds to the disappointment on my face. "I know the historical society on President Avenue houses the school's records and memorabilia. Start there."

Roddy and I look at one of the city maps scattered throughout downtown and determine the historical society is about a mile and a half away. We decide to walk. The sun beats down, and the breeze has stopped. Sweat trickles down my back, dampening my sundress. A mile into our trek, I notice a tiny café up ahead.

"How about a lemonade?"

"Yeah. I'm dying of thirst."

We pop in and order our drinks to go. As I step out of the café onto the sidewalk, I notice the familiar white-haired man with the grizzled beard walking behind us. We lock eyes, and he starts towards me and Roddy. I flinch and grab Roddy's arm. The man looks at my fingers, digging into Roddy's flesh. His shoulders droop, and he shakes his head. Roddy follows my gaze and spots the man just before he swerves down an alley.

"Hey," Roddy says. "I've seen that guy before." He hurries to the alley and disappears around the corner. Less than a minute later, he returns to the sidewalk. "He's gone."

"Gone?"

"Yeah. He must've ducked into a building or something, but the alley is empty."

"What do you mean you've seen him before?"

"Twice. First time, he was hanging on the corner of my apartment building. I figured he was waiting for a prescription from Royer's. But then I saw him again at Gigi's, the day I was spreading the mulch. He was staring at me from across the street."

I shiver. "I think he's watching us 'cause I've seen him too."

"Where?"

"First on my walkway."

"He was at your house? On your walkway?"

"Yeah. I was feeling queasy, and he saw me from the sidewalk. I thought he was just being helpful. And then I saw him again the day I met Marty at the *Intelligencer Journal* office."

"Weird." He rubs his forehead with concern.

We resume our walk with frequent looks over our shoulders.

"Marty thought he might be involved in Gigi's puzzle," I say, sipping my lemonade.

He crinkles his forehead and looks at me with disbelief. "You told Marty about the puzzle?"

"Yeah? What's wrong with that?"

"Considering we have no idea what we're going to find, I didn't think you'd be willing to air our potentially filthy laundry." He tosses his empty cup into a garbage can.

"I didn't share details. Just that we need to solve a puzzle."

"Good," he says with a nod.

"So, do you think Marty could be right? Does the white-haired guy have something to do with the puzzle?"

"That's actually a good guess. We only started seeing him after we opened the box."

"Should I be afraid?"

"I'd say cautious rather than afraid."

I finish my lemonade just as we reach the historical society building. Roddy and I are greeted by the welcoming docent standing behind the reception desk.

"Hello there! I'm Millicent. How can I help you today?" she asks, pushing her red-framed, cat-eye glasses to the tip of her wide nose.

"Hi, Millicent. I'm Ruby, and this is my twin brother, Roddy."

"Twins? I'm a twin, too," Millicent beams. "Myrtle's my sister's name. We look identical. Well, we did until I stopped dying my hair," she says with a laugh, pointing to her shoulder-length silver curls.

"Are you identical?" I ask.

"No, fraternal, but we looked enough alike we could fool anybody but our mom. We had the best time pulling pranks on our teachers. One time we swapped classes. I was supposed to be in English and Myrtle—" She stops mid-sentence. "Oh, mercy me! You're not here to listen to an old lady's ramblings."

Actually, I love to listen to old people. Old people and kids. They tend to be straightforward and genuine. Kids haven't learned to use pretense, and the elderly are wise enough not to bother.

"We've pulled our share of pranks too!" I say. "And our grandmother was a notorious prankster. That's actually why we're here. To research her past. She died recently." My voice catches, and tears prick my eyes. Lately, I'm a leaky faucet.

"Oh, you poor thing," she says, hurrying from behind the desk. She reaches her arms out to hug me and stops mid-lean like she's worried she's overstepping. I close the distance between us.

Squishy arms wrap around me, and loving hands pat my back. It's really nice.

Roddy clears his throat.

Millicent pulls back and rubs her hands up and down my arms. "It gets easier with time. I promise. Now, what do we want to find out about Granny?"

"We actually called her Gigi. We know the Bowman Technical School was important to her, and we'd like to learn all we can about it."

She claps her hands together. "You're in luck. We have a whole exhibit for B.T.S. Follow me."

Millicent leads us to the back corner of the research center. Glass-topped displays hold artifacts, and the walls are lined with books. She swoops her arm across a small side wall of shelves.

"All the books on those shelves are about the Bowman School and Watch Shop. So dig in."

"May I take pictures?" I ask.

"You may. Just no food or drink within the research center. Bathroom's up front and to the right, and you know where to find me if you need me."

When Millicent turns to leave, Roddy rolls his eyes.

"What?" I mouth silently.

He waits to speak until the door closes behind her. "I don't know how you do it."

"Do what?"

"You're like a magnet. People gravitate to you. A perfect stranger ends up hugging you within minutes."

I shrug. "I guess I'm good with people—just not men."

He tugs my ponytail. "You'll be fine with men when you find the right one."

I hang my purse and jacket over a chair. "Let's get to it."

I skim a biography of Ezra Bowman, the founder of the Bowman Technical School. The school taught watchmaking and repair, jewelry work, and engraving. Like the plaque said, from 1912 to 1979, the school occupied the top two floors of the Duke Street building. The bottom floor was Bowman's Watch & Jewelry Shop.

"Any luck?" Roddy asks.

"Nothing jumping out at me yet. Maybe Gigi went to school there."

"Don't think so. It was all men."

"Then Pop?" I suggest.

"Maybe. But if he did, he didn't use his skills."

Thinking of all the college grads waiting tables, I conclude that's not unusual.

I kneel on the floor to scan the lower bookshelves. "Jeez. There's three shelves of student roll books."

"Start when Pop would've been eighteen."

Hauling a stack of roll books to the table, I open the 1924 volume. The record is organized by courses: Fundamentals, Servicing, Repair, Escapement, Engraving, Welding, Design, and Sizing. There are at least forty different courses offered. After reading page after page of students' names in the roll books from 1924 through 1930, my eyes burn.

"Help me with this," I say.

Roddy grabs the 1931 volume, and I take 1932. A few pages in, he yells, "Here it is! Pete Collier."

I look over his shoulder. Pop's name is listed on the class roster for Fundamentals, Engraving, and Welding in 1931.

"I haven't found his name in the roll book for '30 or '32. It's a two-year course. Why is he only listed in '31?"

Roddy shrugs. "Dropped out? Failed out? Kicked out? I don't know."

"And what does this have to do with Gigi?"

Roddy slides the roll books back into their proper place on the shelves and pulls out *The History of Watchmaking in America.* "Keep digging."

I stand and stretch. "Be back in a few," I say to the back of Roddy's head.

He mumbles something unintelligible.

After a bathroom break, I wander out of the research center and into the lobby. Millicent is snacking on chocolate chip cookies and reading *The Autobiography of Benjamin Franklin*.

She extends a tin full of cookies. "Want one? Homemade."

"Please." I eagerly accept the cookie. "Delicious," I say after the first chewy, gooey bite.

"So? How goes it?"

I yawn. "Tedious."

"Maybe I can help. What are you looking for?"

"More than just facts."

"Aah." She rubs her palms together and waggles her eyebrows. "Scandal and intrigue. The juicy stuff."

I laugh at her antics. "Exactly! Know any about the school?"

"I do!" A Cheshire cat grin curls the corner of her lips.

I lean my elbows on the reception desk. "I'm all ears."

"So, you're aware that Ezra Bowman was the founder?"

"Yep. Just skimmed his biography."

"Well." She dramatically tilts her head and places her fingertips on her chin. "It's rumored that Ezra's third son, George, is actually his daughter, Georgette."

"What?"

"Yes, back then, women weren't allowed to learn trades, but supposedly Georgette had an immense natural talent for watchmaking. Her father taught her at night after classes ended for the day. Georgette was shortened to George, and she became the never-seen but highly regarded master watchmaker for the Bowman Watch Shop."

"Wow. On so many levels."

"Any help?" Millicent asks hopefully.

Maybe George/Georgette and Gigi were friends? "Possibly. Keep talking."

"Well, there was an unsolved jewelry heist."

My ears perk up. "Go on."

"In the early thirties, I can't recall the exact year, the Bowman Watch Shop was robbed. The thieves stole everything—including customers' pieces waiting for cleaning and repair. Not only did the Bowmans lose all their merchandise, they had to replace what their customers had lost. It almost bankrupted them."

"Didn't they have insurance?"

"Apparently not. It was during the Depression, so I assume they let it lapse."

I think about Pop's gold pocket watch and Gigi's giant diamond ring. Could they be the spoils of a robbery?

"Can you find out the exact date?"

"It should be in our database. Let me look it up." Millicent's fingers fly over the keyboard. "Aah. Here it is. September 12, 1931. We have the newspaper article on microfilm. Would you like me to queue it up?"

"Please!"

I follow Millicent back to the research center, where Roddy is still plowing through the fusty books. At the microfilm readers, she pulls out the appropriate reel and flips to the article. "There you go."

"Thanks!"

Millicent returns to her desk.

"Roddy, come take a look."

He pulls his head out of a worn ledger and joins me. After reading the article, I snap a photo of it and look at Roddy.

His mouth hangs open in disbelief. "Could he? It'd be a pretty good reason to drop out of the school if you just robbed their store."

It's really disconcerting to think your sweet, fun-loving, sometimes doddery grandpa could've committed a jewelry heist—and gotten away with it!

"Don't forget," I say, grasping at a justification. "It was during the Depression. Maybe his family was starving. Or maybe he was like Robin Hood, robbing from the rich to give to the poor."

Roddy forms his hands into spectacles and holds them up to his eyes. "Rose-colored."

"You know a legitimate motive is just as likely as greed," I say, miffed.

He rolls his eyes.

"Wait." Roddy jumps up. "The date of the robbery was September 12, 1931. I think I saw Pop's name in the rolls past that."

He runs over and pulls the 1931 student roll book from the shelf and flips to the back. "Yep! He was in attendance in welding class on December 20th. More than three months after the robbery."

"See," I say with conviction. "I bet he had nothing to do with it."

Roddy's not the only person I'm trying to convince.

***

After another hour of poring through the school's history, the only additional thing we've found is a 1931 yearbook photo of Pop.

Millicent makes us a photocopy and an offer. "Give me your email. I volunteer here three days a week and would love a project to keep me busy. If I find anything else about your grandparents, I'll let you know."

We give her our grandparents' names and my email, and she gives us a handful of chocolate chip cookies. We think we have gained enough information about the school, but a big dilemma remains. Where are we going to spread Gigi's ashes? Roddy's certain the owner of the house won't want us to spread Gigi on her property.

"It doesn't hurt to ask," I say as we walk to Duke Street. "The worst that can happen is she says no."

"Well, if ever there's a time to get strangers to love you, this is it."

I playfully bump my shoulder against his. "But no pressure, right?"

When we reach the house, I rap three times with the brass grandfather clock door knocker. I hear shuffling inside, and a few moments later, the gray-haired man opens the door.

"You again," he rasps.

"It is," I say with my biggest smile. "We have a huge favor to ask."

"Who is it, Dad?" a woman calls from inside the house.

"Those kids I told you about," he croaks out.

Gotta love his description of us.

A middle-aged brunette appears at the door, looking harried. "Can I help you?" she snaps.

"Hi. We met your dad earlier today. I'm Ruby, and this is my twin brother, Roddy. Our grandmother passed a few weeks ago, and we are on a quest to honor her deathbed wish."

Okay, okay, so I embellish a little.

Her eyes soften, and she puts her hand on her dad's shoulder. "I'm sorry for your loss, but how does it involve us?"

Cue the violins.

"This," I spread my arms to encompass her home, "was where it all began. My grandmother's grand love affair. She met our grandfather, and it was love at first sight."

It absolutely could be true! In fact, I've decided it is.

I continue. "All she wanted was for her ashes to be spread where she met her great love. Where she met the man who changed her life. Is there any chance you'd allow us to fulfill her last wish?"

Excitement lights the woman's eyes. "What were your grandparents' names?"

"Evie and Pete Collier."

She covers her mouth in shock. "Oh, my God! Come with me." She leads us around the corner of the building and through an antique iron gate that opens into a lush courtyard. "You have to see this."

We follow her to a new concrete bench under an old willow tree.

"Look," she says, pointing to the trunk of the tree.

A crude heart carved into the bark encircles the letters PC + EF.

Roddy's eyes widen. "Our grandma's maiden name was Fisher."

I trace the letters and let bittersweet tears fall. "This is amazing."

"When I first moved here and needed a break from the chaos of demolition, I'd sit on this bench and make up stories about the lovers who carved this. And now I know." She clasps her hands in front of her and smiles at Roddy and me. "You may absolutely spread your grandmother's ashes here, but I have one request."

"And what's that?" Roddy asks.

"Would you send me a photo of your grandparents? I'd love to be able to connect faces to the carving."

I'm moved by her sentimentality. "Of course. I have your address, but what is your name?"

"Claire Martin."

"I'll mail it first thing tomorrow, and thank you. This means the world to us."

"Well," she says. "I'll leave you to it. Take as much time as you need; just close the gate when you go."

"I didn't expect to find this." Roddy sits on the bench. "Maybe Pop really doesn't have anything to do with the robbery. Maybe the significance is just like you said—love at first sight."

I sit beside my brother. "Told you. I can see just fine out of my rose-colored glasses."

"For today, but we *are* going to discover a secret about Gigi—and maybe Pop—that may make us not want our inheritance. We may come to question all we thought we knew about them. You need to prepare yourself for that."

"For today, I don't have to. For today, I'm going to sprinkle her ashes under a romantic willow tree and imagine them dancing in heaven."

JUNE 2000

RUBY

After popping a photo of Gigi and Pop in the mail to Claire Martin as promised, I call Mr. Davenport. Roddy and I both have busy days, but we're hoping to work on deciphering the next clue tonight after work.

"Hi, Mr. Davenport, this is Ruby Finch," I say when he comes on the line.

"Well, hello. Delightful to hear from you. May I assume you've gleaned the necessary information?"

"Yes. I believe so. We learned that Pop was a student at the Bowman Technical School in 1931, and we found Pop and Gigi's initials carved in a tree trunk. That leads us to believe the location is significant because it is where Pop and Gigi met."

"Correct. And?"

"And?" I ask. "You mean we need more?"

"Precisely."

Tingles of dismay pulse through my body. I'm afraid "the more" is the robbery. I curl my fingers into a fist and tense my muscles. "Were Pop and Gigi involved in the Bowman Watch & Jewelry Shop robbery?"

I hold my breath waiting for his answer.

"No."

I exhale and relax with relief but tense again when I realize we need more information to receive the next clue. I remember the rumor about Ezra Bowman's third child.

"Okay, does it have something to do with the George/Georgette rumors?"

Mr. Davenport chuckles. "It does not, but I'm impressed with your diligence. As an interesting aside, in the twenties, watches crafted by George Bowman were in high demand, not only because of their superior quality but because of the scandal surrounding her identity."

"So, George was Georgette?"

"Indeed."

"But that has nothing to do with Gigi's puzzle?"

"Unfortunately not. I hope you and your brother didn't expect this to be easy. Your grandmother always emphasized the importance of challenging one's self."

"Believe me; I have years of firsthand knowledge."

"I'm sure you do. We'll speak again when you have more to add." The phone clicks when he hangs up.

Crap! We thought we had gathered enough. I really want to do more digging, but I have a meeting with Janet in an hour, and I'm still in pajamas. After a quick shower, I slip into a comfy green and white checked shirt dress and white canvas slides. I swipe on mascara and a touch of lip gloss and let my damp curls roam free. Grabbing my leather portfolio, I double-check I have everything I need for the meeting: fabric swatches, music playlists, décor ideas, sample menus, and the all-important storyboard. For every shindig I plan, I create a storyboard to help my client visualize how the event will unfold. It assures we're on the same page.

Thirty minutes later, I slide into a cozy cardigan (this time, I'm prepared) and enter the glacial *Intelligencer* building. Janet and I planned to meet over lunch. Shortly after the receptionist rings her office, a frazzled Janet appears.

She runs her hand through her ruffled hair. "Ruby, I'm so sorry. I'm going to have to cancel. An article got pulled last minute, and I've got to write a new one within the next ninety minutes. I should've called, but in the chaos, I forgot we were meeting."

I keep my irritation under wraps. "No problem. How about I leave this with you?" I say, holding up my portfolio. "You can take a look when things calm down."

"Yes, yes. Perfect. Thanks for understanding." She grabs my leather case and heads towards her office. "I'll call you," she yells over her shoulder.

I'm annoyed and hungry. I hate eating in restaurants alone, so I guess I'll go through the Wendy's drive-through on the way home. As I'm stepping through the door, I hear a man yell, "Ruby! Hey! Wait up!" It's Marty.

He trots over to me. "Fancy meeting you here."

He's all smiles in his rumpled shirt and loosened tie. His buoyancy makes it hard to be irritable.

"Hi, Marty. I was here to meet Janet for lunch, but she had to cancel."

"Well, you're in luck. I was just heading out for a bite, and it's my turn to treat. Shall we?" he asks, offering his arm.

I link my arm through his and laugh. "We shall."

"So, have you solved the puzzle?" he asks as we stroll down the sidewalk arm-in-arm.

I roll my eyes and laugh. "Oh, no. Gigi wouldn't dare make it easy. We've only solved one part—five to go."

The sidewalks are bustling with folks taking advantage of the glorious summer day. We pass a pig-tailed toddler whose face is covered in chocolate from her melting ice cream cone. A dog walker tries to rein in her mismatched pack, consisting of a dachshund, a pitbull, a miniature poodle, and a Bernese mountain dog. I hear the clicking of wheels over pavement and then, "ON YOUR LEFT!"

Marty pulls me towards him. A teenage skateboarder narrowly misses me as he bullies his way through the pedestrians.

"Thanks," I say.

He brushes off his imaginary lapels, puffs out his chest, and puts his hand on his hips. "All in a day's work."

I laugh and lift my finger up and down as I point to his stance. "So, you're the town sheriff saving a damsel in distress?"

"Nope." He hoists up his pants and sniffs in a deep breath à la Barney Fife. "Just your garden-variety superhero."

"Well, come on, Mighty Marty-Man, after your brave rescue, let's get you fed."

He rubs his chin between his fingers. "Hmm. Mighty Marty-Man. It's got a nice ring to it."

We continue walking, weaving through the crowd of lollygaggers (Did you hear that, Gigi? Ten points for lollygaggers.) Three food trucks are lined up across the street: Sizzle, Creamporium, and Paul-strami on Rye.

"Marty, have you ever tasted Paul-strami's—" I stop mid-sentence.

The white-haired man is in line at Sizzle. He is definitely following me, and I want to know why. Without thinking, I start to jaywalk across the street. I check for cars but somehow miss a bicycler. As I step out between two parked cars, he runs smack into me. I hear the screech of car tires as I'm knocked to the ground. When I land, I'm on the road beside the biker with my leg stuck between the twisted frame and wheel. A few onlookers, including the white-haired man, run to help me. As he closes the space between us, I see it's not even the same man. Jeez! I got creamed by a bike for nothing.

Marty is by my side before anyone else gets to me. "Ruby! Are you okay?"

"Fine! Fine! Check on the rider!" I yell. I can't free my leg, so I twist my body to face the bike rider. "Oh, my God! I'm so sorry! Are you okay? Should we call an ambulance?"

Marty helps the bicycler stand up. The man dusts off his cycling outfit. "I'm fine. Just a few scrapes. I think *you* may need the ambulance." He points to my leg.

My shin is smeared with blood and gravel, but I don't feel any pain.

Marty pulls out his phone. "I'll call one now."

"No!" I yell. "This isn't ambulance worthy. Will you drive me?"

"Yeah. Sure. Of course. But my car's in the parking garage."

"We'll get her leg out," the bicycler says. "You get your car."

Marty pats his chest and pockets like he's searching his body. "Keys. I need my keys." He pulls them from his pocket. "Got them. Okay. Be back in a jiffy."

A few Good Samaritans are directing traffic around me.

"I'm Michael," the rider says. "I'm going to stabilize the wheel so you can ease your leg out."

"Thanks, Michael. I'm Ruby, and I feel absolutely horrible. I'm so sorry. It was all my fault."

"Accidents happen." He braces the wheel with both hands, and I gently slide my leg out. "Can you stand?"

"I think so. It really doesn't hurt."

He gets behind me and lifts me to standing. "Try to put a little weight on it."

I put my foot down and add a little weight. "Seems fine. I don't think anything's broken."

Now that my leg is free, I can see the damage. Multiple scrapes and cuts crisscross the lower half of my leg. Gravel is embedded in my raw skin, and blood seeps from the wounds. Michael helps me to the front steps of a rowhome, and I sit down. He drags his mangled bike from the street and pulls alcohol wipes from his saddlebag. Traffic on the street starts flowing freely again.

"Thank you," I yell and wave to the gentleman who was directing traffic.

He smiles, nods, and gets back in line for a pastrami sandwich.

"Press this against the cut to stop the bleeding," Michael says, handing me the wipe.

"Yeow! Feels like a thousand bee stings!"

"Sorry. Should've warned you."

With my free hand, I dig my wallet, a pen, and a crumpled Turkey Hill Mini Mart receipt from my purse. I write down my email and phone number and pull out my driver's license. "Here's my contact info." I hand the receipt and license to Michael. "Email me an estimate to fix your bike. Are you sure you're okay? Do you want to go to the hospital just to be safe?"

"No. Really, I'm fine." He returns my license, and I slide it back into my wallet. "I'll get you the estimate in the next week or two."

How was I lucky enough to dart in front of the nicest guy in the world?

"Well, do you need a ride somewhere?" I ask.

"Nope. Got that covered." He wiggles his phone in the air. "Texted my husband. He's on his way."

Marty returns, panting for breath. "Okay, I'm double-parked. Let me help you into the car."

Marty pulls me up to stand.

"Thank you so much, Michael," I say as I limp to the car. "I'm so sorry I ruined your day."

He shrugs his shoulders. "Not ruined, just a blip. Take care of yourself, Ruby."

I climb into Marty's Toyota Corolla, and he straps me in like I'm a child, then jumps into the driver's seat.

"The ER, right?" he asks.

"Yes, please."

He's white-knuckling the steering wheel and driving too fast.

I touch his arm. "No hurry. The bleeding has slowed. I'm going to be fine."

He nods. "Should I call your brother?"

"No. It's not a big deal. I bet I won't even need stitches."

The waiting room in the ER is empty, so a nurse takes me right back.

"I'll be right here." Marty plops into an orange padded vinyl chair.

Since I'm wearing a dress, I don't need to change into a hospital gown. I bite my lower lip and squeeze my eyes shut as the nurse tweezes out the gravel and douses my leg in antiseptic. Once the dirt and smeared blood are wiped away, the injury looks much less serious. One cut is about an inch long, and the rest are only bad brush burns.

"I think Steri-Strips will do it." The nurse applies three to close the cut. When she finishes getting my medical history and account of the accident, she turns to leave. "The doctor will be in shortly."

"Shortly, as in now," the doctor says as she enters the room. "I'm Dr. Grant." She scans the nurse's notes. "Okay, let's have a look." She gives my leg a cursory examination. "The cut will heal fine. Barely a scar. However, because of the nature of your accident, I'd like to get an X-ray. To be safe."

"Sounds good," I agree.

The X-rays take less than ten minutes. When they've finished, the nurse wheels me back into the bay and I ask, "Everything okay?"

"The doctor will take a look. I'm sure she'll be in shortly to give you the results."

"Could my friend, Marty, wait with me?" My leg's starting to ache, and I could use a distraction.

"Sure. I'll buzz for the front desk to send him back."

Less than a minute later, Marty peeks around the curtain. "You rang?" he says in a Lurch-like voice.

He's so dorky—exactly what I need right now.

"Come in." I motion for him to enter the room.

Somehow he gets tangled in the curtains as he tries to push them aside, and I crack up. He's already taking my mind off of the pain. After he settles into the plastic bedside chair, he bops his head and shoulders up and down—all cool and casual—like a pathetic imitation of Eminem.

"So how's things?"

I shake my head in laughter. "You're killing me. You've got to stop with the bad impersonations. They're worse than your jokes."

He grabs his chest like he's pulling out a knife. "I'm wounded."

I reach out and take hold of his hand. "In all seriousness, thanks. You really were Mighty Marty-Man."

He blushes and squeezes my fingers. "In all seriousness, you're welcome."

We sit quietly, holding hands until the nurse pops in. "The X-ray films aren't up yet, but in the meantime, the doc ordered a prescription of Tylenol with Codeine. You can take one now if you'd like."

I want one—the burning pain has changed to a throbbing ache—but I have to drive home, and I'm sure it will make me sleepy. "I'm going to have to drive. Could I have ibuprofen now and take the Tylenol Codeine later."

"Absolutely. Be right back."

"Is the pain bad?" Marty asks.

The nurse scoots back into my bay. "Here you go."

Once I swallow the pill, the nurse is back out on the ER floor.

I shift in the bed. "Like a six. But I know my pain tolerance is really low, so it'd probably be a four for anyone else."

"Not me." He laughs. "Don't tell anyone, but Mighty Marty-Man tears up from a hangnail."

Most guys I've met would *never* admit to being a wimp about pain. I love his self-confidence.

"I like you, Marty Metzger," I blurt out.

"I like you, too, Ruby Finch."

Jeez. Now, what should I say? I heat up with self-consciousness. Thank goodness Mighty Marty-Man once again saves the day.

"Well, since I'm banned from entertaining you with my witty imitations." He leans back in the uncomfortable chair and crosses his right ankle over his left knee. "How about we work on your grandmother's puzzle? I'm pretty good at Clue. Let's give it a shot."

"Clue's my favorite game! I'm always Miss Scarlet, and my grandmother was Mrs. Peacock. Who are you?"

"Professor Plum, of course."

"Naturally," I agree.

I fill Marty in on the specifics of Gigi's last puzzle and what we've found out so far.

"So it's not about the robbery or the stifling of female talent, and it's more than just the location where they met?" he reiterates.

"Correct."

"Maybe it has to do with his classmates or teachers."

"Hmm." I squeeze my lower lip as I think. "Maybe. We do have a copy of a yearbook photo. I could do more research."

"Or maybe." He taps his finger on his chin. "Maybe it's about what he learned while he was there."

Marty's last thought resonates, but I can't figure out why. A memory lurks just out of reach.

The doctor strides into the room, flipping pages on a clipboard. "Good news, Ruby." She notices Marty. "Oh! Hi, I'm Dr. Grant."

"Marty Metzger." He stands up and shakes her hand.

"The X-ray is clean. No breaks. Most likely, the pain will worsen overnight and into tomorrow, so I've given you enough Tylenol Codeine for forty-eight hours. After that, use regular Tylenol and ibuprofen. You should gently clean the road rash, apply antibiotic ointment, and cover it with a fresh gauze bandage daily for a week. Let the Steri-Strips come off on their own, probably in ten to fourteen days. Any questions?"

"No. Thank you, Doctor."

She pats my foot and smiles. "No more running out into traffic. The nurse will bring in the discharge papers. Take care."

Marty gives an exaggerated wipe of his forehead with the back of his hand. "Whew! That was the most exciting lunch I never had."

"I'm a memorable non-date," I say with a wink.

"Without a doubt." He starts to say something else but drops his head and fidgets with his fingers. He clears his throat and looks at me. "Speaking of dates, the Main Theater in Ephrata is screening *Saturday Night Fever* next Thursday. It'd be good research for Janet's party. Whaddya say? Will you go with me?"

I pretend to look aghast. "You're asking me out on a date during an ER visit while I'm still in a hospital bed?"

"What? Bad timing?" he deadpans.

Even in this cold, sterile environment, Marty has me feeling warm and fuzzy.

"Yes. I'll go with you as long as there are no John Travolta impersonations planned."

"Deal," he says.

The nurse enters the ER bay and goes over everything the doctor just told me. Within minutes, I've signed the discharge papers and am in Marty's car on the way back to his office. He drives me to Sally's spot in the parking garage and rushes around his Corolla to open the door for me.

"Well, thanks." I feel shy.

I think he does too. "You bet. Um, see you in a week."

He extends his hand for a shake as I lean in for a hug. I'm embarrassed and pull back. He's embarrassed and leans forward. We laugh at our mutual awkwardness.

"Fist bump it is." He holds out his curled hand.

I bump my hand to his and unlock Sally's door. "Till Thursday."

Why does seven days seem so far away?

***

"I can't believe you didn't call me," Roddy yells as he paces around my living room.

As expected, as soon as he heard about my misadventure, he came rushing over.

"Don't make a big deal out of it. I'm fine. I shouldn't have gone to the hospital. I didn't even need real stitches."

I wiggle into my comfy, white slip-covered couch and tuck my polka-dot throw pillows under my injured leg.

"And who is this Marty guy?" he asks, chest puffed with brotherly concern. "I'm hearing his name an awful lot. Are you dating?"

"Jeez, Roddy. Enough with the interrogation. Do you want to discuss *your* dating life—or, more accurately—lack of a dating life?"

He shoots me a dirty look but gets the point. "Touché."

"Will you fix me a cup of herbal tea?" I ask, milking his concern.

As he putters around in the kitchen, I say, "So, to distract me from the pain, Marty and I hashed out what we know about Bowman Tech."

He pops the tea bag into the mug and waits for sunny Miss Bennet to whistle a happy tune. "And?"

"And something he said struck home, but I can't figure out why."

Roddy leans against the kitchen counter. "What was that?"

"He said maybe the significance of the school is what Pop learned."

"Watchmaking? Engraving? Welding?"

I throw my legs off the couch and sit up. "Welding! That's it!"

"That's what? You're going to have to give me more."

"Do you remember our neighbor, Malcolm's, high school graduation party?"

He scrunches his face to think. "Vaguely. Wasn't his mom Gigi's bridge partner?"

"Yep." I nod. "Anyway. At the party, his parents and Gigi and Pop were discussing what Malcolm was going to do after high school. They said he was going to a technical school to learn to weld."

Miss Bennet announces the water's ready. After Roddy pours the hot water over the tea bag and sets the steeping tea on the crackled powder-blue chest that serves as my coffee table, he joins me on the couch.

"So?" Roddy asks.

"So. Pop responded with 'Solid choice. Welding was responsible for all we have.'"

Roddy furrows his brows. "Pop wasn't a welder."

"Exactly, and that's what Malcolm's dad said. 'Pete, I didn't know you were a welder,' and then Gigi chimed in, 'He's not.' Gigi and Pop looked at each other and burst out laughing, and Gigi said to Malcolm's dad, 'Sorry, inside joke.'"

Roddy looks more confused. "We were like ten. Why do you remember that, and what are you getting at?"

Citrus-scented steam spirals up from my clementine tea. I hold the warm cup between my hands and take a sip.

"I remember because later, I asked Gigi what an inside joke was. When I found out, I thought it was so cool because you and I share so many."

Roddy flips his hands palms up and raises his eyebrows. "Okay?"

"Don't you see? Pop said welding was responsible for all he and Gigi had. That's why Bowman Tech is significant. That's where he learned to weld."

"I still don't get it. He wasn't a welder. How can Pop learning that skill be important to Gigi?"

"Well, I haven't figured it all out yet, but I'm sure I'm right. I'm going to call Mr. Davenport."

"Fine by me. Worst he can say is you're wrong."

My call to Mr. Davenport confirmed the second bit of info we needed to acquire was Pop was trained in welding (specifically acetylene welding) and earned us another clue. Mr. Davenport's email has just arrived in my inbox, and I open it and see two characters. 绿龙

"Jeez, Gigi," I complain to the heavens. "Could you make it any more difficult?"

"Her clues are increasingly abstruse," he says smugly.

"Look at you." I give him a friendly punch on the shoulder. "Way to slip in one of her favored words."

He sighs, "Yeah, but this time it's not gonna earn me any brownie points."

"Well," I say as I study the characters. "I'm guessing it's either Chinese, Japanese, or Korean."

"Yep."

My stomach growls, and I hobble over to the fridge to scrounge for dinner. "Want some scrambled eggs?"

Roddy joins me in the kitchen. "I'll make it. You rest." He grabs eggs, cheese, spinach, and black olives. "How about an omelet?"

"Yum!" I fix myself another cup of tea and limp into the living room. Snatching my pink chenille throw from the back of my aqua-blue chair, I snuggle into the couch and prop up my leg. The wound is really starting to pound.

"Roddy, would you bring me one of the pain pills from my purse and a glass of water."

"Sure." He fills a glass with tap water and grabs my purse from the table. "Here."

I dig out a pill and swallow it and settle back into the couch. Roddy goes back into the kitchen to continue cooking.

"Do any of the teachers at your school teach Asian languages?"

He looks up from the pan. "The school offers only French, German, and Spanish, but Allen Marsdale, he's the Spanish teacher and one of the guys I shoot hoops with on Wednesdays—"

"Yeah, yeah," I interrupt. "The tall guy with the spiky blond hair?"

"Yep. Anyway, I think he speaks a bunch of different languages. Email it to me, and I'll ask him."

I forward the email to Roddy and to Marty. It's possible he or one of his colleagues might be able to translate. Oh, who am I trying to fool? I just want an excuse to contact him.

MAY 1978

EVIE

The buzzer sounded when Evie pushed through the glass door into the Bowman Watch & Jewelry Shop. It was like stepping back in time. The air was still stale and stuffy, and the same glass showcases displayed watches, rings, and brooches. Edwin, an old classmate of Pete's, stood behind the counter. He got squattier and grayer every time Evie saw him.

"Evie!" He waddled from behind the counter to greet her with a hug and peck on each cheek. "You look younger every time I see you. How is that man of yours?"

"Pete's well. I've brought his watch for oiling and cleaning."

Edwin examined the watch through his jeweler's loupe. "His prized possession—1930s decagon-shaped Hamilton. He went to great lengths to get this beauty," he said with a wink.

"He surely did," Evie said and squeezed his hand.

"I'm surprised old Pete won't clean it himself."

Evie chuckled. "You, of all people, know how wretched his watch maintenance skills are."

"True, true." Edwin's beer belly bounced when he laughed. "He failed out of our Fundamentals class and quit Repair and Maintenance within a week. But he was a master at welding."

"Highest score in the class," Evie bragged.

"Yeah, I barely squeaked by. I thought for sure Pete would go into defense contracting or some field to use his skills."

Oh, he used his skills all right, just in unexpected ways.

Evie checked the time. "I hate to run, but I need to pick the twins up from school."

"How are the tykes?"

"Not tykes anymore. They're almost teenagers."

He slapped his palms on the glass counter. "No. Can't be. Don't you wish we could stop time? Or at least slow it down?"

She thought about her madcap life. "Not me. I can't wait to find out what's next! But I really must run." She blew him a kiss. "Call me when I can pick up the watch."

"Will do. Give Pete my best," Edwin called as she strode out the door.

***

Evie pulled her 1974 candy-apple red convertible Ford Mustang into the pickup line at Ephrata Middle School. Knowing how much she hated the wood-paneled station wagon and how much she hated aging, Pete surprised her with it on her sixtieth birthday.

Children rushed out of the school doors into the waiting yellow buses. Their laughter and shrieks jollied the air. Eager little faces peered out the bus window. Evie flicked through the radio stations, stopping when she heard the chorus of "Hot Child in the City." As she sang along, she noticed a red-haired man staggering down Academy Drive towards the middle school. He weaved, stumbled, and would've fallen if a telephone pole hadn't been within his reach. Fully loaded, the buses began their route, and the line of parents' cars inched forward. The man stepped off the sidewalk and into the school's yard. *Dear God, it's Donald.*

Frantic, Evie threw the car in park and flung open the door. Her heels sunk in the mud as she dashed across the grass to stop him.

"Evelyn," he slurred, "Ish marvelush to shee you."

"You're drunk," she hissed. "And you shouldn't be here. We had a deal."

He swayed and pointed a wobbling finger. "I wanna new one. Didja hear me?" he said, taking a lurching step towards her. "I wanna new deal."

"Leave! Now!" she growled and pushed on his chest.

He toppled to the ground. A teacher spotted them and rushed over.

"Mrs. Collier, is everything all right?"

"I'm fine," she said, straightening her shirt. "But this man is obviously intoxicated. I was concerned for his welfare and, of course, that of the children." She gestured to the students waiting at the entrance.

Donald's head rolled from side to side as he tried to sit up.

"I'll get us some help." The teacher used a walkie-talkie to call for assistance.

After a few incoherent mumbles, Donald flopped on his back and passed out. His mouth was hanging open and leaked drool down the side of his cheek. Evie saw Roddy and Ruby exit the school just as the local police arrived to deal with Donald. She returned to her car and pulled up to the curb in front of them.

"Shotgun," Roddy yelled and climbed into the passenger side.

Ruby scrambled in the back seat. "Gigi, is the man you were talking to okay? He looked sick."

"Yes, he's sick." *Inasmuch as degeneracy is a sickness.*

Ruby turned around in her seat and looked out the back window. "Why are the police taking him? Why not an ambulance?"

Evie shuddered at the thought of Donald being so close to the twins. "Because he's also a very bad man."

JUNE 2000

RUBY

"Don't forget her ashes," Roddy reminds me as I tie my Nikes.

I pat the outside of my straw bag. "Already in my purse. It's a beautiful day. Let's walk."

"Are you sure you should," he asks, pointing to my bandaged leg.

I wiggle my leg all around. "Sure am. It feels fine. I didn't even use all of the pain pills."

"Suits me," he agrees.

We head out, stopping on the front porch to lock my cheery yellow door. Feisty wrens chirp from their perch in my lilac bush. The blooms have mostly browned and shriveled, but their sweet scent still lingers in the air.

Roddy's colleague was able to translate the Chinese characters: Green Dragon, which is a well-known market only a mile from my house. It's only open on Fridays and boasts everything from fresh produce, seafood, meats, and candies to T-shirts, handmade crafts, knock-off bags, and dollar trinkets.

"This location's got me stumped. Gigi hated going there." Roddy says.

"Yeah," I agree. "Too touristy for her."

"And too much folderol."

I raise my hand for a high five, "Another ten points. You're killing it!"

He slaps my hand and winks.

"Maybe it has to do with one of the vendors?" I suggest as we turn onto State Street.

He shrugs. "I guess we'll know it when we see it. Let's spread her ashes from the footbridge. You know, the one across the street from the entrance."

"Oh, I love that bridge!" After yoga class, I purposely drive past it because it's so picturesque, especially in the winter. The black limbs of the silhouetted maple trees bow over the bridge, and the water reflects the color of pastel sunsets. "That'll be perfect."

The sidewalk ends, and we're forced to hug the shoulder as car after car from Jersey, Maryland, and New York roll into the market's parking lot. When there's a lull, we cross the street and walk onto the arched stone bridge. Cows graze in the field behind it, and a frog croaks from the bank of the stream. I pull out the sequined pouch, and with each of us holding a corner, we pour Gigi into the water.

"This just makes this spot all the more special." After tucking the pouch back into my purse, I blow a kiss into the air. "Love you," I say to Gigi, wherever she is.

"It's getting easier," Roddy says.

I nod. "It is. It's starting to feel more like we're honoring her rather than losing her."

"Probably her point."

"Probably," I agree. "Onward." I jerk my head towards the crowded market. "Let's see what mysteries we'll uncover."

We cross the street and enter Green Dragon's flea market portion. Rows of pop-up canopies of all sizes and colors are lined up side-by-side for the length of a football field. The din of hundreds of haggling customers, crowding the dusty gravel aisles, grates me. I may hate this place more than Gigi did.

Roddy and I walk up and down the rows, scanning each booth in hopes something will strike a chord. When the boxes of hinges, tarps spread with used sports equipment, tables full of mismatched glassware, and racks full of T-shirts become a giant jumbled heap in my mind, I suggest we move inside.

We stop and buy a green pint box of blueberries from an Amish farmer to munch as we wander inside the long market buildings. Hundreds of scents—barbecue, pies, candles, soaps, seafood—merge into one overwhelming smell.

I cover my nose with my hand. "I gotta get out of here. It's too much." I say to Roddy.

"Find a seat outside. I'll call you when I'm done browsing through all the buildings."

"Just text me."

He rolls his eyes and sighs. "I'll call. Cell phones are new enough; I haven't figured out texting yet."

I shake my head. "And you're the teacher. You've got to get with the times, brother. Okay. *Call* me."

I weave through the mass of people and find an empty picnic table near the Fink's French Fries truck. Their fries—sprinkled with salt and vinegar—are a Lancaster County tradition, and a line of customers snakes around the food truck. Though I love vinegar-topped fries, the pungent scent overwhelms my already over-stimulated nose. As I'm searching for a seat farther away, I spot the white-haired man. (This time, I'm *sure* it's him.) This is more than a coincidence. Concern tightens my stomach, but I'm frustrated with this cat-and-mouse game. He's following us, and—good or bad—I'm going to find out why.

I crisscross through the tourists towards him. He spots me and freezes. I'm close enough to see his intense green eyes and the strawberry-blonde whiskers interwoven throughout his otherwise snowy white beard. He jerks his head to the right, indicating we should move out of the crowd. I follow his lead.

Once we're off to the side, I square my shoulders and jump right in.

"Why are you following us?" I demand.

His handwringing conveys nervousness. He sucks in a deep breath as if girding himself to speak. "My name is Donald Fraser. I was a friend of your grandmother."

"So you are involved in Gigi's puzzle."

Confusion flickers across his face. "Puzzle?"

"Teak box. Clues to locations important to Gigi. Spreading ashes. Ringing a bell?"

"No." He pauses and rubs his chin.

"Well, if not for the puzzle, why are you here?"

"I came because I saw her obituary."

Apprehension skitters up my spine, and I second-guess my decision to move out of the crowd. "Following us around is a strange way to offer condolences."

My phone rings. It's Roddy. "Hello."

"Where are you?" he asks.

"By the stables. In the back."

"Okay. I'll meet you there," he says and hangs up.

I look up at Donald. "That was my brother, Roddy. He'll be here in a sec."

Apparently, in the minute it took for me to answer my phone, something clicked for Donald. His uncertainty is gone, his shoulders are squared, and his voice is confident. "I shouldn't have followed you. I hesitated to speak with you because I'm a stranger to you and your brother, and I didn't want to intrude on your mourning. I hope you'll forgive me because, though I didn't know about the puzzle, I'm sure I can help you solve it."

His eyes are kind, and his tone is sincere. My concern lessens.

"Hey!" Roddy calls to me. "There you are." He spots Donald. For a second, he stops and stares, then—ever the protective brother—hurries between me and Donald. "You're the guy that's been following us. What gives?"

"This is Donald Fraser. An old friend of Gigi's," I explain.

"Okay, but answer the question." Roddy widens his stance. "Why have you been following us?"

Donald smiles and looks at Roddy with an expression I can't quite decipher. Respect? Admiration?

"As I explained to your sister, I wanted to pay my respects, but never felt the time was right to intrude."

Roddy softens his posture, but only slightly.

No longer worried about Donald's intentions, I lay my hand on Roddy's back and shoot him a stand-down look. Stepping forward, I say, "Donald thinks he may be able to help us solve our puzzle since he knew Gigi so well."

Roddy tenses. "I doubt Gigi would approve. The puzzle is for us to solve."

Donald takes a step back and holds his hands up in surrender. "Up to you, but Evelyn and I had a deep bond. I may have insight. Give me a try."

Roddy crosses his arms. "Okay, what's the significance of this place?"

Donald looks up to the right and rubs his chin as he thinks. Roddy scowls at me, and I know he's mad that I shared the puzzle with Donald.

"Hmm," Donald says to us. "I never knew Evelyn came here."

"So much for your insight," Roddy mutters under his breath.

"Yeah," I jump in, covering for my brother's rudeness. "She didn't like this place."

"Delve into the decades before the sixties. That's when I met your grandmother. If she frequented this market, it probably was before then."

I nod. "Okay, thanks."

We stand in a circle with nothing more to say. Feeling awkward, I kick my shoe around in the gravel.

"Well," Donald breaks the silence. "I wanted to lay flowers on Evelyn's grave, but Ruby, you mentioned ashes."

I stop swirling my toe in the dirt. "You know my name? I didn't introduce myself."

He smiles warmly. "Yes, I know a lot about both of you. I watched you grow up."

"Then why don't we know you?" Roddy barks.

Donald's neck and chest flushes. "I, uh, I moved away, but Evelyn sent me pictures and updates."

"So, did you watch us, or did you see pictures?" Roddy presses.

I nudge Roddy with my elbow. Why is he being so gruff?

"It doesn't matter," I say, doing my best to smooth things over. "We've met you now. It was kind of you to offer your condolences. Gigi *was* cremated."

"Where were her ashes spread? In a memorial garden?"

I skirt the question. "No. Probably the best way to recognize her passing would be to donate to Ephrata Area Social Services. She was a big advocate for helping neighbors in need."

"That sounds perfect. Thanks for the suggestion." He turns and takes a few steps but stops and faces us. "You know, I'd really love a chance to reminisce. And maybe my stories would help you with your puzzle. What do you think? Could I treat you to lunch or dinner?"

I can *feel* the capital N.O. emanating from Roddy.

"Umm. Let us think on it," I say. "As you said, we're still grieving, and that might be too hard."

"Can I give you my number?"

I nod. He pulls a pen from his shirt pocket, scribbles his number on the back of an insurance agent's business card, and hands it to me.

"Well," Donald says. I can also *feel* his reluctance to leave. "I, uh, it was really nice to talk with you. I hope you'll call."

Once Donald's out of sight, I backhand Roddy's chest. "What is wrong with you? He's just a lonely old man who was a friend of Gigi's."

"Hmph. Mark my words. There's something off about that guy."

"God, you're cynical."

"And you're a Pollyanna. If he was such a good friend, why did he call Gigi Evelyn? No one who knew her called her that."

Hmm. He has a point. "But he knew she hated Green Dragon."

"Lucky guess. Plus he hemmed and hawed when I called him out on watching us grow up."

"No, he explained that. He moved away."

"What's his phone number?" Roddy demands.

I hand him the card.

"Area code 717. If he doesn't live here, why is his phone number local?"

"I guess he moved back," I say and snatch the card from his fingers.

Roddy throws his hands up in disgust. "I give up. Believe what you want, but—at the very least—be careful around that guy."

I'm a pretty good judge of character, and I saw kindness in Donald's eyes, but Roddy made some good points.

"I will," I agree. "Now, back to the puzzle. What d'you find out?"

"Not a thing. I walked up and down every aisle. I read every booth's sign. I asked a ton of vendors if they knew Gigi. Nothing."

"Maybe Donald was right." I see Roddy roll his eyes but ignore him. "Maybe we need to look at the history of the place."

A stray child zips between us and brushes Roddy's shirt with his ice cream cone. A harried mom, holding a toddler under her arm, appears a few seconds later. "Did you see a—"

"That way," Roddy and I say and point in unison.

We walk over to a food truck selling homemade chicken corn soup and whoopie pies. Roddy steals a napkin and wipes the sticky, melting goo from his shirt.

"That's it." Roddy holds his hand sideways against his neck. "I've had it up to here with tourists. Let's get outta here."

Halfway up the State Street hill, I say, "I think I'll call Millicent and see if the historical society has any records about the history of Green Dragon."

"Millicent?"

"The docent. With the chocolate chip cookies."

"Oh, yeah, yeah. Good idea. We could—"

My ringing phone interrupts Roddy. I don't recognize the number.

"Hello."

"Ruby, it's Marty."

"Oh, hey, Marty. How are you?"

"You okay? You sound out of breath."

"I'm climbing a hill with my brother."

"Climbing? With your bum leg? Who's the superhero now?"

I laugh. "It actually feels fine."

"Oh, good. Well, I don't want to interrupt, but I translated the Chinese character. It means green dragon."

"Yeah. We know. One of Roddy's coworkers helped us out. We're actually walking home from there now."

"Did you find what you needed?"

"Nope."

"Well, maybe I can assist. Did you know Green Dragon used to be a speakeasy?"

"What? No way?"

"Really. And by happy chance, I wrote an article about it last year."

"What did you find out?"

"I have a manila folder bloated with information, including dozens of old photos. Since I don't know what you're looking for, maybe it would be best if you looked through it yourself. Want to meet?"

A tingle of anticipation (or maybe heartburn) flutters in my throat.

"Yeah. That sounds like a great idea. Do you work on Saturdays?"

"Sometimes, but not tomorrow."

"Great. Do you want to meet at my house around ten? I'll fix brunch."

Roddy laughs out loud, and I shush him.

"That sounds just ducky. I'll bring mimosas. Text me the address."

By the time I text the address, we've crested the hill and are on the downside. I'm sweating like I just finished Denise Austin's Boot Camp video, and my leg is getting achy.

"So *you're* going to fix brunch? Let me guess. Cheerios and Eggo waffles?"

I stick out my tongue. "I can cook, and I can also order takeout."

We turn onto Irene Street. A community playground is on the left, and I sit on the swing. "I'm hot," I say. "I need a break."

His brows knit with worry. "It's your leg, isn't it?"

"No," I fib. "It's the humidity and the hill. I just need a minute to cool down."

He shimmies into the swing beside me, and we sway back and forth.

"So what did this Marty dude have to say about Green Dragon?"

"He has a file full of stuff from research he did for an article, with photos. That's why I invited him to brunch. He'll bring it with him."

"From your flirty voice, I'd say it has to do with more than info."

"I wasn't flirting," I snap.

"Oh, but you were," he teases.

"Was not," I throw back my head and crack up, laughing at our juvenile bickering. "We may be heading towards old, but at least we can be immature forever."

"Amen to that, sister," he says, rocking his swing to gently bump mine. "So, as your older brother—"

"By five minutes," I interrupt.

"Still older." He shrugs. "Anyway, as your older brother it's my duty to rescue you, so I'll cook brunch."

My mouth falls open, not sure how to respond. At the thought of my brother chaperoning, my excitement fizzles to dulled anticipation.

"Unless you *were* flirting, and you want privacy?" he taunts.

No way I'm giving him the satisfaction of being right—even if he is.

JUNE 2000

RUBY

Roddy arrives at nine, schleppin' a freshly baked veggie quiche and a plastic bag full of groceries.

"Plastic," I grumble as I unpack the bacon, fruit, and greens.

He holds his hand up like a stop sign. "Don't start."

I stuff the bag under my sink to use later as a bathroom trashcan liner. "Okay, what can I do to help?"

"Don't touch anything," he teases as he heats up the oven and grabs a pan from the cabinet.

I roll my eyes and set the table with the green Fiestaware plates Gigi gave to me and purple polka-dot napkins.

"Be right back," I tell Roddy and dash out to my backyard to cut a few pink hydrangeas. As I'm choosing the showiest blooms, I hear a truck idling out front. Walking around the side of my house, I catch a glimpse of a black Ford pickup zooming away. Donald. Apparently, he wants more than to offer condolences. Maybe the best way to find out what he's after is to take him up on his lunch offer. I decide not to tell Roddy my plan. He won't like it, and I don't want to argue. Plus, his curtness could make Donald clam up.

I head back inside, grab a cut crystal vase from my kitchen cabinet and arrange the flowers for a centerpiece.

"Getting pretty fancy for research, doncha think?" Roddy asks.

"I *am* a party planner, Roderick." I use his full name because I know it annoys him. "Details *are* important when entertaining."

He gives me a dismissive wave and flips the sizzling bacon strips in the pan. I run upstairs to change. I pull a button-front, yellow-and-white gingham dress from the hanger and slip my arms through the sleeves. Nah. Looks like I'm trying too hard. Next, I throw on a Coexist T-shirt and jean shorts. I check my reflection in the mirror. Nope, too working-in-the-garden. Leaving a trail of crumpled clothes on the floor, I dig through my drawers until I find my blue and white striped T-shirt dress. I pull it over my head and tug it over my body. It's casual, but cute. Bellissimo! Shuffling my feet into my navy-blue canvas sneakers, I head to the bathroom to tame my now staticky hair. Looking into the round scalloped mirror above my vintage pedestal sink, I squirt a dollop of defrizzer onto my palm and work it through my curls. A swipe of color for my lips and lightly freckled cheeks, a spritz of Clinique's Happy, and I'm ready.

The doorbell chimes as I'm skipping (not an iota of pain in my leg) down the stairs. "Be right there," I trill.

I duck my head into the kitchen before I open the front door. "Behave!" I warn Roddy.

He gives me a goofy, I-knew-you-liked-the-guy smile.

I swing open the door and welcome Marty inside. A bulging file is tucked under his arm. In one hand, he's holding a pitcher of fresh OJ, and in the other, a bottle of champagne.

"Mimosas," he grins.

I grab the pitcher and bottle from his hands. "Just put the file on the coffee table and come meet my brother."

Marty's smile falters for a split second. "Righto."

Marty lays the file down and follows me through the living room into my kitchen. "Marty, this is my twin, Roddy. Roddy, Marty."

"Hey, man. Good to meet you. Thanks for getting my sis to the hospital the other day, and thanks for helping us with our research."

"My pleasure. I've got to admit, your grandmother's puzzle has me intrigued. She must've been quite a rare bird."

Roddy clears his throat. I can tell he's touched by Marty's description. "She was."

Gigi would've loved it too. To her, ordinary was a cuss word.

***

After a delicious brunch, we settle in my living room to savor our cocktails and peruse Marty's file. His article details how the Green Dragon was originally called Schreck's Tavern. Inspired by a Chinese restaurant he saw in Atlantic City, Schreck changed the name to Green Dragon and decorated the speakeasy with an Asian theme. Noah Burkholder took possession of the tavern after it was raided in 1932 and turned it into a livestock auction. The Rohrbach family created the market that operates today.

"I interviewed Nevin Burkholder, Noah's son. He was in his eighties and quite the chinwagger. If he's still alive, I'm sure he'd jump at the chance to talk with you. I'd be glad to set it up," Marty offers.

I rub my fingers across my chin. "I have a feeling it might have more to do with a speakeasy than a livestock auction."

"Agree," Roddy says. "What can you tell us about its Prohibition days?"

"Well." Marty rifles through pages of notes. "The Green Dragon wasn't just a small-town dance hall. It booked big-name acts like Salt and Pepper—the Black female tap dance duo—and Blanche Babette. Its customers came from as far as Philly. In fact, the notorious 'Boo Boo' Hoff spent more than one night at the Dragon, and Lancaster's own Fred 'Farmer Boy' Hanson was a regular. Let me find the photos."

"I read about Hoff when I was looking through the microfilms at your office. Wasn't he a big-time bootlegger in Philly?" I ask.

"He was," Marty says as he flips through a stack of photos. "He was also a boxer and boxing manager for a while." He stops at a yellowed black-and-white image of three men smoking cigars around a table. "See." He hands me the photo. "The middle guy is Max 'Boo Boo' Hoff. That's Schreck." He points to the jowly, bald guy on the right. "And the man on the left is Charles Frawley, the Lancaster City Chief of Police."

"Corruption at its finest," Roddy says.

"Oh yeah, colossal palm-greasing," Marty agrees. "There's another shot of Frawley with 'Farmer Boy' Hanson."

"What did 'Farmer Boy' Hanson do?" I ask.

"Here it is," he hands us the picture. Frawley's got his meaty arm around a scrawny, light-haired, freckle-faced man.

"He looks like a kid," I blurt.

"He does, but don't be fooled by his looks. He wasn't innocent. Hanson set up dozens of local farmers with one-gallon copper 'alky cookers,' or stills, to make small batches of liquor in their kitchens. Every week he'd make his rounds, buy the homemade booze from the farmers, and then turn around and sell it to the speakeasy and tavern owners for a hefty profit. To cover his tracks, he also bought their produce and sold it to local grocers."

"It must have been so hard to survive back then. Why else would farmers risk losing their land?" I ask.

"They say you can credit Prohibition for making criminals out of regular people. Is any of this info helping?"

Roddy shrugs. "That's the problem. We don't know what we're looking for."

"Can I look through all the pictures?" I ask.

He checks his watch. "Sure. You know what? Why don't you keep the whole file until you've found what you need? I promised Brad I'd take him to North Museum today. They have a new interactive dino exhibit."

"That's his nephew," I explain to Roddy. "The boy who had the paleontologist party."

"Yeah? Sounds like a cool kid," Roddy says.

"He is," Marty and I say at the same time.

"Jinx," I shout out a second before Marty. "You owe me a Coke."

Roddy rolls his eyes at our silliness. "How can there be two adults who still play this game?"

"I play Punch Buggy, too," Marty offers, laughing.

"Me too! And I have one!"

Marty stands and extends his hand to Roddy. "It was good to meet you. Thanks for brunch."

"You bet. Good to meet you, too. Thanks for bringing all of this stuff." Roddy motions to the photos and notes scattered across the table.

"I'll walk you out," I say, leading him to the door.

We step out onto my front porch. Marty pats his stomach. "Good food, good fun."

My stomach flutters like a schoolgirl's at the end of a first date. "Thanks for coming."

"We're still on for Thursday, right?" he asks.

I point my finger in the air and do a few John Travolta moves. "You bet!"

"Your impressions are much better than mine," he says, as he shakes his head in an exaggerated no. "Okay, I'll pick you up at seven. See you then." He waves and walks to his car.

Hmm. Not even a peck on the cheek.

While I was outside, Roddy loaded the dishwasher and poured himself a glass of lemonade. "Want one?" he asks as I settle back on the couch.

"No thanks," I sigh.

"What's with the hangdog face?"

I blow out a raspberry. "I think Marty's just a pal."

Roddy plops into the comfy chair across from me and swipes

his hand across his forehead. "I'll get whiplash trying to keep up with you. You told me this was not a date, so..."

"It wasn't a date. I mean *you're* here. What kind of date includes a twin brother?" I cross my arms and pout in the corner of the couch. "I'm just saying, I don't think he wanted it to be a date."

"Wait. Let me get this straight. This wasn't a date, but you *want* Marty to have *wanted* it to be a date?" he asks.

"Precisely."

He pulls himself further back into the chair. "You know what? I'm not touching that. How about we look through this info?"

"Fine," I snap and grab a stack of photos.

Roddy pages through Marty's research. I flip through black-and-white shots of stage acts, tables full of drunk revelers, and couples on the dance floor.

"Oh, my God! Look at this!" I shout.

Roddy scoots beside me on the couch to look over my shoulder.

"That's Hanson," he says.

"Yes, and he's with Gigi and Pop!"

"Damn!"

"And that's Elizabeth Fry. You know, Gigi's friend from the hat factory."

"Wonder who this guy is?" Roddy says, pointing to the man with his arm around Elizabeth.

"Don't know. Maybe we can find him in other pictures. Do you think Gigi and Pop were bootleggers?" I ask. "Is that what we're supposed to learn? That our inheritance comes from bootlegging?"

"Maybe."

"That's not so bad, right? Making alcohol? I mean Prohibition was a stupid law. Everybody broke it."

"No. Bootlegging's not that bad, but that can't be all of it. We still have three bags of ashes left. There's got to be more to it," Roddy says.

I grit my teeth, annoyed by his constant pessimism. "Well, it's probably enough to call Mr. Davenport."

Roddy shrugs. "And tell him what?"

"I guess tell him Gigi and Pop made liquor for Farmer Boy, and maybe Beth Fry and her beau did too."

Roddy snaps his fingers. "Or what if Gigi and Pop sold it for him? Through the store."

"Oh, yeah. That makes a lot of sense! Should I call him?"

He pulls his flip phone out of the pouch on his waist. "I'm already dialing."

Roddy switches to speakerphone when Mr. Davenport's secretary puts the call through.

"Roderick, nice to hear from you. What have you uncovered?"

"The location is Green Dragon, and we found out its pertinence stemmed from its time as a speakeasy."

"Correct. Continue."

"Ruby and I believe that our grandparents sold bootleg liquor in their store."

"I'm sorry. That's incorrect. Call me—"

"Okay, wait," Roddy interrupts. "They made booze? Is that it?"

"Incorrect."

I pipe up. "Hi, Mr. Davenport. It's Ruby. Is Green Dragon significant because that's where Gigi met 'Farmer Boy' Hanson?"

"Precisely. I'll email you the next clue." The phone clicks when he hangs up.

"Way to save it," Roddy says. "But, if they didn't sell or make booze, why is it important that they knew 'Farmer Boy'?"

"No idea," I say as I boot up my computer. "I guess that's why there are three locations left."

I gather Marty's information into a tidy pile on my coffee table and pour a glass of lemonade for Roddy and me.

"Put on your thinking cap," I say, printing out the puzzle. "The email just came through."

1. 1931 Aldous Huxley: 4, 10
2. Charles Dickens 13th novel: 1, 4, 16, 17
3. Murder inspired by a demonic hound: 17, 18, 19, 20, 21
4. Prequel to *Jane Eyre*: 8, 14
5. 1951 J. D. Salinger: 9, 12, 13
6. Get lost down a rabbit hole: 1, 2, 6, 12, 20, 24
7. Friedan's landmark book: 3
8. V. C. Andrews best seller: 13 through 17
9. Think *The Tell-Tale Heart*

Quintessential Gigi.

1931

EVIE

Evie and Bess slipped their false bravado over their sleeveless dresses and the red cloche hats they nicked from Tollman's and strolled into the Green Dragon like they owned the joint. Pete looked up as they entered. He and his brawny friend sauntered over to meet the girls.

"Watch delivered into the hands of Mr. John. Promise kept. Eager dance partner at your service." Pete bowed to Evie. "Condition met."

His blue eyes zinged through Evie like the rush from the first sip of alcohol.

"A man who keeps his word," Evie casually replied, keeping her flutters concealed. "This is my friend, Bess."

"And this is my friend, George."

Introductions were superfluous. Bess and George were already engaged in a steamy stare.

"Let's find a seat, and we'll get you gals a drink," Pete said, guiding Evie, George, and Bess to a corner table.

Performing on the Dragon's bright red stage was the wildly popular chorus line from Babette's in Atlantic City. Snazzily dressed customers jitterbugged on the dance floor. Booze flowed like open faucets, and laughter sang through the room. The unbridled gaiety was exactly what Evie needed.

Lately, her life had been dark and wearisome. Her mother's health had deteriorated to the point where she could no longer complete her laundry jobs. With the added cost of medicines, the family couldn't survive on Evie's wages alone. So, after working long days at the Caldwells', not only did Evie have to care for her mother and handle her drunk father, she also had to finish customers' laundry.

When Pete and George return with their Mary Pickfords, Evie shoved away grim reality and clasped the merriment. The hooch mixed with the pulsing beat of the music had Evie and Bess straining in their seats like racehorses waiting in the gate. Unable to contain themselves, they dragged the boys onto the dance floor. Evie twirled and shimmied till she was panting—in love with the music, the rum, and the possibilities of life.

"Oh, I need a breather and another drink," Evie said when the boogie-woogie ended.

Pete and George headed to the bar as Bess and Evie made their way back to their table.

"He's the cat's pajamas," Bess gushed about George. "I'm so glad we came here tonight." She dabs the sweat from her forehead with an embroidered handkerchief.

"Me too."

Evie smiled and slid her eyes to the bar to watch Pete. He dug a crumpled bill out of his pocket and shrugged his shoulders as he showed it to George. George waved his hand dismissively and pulled out a thick wad of cash. He grabbed a few bills from the gold money clip and threw them on the bar.

"Here you go, more giggle juice for two dishes," George said, handing Evie and Bess the drinks.

Evie popped the maraschino cherry in her mouth and sipped the fruity cocktail. The rum warmed her belly with contentment. George shifted his chair closer to Bess and wrapped his arm loosely around her shoulder. She leaned into him and they giggled.

Pete bent towards Evie's ear and whispered, "Looks like a match."

"Yeah, she's smitten," Evie agreed.

"I am, too," Pete said with a brazen wink.

His words warmed her much more than the rum, and she felt her cheeks flame red.

"Hey, Georgie Boy!" A skinny man with hair so light it bordered on white gave a few friendly smacks to George's back.

"Hey-yo, Mr. Hanson," George said, standing to shake the gentleman's hand. George towered over the guy. "This is my friend Pete."

Mr. Hanson shook Pete's hand. "Georgie here told me a bunch about you. I'm always looking for hard workers. You fail outta watch school, look me up."

"That might be sooner than you think." Pete said, laughing.

George waved his thick, muscled arm across the table towards the girls. "And this is Bess and Evie."

"Ladies," Mr. Hanson said, tipping his tan, silk-banded fedora. "You can nibble one on me." He points to our almost empty glasses. "I happen to know they just got a swell batch of booze," he said with a stage wink. "No bathtub gin for these kittens." His grin was so wide his freckled cheeks almost touched his eyebrows. He flipped two Lincolns from his billfold onto the cocktail waitress's serving tray. "Get my pals whatever they want, and keep the rest for yourself, doll," he said, patting her bottom.

"I'll be round on Wednesday, Georgie. Be sure you got plenty of corn for me." As Mr. Hanson strode through the drum, men and women swarmed him for a shot at his attention.

"You work for him?" Bess gasped. "For 'Farmer Boy' Hanson?"

Evie wasn't certain whether Bess's expression was awe or dismay.

"Shh!" George warned. "Don't let him hear you say that. He hates that nickname."

When Bess sidled a little closer to George, Evie had her answer.

"So you do work for him?" Bess asked.

George raised his eyebrows up and down. "I'm just a simple farmer."

Evie never saw a simple farmer with a wad of cash, and she knew better than to think corn meant the on-the-cob kind.

Evie sat taller in her seat, squared her shoulders, and looked directly at George. "So, how can I be one of Mr. Hanson's farmers?"

JULY 2000

RUBY

Fairies float in the rays of the morning sun shining through my window. (Okay, maybe it's more dust than fairy.) Pink pansies smile from their pot on the vintage baker's crate that serves as my bedside table. I crawl out of my comfy bed and twist and twirl with the fairies to loosen up the kinks. It's going to be a happy day.

And busy. Normally I keep my Sundays lazy, but today is jam-packed. I have an early call with Janet to finalize party details. Brunch with Donald is set for eleven. And in the late afternoon, Roddy and I plan to solve the next puzzle.

I stare into my closet, searching for the cheeriest outfit. A bright yellow tunic with white embroidered flowers catches my eye, and I slide it off its hanger. Rooting through my drawers, I find my purple yoga pants. Perfect. I throw on my clothes, complete my daily ablutions, and start a pot of coffee.

As the coffee brews, I check my emails. I have thirteen from Janet, three spam, and one from the historical society. Janet can wait until after coffee. I open the one from Millicent.

Dear Ruby,
I found a gem about your grandfather. He's a hero. See attached. Visit soon. I'll have cookies waiting.
Millicent.

A hero? I click to open the attachment, and a copy of a *Lancaster Journal* article pops up on the monitor.

CEREMONY HONORS QUICK-THINKING BOWMAN TECHNICAL SCHOOL STUDENT

During their annual gala at the Hotel Brunswick, Mr. John Bowman presented student Peter Collier with free tuition and a diamond and gold Hamilton pocket watch in recognition of saving his son Edwin's life.

During a lecture in Fundamental, Edwin Bowman became short of breath and felt what he later described as "chest flopping." Peter noticed his classmate's gray pallor and panting. When Edwin fell unconscious to the floor, Peter took swift, heroic action. With one decisive thump to the chest, Edwin's eyes fluttered open.

The Bowmans' family physician said, "Without Mr. Collier's intervention, young Mr. Bowman would not be alive."

When asked to comment on his actions, Mr. Collier said, "It was just instinct, I guess."

Wow! How cool is that? I type a quick thank-you to Millicent for sharing the information and forward the email to Roddy. At least some of the secrets we're uncovering are good ones.

I check the time. Jeez, fifteen minutes before I have to call Janet. I scramble an egg while I slug back my coffee. After wolfing down my breakfast, I read through her emails. Changes, changes, and more changes. This is going to be a taxing phone call.

***

Our call actually went smoothly. After I provided Janet with the reasoning behind each of my suggestions, we got on the same page. Only a few loose ends remain for her big event.

Now Sally's ferrying me to Zinn's Diner. The two-story statue of a barefoot Amish farmer holding a wooden pitchfork welcomes me as I swing Sally into Zinn's parking lot. Donald's already waiting on the bench in front of the statue.

"Hi," I say, walking up to him.

His broad smile makes rosy plums of his cheeks, and I'm again struck by a sense of familiarity.

"Ruby, thanks so much for meeting me."

We're led past the old-timey diner counter to a tan vinyl booth in the corner. The just-cleaned, aluminum-rimmed Formica tabletop is still damp, so I fold my hands and rest them in my lap.

"I'm treating," Donald says, picking up his menu.

I don't have to look. My mouth's already watering, thinking about my order.

"What can I get you folks?" a spry server asks.

"I'll have Gene Wenger's ham loaf and an iced tea," Donald orders.

"Could I have a tuna melt, dandelion greens with hot bacon dressing, and a lemonade please?" Zinn's homemade bacon dressing is ah-mazing!

The server hurries behind the counter to get our drinks.

"Your mother loved hot bacon dressing, too," Donald says.

"You mean my grandmother," I reply.

"No, your mother, Ella."

My mouth drops open. "You knew my mother?"

"I did. That's how I met Evelyn, because of Ella."

My stomach somersaults. I know very little about my mother. Gigi and Pop were devastated by her death, and talking about her was too painful.

The server brings our drinks, and I try to narrow the dozens of questions pinballing in my brain to one.

"Why, when? I mean, how did you know her?"

"I was her boss. At JCPenney, when it was still in downtown Ephrata."

"Her boss? She worked?"

"For the summer after she graduated high school. Then she got married."

"Were you close?"

His green eyes stare past me with what looks like regret.

"I was twice her age."

He physically draws into himself—leaning away from the table, rounding his shoulders, and crossing his arms—so I let the non-answer slide.

"Tell me what she was like. I don't know a lot about her."

"Well, you look a lot like her, but her hair wasn't red. More of a dark blonde. But, I'm sure you've seen photos."

I nod.

"She was whip-smart and eager to please. Always striving to be the best of everything—employee, daughter..." He trails off, lost in memories. He blinks a few times and takes a sip of tea. "I'm sure Evelyn shared tons of stories with you and your brother."

"Quite the opposite. I think our grandparents thought talking about our mom would make us miss her."

"When your mother died, protecting you became Evelyn's sole purpose. She was fiercer than a mama bear."

The OG helicopter parent. God, I miss her.

The server brings our meals. Donald picks at his ham loaf as I dive into my salad. Hot creamy dressing covers the wilted greens, and I munch a forkful. The salty-sweet flavor coats my mouth in heavenly goodness. (It's bacon. Enough said.)

"Good?" he asks.

"Scrumptious. How about yours? Not good?"

He's pushing it around his plate.

"I'm sure it's great, but I've lost my appetite. Memory Lane is thornier than I expected."

The poor guy looks bereft. Apparently, Gigi and Pop didn't have dibs on the pain caused by my mother's death. I put my fork down and wait for him to look up.

"Did you love her?" I ask gently.

"Your mother?"

I nod.

"I hardly knew her."

"Then what about the past makes you so sad?" I prod.

He pushes his untouched plate of food to the side and holds his hands out, palms up. "Look at me. I'm a lonely old man. A lifetime of bad decisions got me here. The woulda, coulda, shouldas are eating me alive."

"What about family? A wife? Kids? Siblings?"

"I traded my chance at a family decades ago—for booze. I'm a drunk. A dry one. Been sober for nineteen years, but I'm still a drunk."

It's exactly like I told Roddy. Donald's lonely and grasping for connection.

"Everyone deserves a second chance," I say.

He looks up and holds my gaze. "Do you really believe that?"

"I do."

"Then maybe there's hope."

He pulls his food back in front of him and digs into his ham loaf.

***

Donald and I let the past rest for the remainder of the meal but planned to get together again soon. Our brunch took a lot out of me, and I'm just dozing off on my comfy couch when my doorbell chimes. Too tired to move, I yell, "It's open."

Roddy's scolding me as he comes through the door. "Are you crazy? Never say that unless you've checked who's at the door. I could've been anybody." He sees me snuggled under the chenille throw blanket. "Are you sick? What's wrong?"

Roddy knows I never nap. "Not sick, just tired."

"But you're okay?"

"I'm fine." Yawning, I push up to sitting and rub my eyes. "How about pouring me a lemonade while I pee?"

"Sure. Unless you want one of these," he says, pointing to the six of Bud he's carrying.

The thought of beer (which I normally like) makes me queasy. "No thanks."

After I pee and splash some cold water on my face to wake up, I grab pencils and paper and join him at my kitchen table.

"Let's solve this." I position the email printout of the clues between us. "Okay, first clue is 1931 Aldous Huxley."

"*Island*?" Roddy suggests.

"No, I'm pretty sure that was written in the '60s. Think earlier."

"Oh, duh! *Brave New World.*"

"Bingo! I'm sure that's it. So what do the 4 and 10 mean?" I wonder.

"Chapter numbers? Do you own that book?"

"Definitely not," I say, shaking my head. "I'm not keen on science fiction, but I bet I have the next one on my shelves."

Roddy reads the clue. "Charles Dickens 13th novel."

"*Great Expectations.*"

He flicks his fingers towards the hallway. "Well, go get it."

I scan the overcrowded bookcases lining the back wall of my guest bedroom and pull Dickens' novel from the shelf.

"Got it!" I yell, jogging back to the kitchen.

We open to chapter one. "Now what?" Roddy asks.

I read the first line, "*My father's family name being Pirrip, and my Christian name Philip, my infant tongue could make of both names nothing longer or more explicit than Pip.*" My eyebrows raise as I look up at Roddy. "First word *my* and fourth word *name*?"

He shrugs. "Maybe. Keep going. The next number is 16."

I count to the sixteenth word. "*Make.*"

"Hmm," Roddy says, chin resting in his hand. "Next number is 17."

"*My name make of.* It's not making sense. Oooh, I know," I say, snapping my fingers. "Maybe it's the letter, not the word. The first, fourth, sixteenth, and seventeenth letters."

"Of the title!" Roddy chimes in. "Let's try that."

We jot down the eight book titles. Gigi's ninth clue tells us a title name and has no numbers, so we put that aside for the time being. Roddy counts and underlines the appropriate letters in each title.

1. Bra<u>v</u>e New W<u>o</u>rld
2. <u>Gr</u>e<u>a</u>t Expectation<u>s</u>
3. The Hound of Basker<u>v</u>il<u>le</u>s
4. Wide Sargasso S<u>ea</u>
5. Catcher <u>in</u> the <u>R</u>ye
6. <u>Alice's</u> Adve<u>nt</u>ure in W<u>o</u>nde<u>r</u>land
7. Th<u>e</u> Feminine Mystique
8. Flowers in the <u>Attic</u>

I write each underlined letter on my paper: *Vogansville General Store Attic.* I barely remember our grandparents' store.

"Looks like we're going back to our roots," I say.

"What about the ninth clue?" Roddy asks.

I read the last clue out loud. "Think *Tell-Tale Heart.*" Dread commandeers my gut. "Is she telling us we're going to find a body buried in the floor of the attic?"

Roddy's jaw tenses, and he rubs his temples. I can tell he's just as freaked out as I am. "Well, that *would* be a secret that would make us not want our inheritance."

I wrap my arms around myself to stop my shivers.

"Some secrets are meant to stay that way."

JUNE 1931

EVIE

Evie sprawled across Bess's bed, grateful for the respite. Things at home were considerably worse. Evie was forced to quit her job at the Caldwells' after her father took a drunk tumble down the basement stairs and snapped his leg bone in two. Her mother, weak from consumption, was unable to even lift a spoon to feed herself. She needed the healing climate of a sanitarium, but with not enough money for food, that was out of the question.

On the radio, Mrs. Pennyfeather, from *The KUKU Hour*, was giving nonsensical advice on how best to iron a shirt. Bess and Evie giggled at the absurdity.

"It feels good to laugh," Evie said.

Bess flopped across the bed beside Evie. "It'll get better. It has too."

Bess had her own problems. She was constantly dodging a handsy boss. Though her bank job paid well, she wasn't sure how much longer she could put up with his groping.

"Well, once you and George get hitched, you can quit that job."

"If he ever asks me," Bess whined. "I barely see him."

George was flush with cash but short on time. Mr. Hanson had taken a shine to him and promoted him to be his driver and muscle.

"Don't pout," Evie said. "You know he's got to make hay while the sun shines." Evie rolled on her side to look at Bess. "I really wish I could talk him into letting me have his still."

Seeing no other way to raise enough cash to help her ailing mother, Evie badgered George every time he saw him.

Bess shrugs. "You know George. Thinks women are too fragile for something like that."

"I'd like to see a man push out a baby," Evie fumed. "*Then* talk to me about women being fragile."

Bess laughs and shakes her head. "He's no match for Evie Fisher. I have no doubt you'll wear him down. Speaking of matches, what about you and Pete?"

Evie flipped on her back and stared up at the cracked ceiling. Sighing with frustration, she said, "What about us? We're both flat broke. He's got school, and I've got my parents."

"Now that he saved rich old Mr. Bowman's son, he's got good connections."

"We'll see if it gets him more than schooling and a watch," Evie grumbled.

"Gloomy Evie is no fun." Bess tapped her head against Evie's. "Where's my friend who can take on the world?"

"In hiding," Evie grumbled.

"BREAKING NEWS," the radio host announced in a strident voice. "Al Capone pleads guilty to tax evasion and prohibition charges."

Both girls scrambled up to sitting.

"Today," the radio announcer continued, "Mr. Capone's bold assertion—they can't collect legal taxes from illegal money—was proven patently false."

"It's crazy, after all the things he did, tax evasion is what's bringing him down," Bess said.

"Yeah. You'd think he'd be smarter." Evie turned towards Bess and took her friend's hands. "I hope George is. Being smart, I mean. Especially if you two marry."

"And in local news," the newscaster continued. "The suspects in the Farmers National Bank robbery are still at large. Having stolen more than $300,000, the three armed men are assumed to have crossed the border into Mexico."

Evie whistled. "Three hundred grand. That's a lot of cabbage."

"Yeah, but who wants to live in Mexico?"

"Mexicans," Evie quipped.

Bess threw a pillow at Evie, and they both collapsed back on the mattress laughing, savoring the brief moment of joy. Bess propped herself up on her elbows and gave Evie a loud kiss on her cheek.

"Evie Fisher, I'd be lost without you."

"Well, don't trouble yourself," Evie replied. "You're stuck with me."

The radio broadcast returned to its regular programming.

Mrs. Pennyfeather was prattling about dandelion leaves making a tasty meal. "And if you happen to add a bit of baker's yeast to the leaves and let them ferment for a few weeks, they might just turn into wine."

Galvanized, Evie jumped out of Bess's bed and paced around the room. "I don't need George's still. There's more than one way to grow cabbage."

JULY 2000

RUBY

Roddy and I cooked up a cover story, and I'm dressing the part. I slide into a pair of worn baggy jeans I picked up at the Re-Uzit Shop (along with some really cute fall clothes) and a mustard-colored T-shirt sporting a giant honeybee with the word *kind* written under it. I braid my hair and top it with a blue baseball cap. As I'm slipping into my Nikes, I hear Hank idling outside. We're taking him to stay in character. Tiny Sally would be ridiculous. I grab my macramé crossbody bag with Gigi inside and jog out to meet Roddy.

"Do you have all the tools?" I ask as I hop into the Jeep.

"Why are you so perky? You know what we might find today," he grumps.

"I've thought about it, and it's not possible. No way Gigi was involved with murder or hiding a body."

"So, you think that just because you decided, it can't be true?"

"Exactly." I nod and push away a tiny twinge of doubt.

"Okay." Roddy sighs and shakes his head. "I hope you're right." He pats a leather messenger bag he has stowed between the seats. "Hammer, screwdriver, and flashlight. To Vogansville."

Because Lancaster County is known for reasonably priced antiques, dealers flock here from every state to find merchandise.

We're hoping the Amish guy who owns the store buys our picker disguise and lets us scrounge around in his attic.

We wind around the twisty country roads, passing a few buggies on the way. As we enter Vogansville on Wissler Road, the little white church, with stained glass windows and a bell tower, is on our left. A chest-high wide stone wall surrounds its cemetery. At the back right corner, branches from the neighboring farm's mulberry tree hang over the wall.

"Remember walking the wall?" I ask.

He rubs his stomach. "And eating too many mulberries."

Across from the church, three two-story houses sit in a row.

"That was Mrs. Buch's house." He points to number 34 mounted beside the front door of the moss green house with board and batten siding and a welcoming front porch.

After filling up on mulberries, we'd stop at Mrs. Buch's for meadow tea.

"I wonder if she's still alive?" I say.

"Can't be. She was old when we were little."

Once we pass the houses, we arrive at the crossroads in the center of the tiny village. *Smucker's Dry Goods* is painted on a piece of scrap wood in uneven lettering and staked in a patch of grass in front of the business that was formerly our grandparents' general store. A hitching rail, large enough for three horses, runs alongside the clapboard building. We drive by the store and park on the gravel shoulder of the narrow road. Roddy will stay in the Jeep until I give him the all-clear. If I can't charm my way into the attic in my role as a picker, we'll need the store owner not to know Roddy and I are together for plan B.

As I'm walking behind a buggy, the sweat-slathered horse whinnies. A stout Amish woman climbs out of the carriage and ties the reins to the hitch.

The screen door squeaks when I open it. A young Amish girl—maybe eight or nine years-old—greets me from behind the counter of the dimly lit store.

"Hallo," she says.

I walk up to the wooden counter with its pieced-together Formica top. "Hi."

A barefoot toddler runs out from behind the counter and stares up at me. I wave but don't talk to her. Amish children only learn English when they start school.

"Rebecca! Hock dich naah."

The little girl waddles to a chair behind the counter, crawls up on it, and pops her thumb in her mouth.

"Is that your sister?" I ask.

"Ya."

"Well, my name is Ruby. I'm on a buying trip to find all kinds of antiques and collectibles. One of your neighbors told us you might have an attic and barn to root through."

"Du bringscht zerick Daed. Dapper schpring," she says to her sister.

"She'll get my dad," she tells me.

"Thanks." I browse around the store as I'm waiting. Battery-powered lanterns hang from hooks in the ceiling, lighting shelves full of everything from canning supplies and kitchen utensils, bolts of fabric and notions, to children's books and puzzles, and men's straw hats and ladies' net coverings.

I don't have vivid memories of my grandparents' store, but I do know it was nothing like this. Gigi and Pop stocked popsicles and penny candy, flour and yeast, wheels of cheese, and jars of red-beet eggs. I'm sure they sold other things, but I mostly remember the food.

The door creaks, and the woman who had crawled out of the buggy enters, moving slowly to the counter.

"Wie bischt?" she asks the young girl.

"Gut," the girl responds.

They continue their conversation, but since I only remember two Pennsylvania Dutch phrases: kumme esse (come eat) and ach du lieva Gott in Himmel (oh my goodness God in Heaven—which counts as a curse, so, of course, I remember it), I tune out.

A few minutes pass, and a lanky, bearded man in black suspendered pants and a bright purple shirt strides through the back door of the store. His daughter points at me. I walk towards the counter to meet him.

"So vut cha need?" he asks.

V and W sounds are switched in Pennsylvania Dutch. It carries over when native speakers use English, too.

"I, uh, your neighbor told me you might have some old stuff hanging around in your attic that you might want to sell."

He shrugs. "Not much up there, yet. Mebbe some chairs waitin' on fixin', a few rusty parts. Prolly some boxes of old papers and a sign or two from the store that used to be here."

"Oh, I love signs and broken stuff. I make it into garden sculptures and that kind of thing," I say, improvising. "Can I take a look?"

He pulls off his hat and scratches his bowl-cut hair before replacing it on his head. I can see his amusement at the crazy "English" (that's what they call us).

"Yeah, vell, okay. Bring down vut you vant, and I'll give you a price."

"My brother's with me. Can he take a look too?"

"Suit yourself." He gestures to his daughter. "Anna vill call for me ven you're done, then."

He says something to his daughter, and she nods her head. I run out to the Jeep to wave Roddy in.

"We're in?" he asks, giving me a thumbs up.

"Yep. Grab the tools."

He pulls the bag from between the seats and slings it over his shoulder. "Ready."

Once back in the store, Anna leads us to unrailed, wooden steps.

"There you go, then," she says, pointing up.

Our sneakers make imprints in the thick dust on each tread. I sneeze.

"Bless you," Roddy says. "Hey, be careful there."

At the top of the steps, he points his flashlight beam at the head of a broken pitchfork sticking up in the air. I step around it. Tiny windows on each end of the long attic let in traces of light. My eyes adjust to the dimness. A jumble of table legs and chair seats is in the far corner. A few empty wooden Reading Soda Works crates are tucked in the eaves. I remember drinking their birch beer.

"Look. I bet these are from when Gigi and Pop had the store."

"That's cool. We should buy them."

I pull out two and stack them in the center of the attic. "Good idea."

Roddy shines the light along the other side of the attic. A four-foot sign spans part of the wall. Its background is worn green with fading white letters, *Vogansville General Store.*

"Oh," I say excitedly. "I've got to have that. I would love to hang that above my sofa!"

"I'll put it on the pile," Roddy says. "I guess we really are pickers."

"We are!"

I keep looking. I open a beat-up trunk and find a stained handkerchief with a sprig of lavender stitched on the corner, a silver hat pin, and mouse poop. A scooter with a missing wheel is propped against a stack of cardboard boxes. I lay the scooter to the side and open the boxes one-by-one, finding nothing more than canning jars, clothes pins, and assorted rusty hinges.

"Should we look for...should we check the floorboards?" Roddy asks.

The attic grows darker and creepier.

I swallow hard. "I guess. How do you want to do it?"

"Let's do it like a grid search, you know, like the way cops look for, um, evidence."

I squeeze my eyes shut, unwilling to entertain the possibility that we're about to find human remains.

I breathe in courage. "Okay."

We start at the far end of the attic and begin a slow walk to the other side, watching for loose or replaced boards. Only a quarter of the way through our search, my back protests at being hunched over for so long. Changing positions, I drop down to my hands and knees to crawl. Dust and dirt coat my hands and the knees of my jeans. I'm really glad I wore long pants to keep the grime out of my cut.

"Can you see better?" Roddy asks.

"Yeah, and it hurts my back less."

Roddy joins me in our slow crawl. At about halfway, I spot a different color plank off to my left.

"Look," I say, "This plank's much lighter."

Roddy shines the light on it. "You're right. Think that's it?"

"Beats me." I shrug. "But worth a try."

Roddy pulls the tools from his bag. He wiggles the edge of the straight-edge screwdriver into the slight gap between boards and tries to pry it loose. It cracks and the edge of the board splinters off, leaving a small opening.

"Damn!" he says.

We both freeze and hold our breath, afraid Anna heard our destruction. Thirty seconds pass, and I exhale.

"See if you can see anything before I destroy it anymore," Roddy says.

My palms are sweaty, and my heart is pounding. He shines the beam into the three-inch opening.

"Jeez, Roddy. I can't tell. It's too dark."

He sucks in a big breath. "Okay, here goes nothing."

This time he taps the screwdriver into place with the hammer then slides the claw end of the hammer into the small opening and pries with the hammer and screwdriver at the same time. The board lifts.

Under the glow of the flashlight, we see it—a canvas book with a cracked leather spine.

"Oh, thank God! I knew it wouldn't be bones." My heartbeat normalizes as I lift the book from its hiding place. I flip through the yellowed pages. "It's a ledger of some sort. It's got dates and dollar amounts, and—"

Roddy interrupts, "Slip it into my bag. We don't have time to look at it now."

"Are we going to steal it? Shouldn't we pay for it?" I ask.

"It belonged to Gigi, so now, legally, it belongs to us."

I slip it into his messenger bag.

"Let's put her ashes in the floorboard," he suggests.

I shudder. "But it's so gloomy up here."

"This place was in Gigi's bones, and now she'll be in its bones."

Can't argue with that, so I pull out the sequined pouch, and we pour her ashes where the ledger had laid. Roddy replaces the plank as best he can, and I drag the cardboard boxes on top of it to hide the damage.

I grab the soda crates, and Roddy carries his bag and the sign.

"Rest in peace, Gigi," I whisper before carefully walking down the rickety steps.

"So you found some stuff, then?" Anna says when she sees what we brought down. "I'll get dad." She hurries out the back of the store into the attached house. A few minutes later, she's back with her dad.

"Vell, vut didja find?" he asks.

"A sign and two crates," Roddy says.

He strokes his long beard. "Store signs are pretty poplar these days," he says, dropping the u from popular. "I guess I need a hunderrd for that."

"A hundred?" I say, shocked at the high price.

"Ya." He nods. "And thirty each for the crates."

"Jeez," I say.

"Do you want them?" Roddy asks me, "Or shall we leave

them?"

I hem and haw, hoping for a reduction in price.

"Tell you vut," he says, stroking his beard some more. "Give me von-fifty for everything."

"Deal," I say. These pieces are part of my history. I can't walk away.

We load the sign, crates, and ledger into Hank and head to my house.

"Well," Roddy says. "A ledger's a damn sight better than what I thought we'd find."

"Oh, I knew it couldn't be a body."

He gives me the side-eye.

"It's classic Gigi—upping the drama with the *Tell-Tale Heart* reference."

"You know, it's the fourth place we've spread her ashes, and I don't feel any closer to learning her secrets."

"Roddy, we've learned a lot. Think about it. We know Elizabeth Fry was Gigi's best friend, and they were fired from Tollman Hat Factory on the same day. We sat at the very spot where Pop carved a profession of his love for Gigi into a tree. If you ask me, that made this whole adventure worth it."

"Yeah, that was cool," he agrees.

"We also learned Pop was trained in welding, and his skills were somehow responsible for their good fortune."

"And," Roddy adds. "We have photographic evidence our grandparents cavorted with the notorious 'Farmer Boy' Hanson."

"Delightfully scandalous!"

Roddy laughs and shakes his head. "You really are so much like Gigi—finding the fun and wonder in everything."

Tears well in my eyes thinking of Gigi's irrepressible joy.

Choked up, Roddy clears his throat. "Enough of the sappiness," he says, pulling into my driveway behind Sally. "Time to get to work. Maybe the ledger will tie all we've learned together."

As Roddy unloads the car, I notice a huge bouquet of vibrant yellow, pink, and orange Gerbera daisies on my porch. A plastic pick stuck in the vase holds a card. *Thanks for lunching with me. Hope we can do it again. Donald.* How sweet. I quickly tuck the card into my pocket. I absolutely want to meet Donald again (he knew my mom), but I'm not ready to share it with Roddy.

Roddy carries the store sign through my open front door. "Are those from Marty?" he asks, pointing at the flowers.

"No, no. A thank-you from a client," I lie.

I grab one of the soda cases and the ledger and join Roddy in the living room. "Before we dive in, will you help me hang the sign?"

"Sure. Wipe it off while I get my tools."

Ten minutes later, the sign hangs above my couch.

I do a little jig around my living room. "I love it! A little piece of our childhood on my wall."

"I'm glad you bought it. What are you going to do with the soda crate?"

I clap my hands together, excited about the project. "I'm going to hang it on my kitchen wall and use it as a spice rack. I just have to find jars to fit."

"Kudos. You're so creative."

"Thanks." I swirl my hand around my chest. My brother's full of compliments today, and I'm rubbing them in! "Lemonade?"

"Water for me," he says.

I pour our drinks and grab the ledger. Roddy sits beside me at my kitchen table.

"Ready?"

He nods. The musty scent of old paper tickles my nose. A silverfish scuttles across the page as I lay the cover open. Roddy smushes it.

After a deep inhale, I flip to the first page of the ledger. "Here we go."

Date	Name	Received	Deposit	Payment	Fee
1933 04/09	Fred Hanson	Cash $1000			
1933 04/10	Ephrata Natl Bank		$100		
1933 04/15	Ephrata Natl Bank		$325		
1933 04/18	Fred Hanson			Ck #402 $361.25	$63.75
1933 04/18	Ephrata Natl Bank		$50		
1933 04/21	Ephrata Natl Bank		$250		
1933 04/24	Ephrata Natl Bank		$100		
1933 04/24	Fred Hanson			Ck #413 $340	$60
1933 04/28	Ephrata Natl Bank		$175		
1933 04/01	Fred Hanson			Ck #428 $148.75	$26.25
	April Profit				$150
1933 05/05	Fred Hanson	Cash $1500			
1933 05/05	Ephrata Natl Bank		$300		
1933 05/08	Ephrata Natl Bank		$250		
1933 05/10	Ephrata Natl Bank		$100		
1933 05/11	Fred Hanson			Ck #450 $552.50	$97.50
1933 05/12	Ephrata Natl Bank		$395		
1933 05/14	Ephrata Natl Bank		$185		
1933 05/15	Fred Hanson			Ck #459 $493	$87
1933 05/20	Ephrata Natl Bank		$270		
1933 05/22	Fred Hanson			Ck #464 $229.50	$40.50
	May Profit				$225

"It's Gigi's handwriting," I say.

"Yep," Roddy agrees. "And she wrote *Fred Hanson*—'Farmer Boy.'"

We let his names and the entries sink in.

"I don't get it. He gives her money, and then she pays him? Was she buying booze from him? I thought Mr. Davenport said she didn't sell bootleg liquor."

Roddy runs his fingers through his hair. "Nope. This isn't about buying booze. It's worse. She's laundering money for Hanson."

"Laundering money?"

"Yeah, see the fees?" he says, pointing to the last column. "Gigi was charging Hanson fifteen percent to clean his dirty cash."

My chin is resting on the floor. "I, uh...Are you sure?"

"Trust me, I'm right. Hanson gave her bundles of cash. Gigi made small deposits into her bank and paid him by check from her account, less her fee. Hanson probably gave her phony receipts for her checks, like she was buying potatoes, or corn, or whatever else he was pretending to sell."

"How would she explain the money she deposited?" I ask.

"I'm sure she fudged her receipts, too. Made up extra sales to cover the extra income."

"Wow!"

"Yeah. This was no small-time operation. Considering inflation, a thousand dollars in 1933 would be worth about $13,500 today."

I massage my temples. "I don't even know how to feel. Gigi was a criminal. I guess I should've assumed...I mean, she said it could change how we felt. Oh, I..." I trail off, finding words difficult.

Roddy pushes his chair back and strides to the fridge, grabbing one of the beers he left here the other night. He cracks open the can and takes a long swallow.

"It's not murder," he says. "So that's something."

I'm eager to jump on the justification bandwagon. "Besides, like I said when we thought Pop might've robbed the jewelry store. It was during the Depression. Gigi was probably desperate and doing what she needed to do to survive. Can we really hold it against her?"

He shrugs, "I think the real question is, if that's where our inheritance came from, will we keep it?"

I bite my thumbnail. "Jeez, I don't know." I get up, fill Miss Bennet with water, and put her on the stove to heat. "Let's not get ahead of ourselves. We don't know what our inheritance is. It might not be money. Maybe it's just knowledge or Mirabella. And we don't know what else we're going to find. We still have two bags left."

"Yeah," he says with dread. "Two bags left."

NOVEMBER 1933

EVIE

CRACK! The bat connected with the baseball and sent it flying through the bright red maple leaves to the far back corner of the yard. Gangly Mary Buch, in her mid-shin floral dress and bare feet, ran to each of the improvised bases while her younger brother, Earl, cheered her on. The village children were taking full advantage of the autumn warm spell.

Wearing only light sweaters, Evie and Bess watched from wooden rockers on the back porch of Evie's giant, six-bedroom farmhouse.

"It's nice to see the Buch kids smiling," Bess said to Evie.

"It is. They haven't had much to smile about as of late."

"No, they haven't. Last month it was their father's...incident." Bess shudders. "The way George described it...so, so awful." She gulped a swallow of her spiked lemonade and shook her head to clear away the image.

Evie patted her friend's hand. "And this month, their father's death. Poor kids."

Tow-headed Isaac Johnson ran up onto the porch interrupting their conversation. "Mrs. Collier, Momma's calling me home."

"Well," Evie said, straightening the collar on his threadbare cotton shirt. "What'll it be today?"

"Can I have a Popsicle?"

"You may. Take it from the store freezer and be sure to give my regards to your mother."

"Thanks awfully much," he said and dashed into the general store for his treat.

Bess laughed at the ten-year-old's enthusiasm. "What do you get in exchange for all the candy and ice cream you give them?"

The sales of the merchandise they stocked in the store weren't Pete and Evie's main source of income, so they could be generous.

"Smiles," Evie chuckled.

When Pete and Evie bought the property in the summer of '32, the neighbors were less than welcoming. Evie's short hair, trousers, and form-fitting blouses were seen as immodest amongst the Amish and Mennonite community. Evie knew, at the very least, the store needed to appear to be successful, so it was important for her to fit in.

The large garage, in its conversion to a store, was not the only thing to get an overhaul. On opening day, November 15, 1932, Evie greeted her first customers in a loose floral dress, a plain blue apron, and brown lace-up shoes.

Now, almost a year later, business was booming, and a visit to Vogansville General Store had become a weekend tradition for the two dozen kids that lived in the village and on the surrounding farms. After chores, on pleasant Saturday afternoons, they'd play kickball or baseball in the giant yard behind the general store. Before their walk home, every child—whether they had a nickel or not—would get a soda, a chocolate bar, or an ice cream cone.

"You gals want some apple cider?" Evie's mother, Hannah, asked Evie and Bess.

Evie's dad died a few months before Evie and Pete married. In June, after eighteen months in a sanitarium, Hannah was pronounced cured. She returned to Pennsylvania and moved in with her daughter and son-in-law.

"That'd be great, Mrs. Fisher," Bess said.

Once Hannah was out of earshot, Bess said, "You know, sometimes I wonder if my big house and fancy car are worth living with the constant fear of getting caught, but when I see the rosy color in your mom's cheeks, it makes the risk worth it."

Evie watches her mom walk across the yard into the house and smiles. "I never doubt if it was worth it. What was I going to do? Just let her die?" The autumn breeze rustles the red, yellow, and orange leaves, and she pulls her cardigan tight around her. "But, speaking of your big house, you and George need to be careful. Tone it down. Your flashy spending might give them a reason to look."

"You're probably right, but I do love the good life." Bess laughed.

"Here you are," Hannah said, returning with the drinks. "So, Bess, when's that sweet bundle of joy due?"

Bess rubbed her eight-month pregnant belly. "Christmas Day."

Hannah claps her hands in delight. "How wonderful. Wouldn't I just love a grandbaby for next Christmas," she said, looking directly at Evie.

"Mother," Evie warned. "It will happen when it happens."

Hopefully, no time soon. Evie did everything possible to prevent it, making the Lysol douche a required part of her post-coitus regimen.

A Model A Roadster pickup puttered into the circular, gravel driveway at the back of Pete and Evie's house. Freckle-faced "Farmer Boy" Hanson stepped out of the car and walked over to the three women.

"Ain't you three some ripe-looking tomatoes," he said.

Bess tensed but batted her eyelashes at her husband's boss. "Hi, Mr. Hanson."

"Can I get you some cider?" Hannah asked him.

"No thanks, Mrs. F."

"Well, I've got bread in the oven," Hannah said and excused

herself. Evie had made it clear Hannah was to make herself scarce when Mr. Hanson arrived. With his reputation, Hannah didn't argue.

"Surprised to see you," Evie said, standing. "Didn't expect you for another two weeks."

"What can I say?" he said, spreading his arms wide. "We got us a bumper crop."

Bess stands and smooths her high-waisted, wide-legged trousers. "I'll leave you to it." She gave Evie a kiss on the cheek and an extra tight hug. "See ya tomorrow, doll. Bye, Mr. Hanson." She waved. "I'll tell George I saw you."

"Yeah, okay. Give that palooka my best."

Hanson walked out to his truck, hoisted a wooden crate full of apples out of the back, and followed Evie into the store.

Pete was behind the counter, wrapping a wedge of cheddar in cheesecloth for a regular customer.

"Hey, Pally!" Hanson said to Pete. "Where you been hidin'? I ain't seen you the last few times I came around."

"Yeah, you know, keeping my nose to the grindstone."

Pete usually made himself scarce when Hanson showed up. He hated dealing with the loud-mouthed goon. Evie was better able to handle Hanson's obnoxious behavior and was smart enough never to let her guard down. She knew his chumminess was only a paper-thin veneer.

Jacob Cartwright—one of Hanson's "farmers"—dared to sell a little moonshine on the side, and Hanson sicced the coppers on him. They raided the poor sap's farm, confiscated his still, the money he stashed under his mattress, and all of his legitimate crops, and threw him in jail. If Hanson ever turned on her, she wouldn't mess with the local law—he's bought them off—she'd deal directly with the Feds. Evie was confident her secret ledger would provide enough evidence to nail Hanson, enabling her to cut a deal with the FBI and save her and Pete's hides. Though, if Hanson ever discovered where the windfall—that let her and

Pete buy the store—came from, all bets were off. She and Pete would be as big a catch for the Feds as Hanson.

Hanson carried the crate of York Imperials into the storeroom, and Evie locked the door. Halfway through transferring the lopsided, red apples into a wooden store display bin, she reached a burlap bag. She plucked it out of the crate and slid its contents onto her work table. Stacks of twenty-dollar bills fanned out across the wooden surface. Evie counted them in a flash.

"One thousand." She looked to Hanson for confirmation.

"You know it, doll."

"You brought a thousand last week. We can't clean it that fast without causing suspicion."

His happy-go-lucky demeanor turned stony. "That ain't my problem. Expand the store, open another business. I don't care how you do it; just get it done."

Evie swallowed her trepidation and nodded. Hanson dumped the remaining apples into the bin and stormed out of their store. The wheels of his Roadster flung gravel behind him as he peeled out of their driveway.

"What was that all about?" Pete asked Evie as she situated the bin of York Imperials on a shelf at the front of the store.

Between Hanson's increasing amounts of cash and the stacks of their own dirty money, their fake receipts had ballooned to justify frequent bank deposits. Evie knew they were showing more sales than would be feasible for a tiny village store. But no need to worry Pete. She would figure it out—like she always did.

She picked an apple out of the bin, took a big bite, and shrugged. "He doesn't like apples."

JULY 2000

RUBY

My red curls are whipping in the wind, and the July sun nuzzles my cheeks. I slide on my Dezi aviator shades and crank up the radio. "Livin' La Vida Loca" blares from Sally's speakers, and I sing along.

The low humidity and eighty-degree temps have coaxed folks from their air-conditioned homes and offices. Downtown Lancaster's sidewalks are teeming with humanity. Suited women and men mingle with yogis wearing Lululemon capris and bedraggled bag ladies enjoying the temperate weather. At a red light, a young mother and toddler join Ricky Martin and me in belting out his chart-topping hit. I wave goodbye when the light turns green.

Britney Spears' throaty voice rings out just as I pull into the parking lot of the historical society. I cut the engine and her song. (Sorry, Britney. You know I love you.) As I raise Sally's convertible top, I muster my determination. I'm on a mission to learn more about Fred "Farmer Boy" Hanson.

Gigi had to have a good reason to work with him. Maybe he was the local Robin Hood, fighting the establishment to help the poor. After all, according to Marty's research, his enterprising spirit was putting money into the hands of struggling farmers.

I grab my crocheted bucket bag, lock Sally, and head into the building.

"Well, look who it is." Millicent zips out from behind her desk to hug me. "Don't you look cute as a bug?"

I twirl to show off my new-to-me dress. It has a ruffled, off-the-shoulder top and flowy skirt, and the fabric looks like red, blue, and yellow paint spatters.

"Thanks! The primary colors drew me like a moth to a flame."

"Suits your personality—bright and cheery. You know, colors say a lot about a person. I mean, take me, for instance." She waves her hand up and down her gray and tan outfit. "Neutrals. I'm the kind of person who doesn't mind fading into the background. In fact, I prefer it. Now my sister Myrtle, she's another story. The more outrageous the outfit, the better."

I think about Gigi's leopard print leggings and sequined shirt and smile.

"When we were girls, Myrtle was always the star of the show and as popular as buttered popcorn at the movie theater. She had beaus lined up and down the street. She married Rick Van Housen, the love of her life, and birthed her own baseball team—"

"Nine children?" I interrupt.

"Yes indeed! Every one of"em is my favorite." She chuckles. "I wasn't blessed with children of my own or a husband for that matter. I was engaged once to a dashing, dark-haired Adonis. Let him slip right through my fingers...oh, but that's another story," she says with a big sigh. "I'm sure you don't have time for an old lady's nostalgic meandering. Suffice to say, I learned—unfortunately too late—that you've got to be brave enough to grab what you want."

Her words slap me, and I feel the sting of loss. I desperately miss Gigi. Tears well up.

She takes my hands in hers. "Oh, dear! I didn't mean to upset you."

I blink, and a few salty drops slide down my cheek. "No, no. It isn't you. I mean, it's what you said. Gigi always used to tell Roddy and me, 'You only get what you have the courage to take.' I just miss her so much."

She walks around her desk and wraps her jiggly arms around me. Patting my back, she says, "There, there. I know you miss her." She pulls away and lifts up my chin to look me in the eye. "You're lucky. You feel great pain because you felt great love."

I nod and wipe my tears on the back of my hand. I'm embarrassed by my blubbering. "Sorry, I don't know why I'm so weepy."

"No apologies! It is okay to cry! It's also okay to seek comfort. How about a cookie?" She moves behind her desk. A Tupperware container lies beside Booker T. Washington's *Up From Slavery*. Millicent removes the lid and offers it to me. "Hershey Kiss and peanut butter."

"It feels like a two-cookie day," I say, mustering a smile. I take a bite of the peanut-buttery goodness. "Mmm. So good!"

Millicent pops the lid back onto the container. "So, my dear, what's on the agenda today?"

"Research on an infamous Lancaster County criminal—Fred 'Farmer Boy' Hanson."

Millicent cocks her head. "Hmm. Never heard of him." She types something into her computer. "Well, looky here!"

I peek over her desk to scan her computer screen. There are six entries containing his name. Millicent writes down each source and hands me the notepaper. "Do you want me to help you find them?

I shake my head and smile. "You've helped enough," I say, raising the second cookie.

After finishing my treat, I dive into the readings. In the first three sources, I find the same things I already know about Hanson, but the fourth book is a goldmine! Each chapter in *Prohibition Pennsylvania* is dedicated to a county. I flip to Lancaster, and

"Farmer Boy" Hanson's freckled face smiles out at me. I skim the chapter.

To those on the verge of losing their family farms, Hanson was a savior. See, just like I suspected. Even though what he and Gigi did was illegal, it really was helping regular people survive. I knew she had a good reason to involve herself with him. I continue reading.

> While tone-deaf local government demanded payment of property taxes from destitute men, Hanson provided a way to save their land and feed their families. All was rosy—until it wasn't. Produce too little or low-quality liquor and receive a warning. Do it again, and Hanson would turn on you faster than a striking rattlesnake. Unproductive farmers would end up in jail—if they were lucky—or maimed if they were not. It is widely believed Hanson was responsible for over fifteen amputation "accidents."

Jeez! Maybe not. My stomach roils at the thought of Gigi interacting with this monster. She probably got entangled before she knew how horrible he was and then couldn't figure a way out. I root around in the bottom of my purse for a ginger candy. I suck on it and continue reading.

> Predicting the end of prohibition, Hanson diversified. While still producing illegal alcohol, his farmers were givon oceds to yrow and harvest marijuana.

Great, so he's a drug dealer too.

> Hanson's meteoric rise in the criminal underworld was cut short by his murder. He was found dead from cyanide poisoning on December 1, 1933—four days before Prohibition ended. His killer was never found.

A cold shudder rattles me. Did Gigi find a way out? No, no! It's too horrible to even think. I slam the book shut. Enough research.

I slide my tablet into my bag, return the materials to their proper location, and head into the lobby area. Millicent is munching a cookie and reading her book.

"I'm done for today," I say as I approach the desk. I don't want to startle her.

She pushes her red glasses up on her nose and sets her book on her desk. "What's wrong? You're pale. Need another cookie?"

I love her solution for paleness. "No thanks. Just tired, I guess."

"Grief can do that. When my mother passed, I felt like I was dragging around Marley's chains. Now, Myrtle, she was just the opposite, like the Energizer Bunny." Millicent holds her finger to her lips. "Come to think of it, she was like that when she was pregnant too. When she was seven months pregnant with her fifth, no, maybe her fourth, no, no, it was her fifth. Anyway, she took a sledgehammer and knocked out a wall between her kitchen and dining room. Open floor plans were all the rage...Oh, mercy me! Here I am babbling again." She walks from behind her desk and puts her arm around my shoulder. "You go on home and get a nap." She guides me towards the exit.

"I think I'll do exactly that," I say.

At the door, she gives me another grandmotherly squeeze. "You come visit anytime you need a cookie—or a hug."

***

After a long nap, I'm refreshed, and I call Mr. Davenport with Roddy and my discovery from the Vogansville General Store. He confirms Gigi wanted us to learn she had laundered money for Fred Hanson. I used to enjoy solving Gigi's puzzles, but this recent one I could do without.

"Ruby, I am emailing the next puzzle. Once you decipher the location, visit, spread a bag of your grandmother's ashes, and follow the instructions. There is no information to glean from this spot. Please call me when you and Roddy complete the task, and I will send you the next puzzle."

"Okay, thanks, Mr. Davenport."

A few seconds later his email arrives in my inbox.

"Death ends a life, not a relationship." ~Mitch Albom

1. *Lebanese national emblem.*
2. *What is alive with the sound of music?*
3. *Kirkyard.*
4. *Anne Brown played which character in the premiere Broadway cast of George Gershwin's famous opera?*
5. *Cook in hot fat or oil, typically in a shallow pan.*
6. *Surname of the 10th Surgeon General of the United States Army.*
7. *Title IX was signed into law, and my soulmate died.*

Spread my ashes and read poem 809.

Numbers two and five are a breeze, but the rest—I'll need reinforcements (or, at the very least, encyclopedias). I check the time. Jeez, it's already four-thirty. No time to solve the puzzle. Marty's picking me up in an hour. We're eating at Oriental Kitchen (my suggestion, Marty's never been) before the movie. They have the absolute best eggrolls—fresh vegetables wrapped in flaky goodness. My mouth's watering thinking about them. I forward the email to Roddy with a quick note. *2 is hills, 5 is fry. You figure out the rest. :)*

I jump in the shower and squirt clementine-scented, sulfate-free shampoo into my hair, lathering my thick curls into a frothy halo. After rinsing, I suds up my body with Dr. Bronner's pure castile citrus scent soap. (Yep, I'm a sucker for all things citrus.)

The hot water taps my back like a hundred gentle fingertips. I relax into it and let my worry over what Gigi might have done follow the bubbles down the drain. Only when the water at the hottest setting becomes lukewarm (blasted old plumbing) do I towel off. I'm wearing another new-to-me outfit tonight, green capri leggings and a daisy-print A-line tunic. I leave my curls loose to air dry, swipe on minimal makeup, and am ready with fifteen minutes to spare. Good thing, because Marty knocks on my door ten minutes early. My stomach flutters and my palms are damp. I take a deep breath and open the door. As soon as we see each other, we crack up.

"So, you got my memo?" I joke.

"Obviously," he says, voguing like a runway model.

His green Bermuda shorts are a shade more subdued than my Kelly-green capris, and the graphic flowers on his polo shirt are white hibiscus instead of daisies, but we're basically wearing the same outfit.

"Should I change?" I ask.

"Why? I think we look spiffy."

I love how unselfconscious he is. If he's game to look like the Bobbsey twins, I am. Grabbing my purse and a yellow sweater, we head out the door.

Less than ten minutes later, we arrive at Oriental Kitchen. The décor is one step up from cafeteria chic. Utilitarian tables and chairs are separated by bamboo screens. A row of red paper lanterns dangles from the ceiling, and a gold and black mural of Asian women covers the back wall. We choose a table by the window, and Mr. Khai (server, cook, and owner) brings hot tea and a bowl of grocery-store rice cracker mix. Marty raises an eyebrow. When the Asian elevator music switches to NSYNC's *Bye Bye Bye*, he nearly spits out his tea from laughing.

"I know, it's quirky, but believe me, the food is delish," I assure him.

We both order an eggroll and chicken with vegetables.

Marty pops a few crackers in his mouth and takes a sip of tea. "How's the puzzle going? Are you close to finding your grandmother's secret?"

Worry joins us at the table and my muscles tighten.

"That bad?" Marty says, noticing my tension.

I frown. "It could be. My grandmother may have been a murderer."

Marty grips the edge of the table. "What? How? Why?"

"We know she laundered money for 'Farmer Boy' Hanson."

"Wow. Did she meet him at Green Dragon?"

I nod. "She did. Roddy and I found a photo of my grandparents and Hanson in the pile you gave me."

"So how does laundering turn into murder?"

"Hanson was murdered with poison. The crime was never solved. I also learned it wasn't uncommon for Hanson to turn on the people he worked with." I'm wringing my paper napkin in my hands. "What if he turned on Gigi? What if poison was her reaction to his threats?"

Marty reaches across the table and gently pulls the crumpled mess from my hands. "What-ifs eat your peace, like Pac-Man gobbling dots."

"Pac-Man?" I laugh. He has a knack for easing tension. "You're giving away your age."

"Worth it to make you smile."

Another belly flutter (I'm chalking it up to hunger). With perfect timing, Mr. Khai brings our eggrolls.

"This will make *you* smile," I say, biting into crispy, flaky goodness.

"Mmm," he says. "Better than a blue ghost."

"Blue ghost?"

"You know, from Pac-Man." He munches away on his eggroll.

I roll my eyes. "Oh, we're still on Pac-Man."

"Yes. Remember, when Pac-Man ate the power pellet, the ghosts turned blue, and he could eat them."

"I was a Donkey Kong girl."

"Donkey Kong?" He shakes his head in mock disgust. "I don't think we can date."

And I thought the possibility I was raised by a murderer would be what scared him away.

"So, we're dating?" I razz.

His face turns as red as Donkey Kong's tie. "I, uh, well, I'd like to. I mean, if you, uh..."

I take hold of his sweaty hand and gaze past his round lenses into his blue eyes. "We're dating."

***

"You should be dancing, yeah," we sing out of tune. Mimicking John Travolta, we dance our way to Marty's car.

"That was fun!" I say as we round the corner onto State Street. I point to the third floor of the Royer building. "Roddy lives here."

"Oh yeah? It's nice you two live so close to each other."

A white-haired man darts furtively out of the tenants' entrance just before we reach it.

Marty grabs my arm and pulls me behind him. "That's the guy who was following you."

Marty scowls, and I grin.

"Hey, Donald!" I yell and wave.

Donald stops and looks at us. His deer-in-the-headlights expression changes to delight.

"You know him?" Marty asks.

"Long story. I'll tell you later."

"What are you doing here?" I ask, catching up to Donald.

"I, uh." He scratches his neck and shoves his hands in his pockets. "I was looking at an apartment."

Marty looks at his watch. "They show apartments at nine at night?"

Donald flicks his gaze between me and Marty.

"Oh, sorry. How rude of me. Donald, this is my..." Thoughts zing through my brain. Do I say *friend*? We are, after all, dating. But if I say *boyfriend*, that may add too much pressure. Oh, Jeez! Why did I say *my*? Heat slithers up my chest, past my neck, and onto my cheeks. "This is Marty. Marty, this is Donald." The men nod warily at each other. "So, did you like it?"

"Like it?" Donald asks.

"The apartment."

"Yeah, yeah," he says quickly. "It was okay. I have some other places to look at."

"I didn't know you were looking or that you wanted to live in Ephrata. You know Roddy lives here, right?"

Donald rubs his nose and chin. "No, no. I didn't. What a coincidence."

Coincidence? I'm sure Roddy saw Donald loitering around his apartment. Why is he being so cagey?

"Thanks for the flowers, by the way. They were gorgeous. How did you know I love Gerbera daisies?"

Pink blooms on Donald's face, and his shoulders tense. "A good guess," he says. "Well, I'll let you two be on your way." He shoves his hands back in his pockets and walks in the opposite direction of us.

"Hey, Donald," I call.

He stops and turns towards me.

"I do want to meet for lunch. I'll call you, okay?"

His shoulders release, and he smiles. "I'd like that." He gives me a backward wave and heads down the street with a spring in his step.

"Lunch?" Marty asks. "Is that a good idea? He's dodgy."

I link my arm with Marty's and move towards the car. "He knew my mother."

"Okay?"

"I didn't. She died giving birth to Roddy and me."

"Oh, Ruby." He pulls me into a hug. "I'm so sorry."

I sniff back a few tears. Before losing Gigi, I barely thought about my mother, but lately, I can't stop. Marty and I hold hands and walk. Comfort seeps from his palm.

"Gigi and Pop were devastated by their loss and would barely talk about my mom—even if I asked questions." I lay my hand over my heart. "Maybe Donald can fill in this empty hole."

Marty takes both my hands in his. We're facing each other, only inches apart. He lifts my hands to his mouth and presses a kiss on each one. Tingles frolic in my belly.

"I hope he can, but promise me you'll be careful. I don't think Donald is completely above board."

Roddy said the same thing. Why are men so cynical?

Making light of his concern, I twirl a curl around my finger. "Okay, I'll promise, on one condition."

"A condition? And what's that?"

"You'll be my plus-one to Janet's party."

"Won't you be busy working?"

"Yes, but leading the fun is part of my job. Gets everyone in the spirit."

He laughs. "My finger-pointing boogie will knock their socks off."

"Oh, and just one more thing."

He raises his eyebrows and waits for my request. I pull him into the alley at the back of the building. Lifting my chin, I lean in close. When our lips touch, my belly tingles intensify to head-to-toe electric zings. Marty wraps his arms around me but pulls his head back to gaze into my eyes. He rubs the tip of his nose against mine. I reach around to the back of his head and pull him close, kissing him.

A passing stranger yells down the alley, "Get a room."

We part, both red from embarrassment. (Okay, okay—and heat.) Tongue-tied, I straighten my shirt and look anywhere but at Marty.

Marty runs both hands over his bald head and, with a bad Italian accent, quotes the "Saturday Night Fever" lead character. "Would ya just watch the hair? Ya know, I work on my hair a long time, and you hit it. You hit my hair."

I burst out laughing. He's too cute, and I absolutely can't help it. I kiss him again.

AUGUST 1963

EVIE

Evie fluffed the pillows on the guest bed and opened the window. The scent of sweet corn growing in the field across the road floated in on the warm summer breeze. She grabbed a lilac coverlet from the linen cupboard and folded it across the bottom of the bed.

"Ella," she called down the hallway. "Have you made up the trundle bed for Lynn?"

Sixteen-year-old Ella popped out of her bedroom into the hallway. Shapely tan legs jutted from her super-short dress. "All set."

Once a month, Evie and Ella hosted a sleepover for Bess and her youngest child and only daughter, Lynn. With four sons/brothers, the Finley females needed an escape from their testosterone-filled household.

"I'm off," Pete said, carrying his overnight bag. He used the monthly tradition as a chance to visit his older brother in Philly. "Be good," he said to Ella, chucking her under the chin. Turning to Evie, he took her in his arms and dipped her, giving her a loud, dramatic smooch. "Until we meet again."

Evie laughed, then kissed him back. Ella rolled her eyes and retreated to her room.

After adding fresh towels to the guest bath, Evie hurried down the stairs, through the kitchen, and out the covered walkway to their store. She scooped two tubs of popcorn from the cart and grabbed a few packs of Lemonhead candies and a jug of Mrs. Buch's homemade root beer. Now that the girls were fixed with their treats, it was time for the women. Back in the kitchen, Evie fished two cocktail glasses from the cabinet and a bottle of Gilbey's gin and Rose's lime juice from the pantry. As she was slicing a fresh lime into wedges, Ella bounded into the kitchen.

"What are you girls up to tonight?" Evie asked. She and Bess were thrilled that their daughters were such good friends.

"Eyelashes. Lynn's bringing a few sets, and we're going to practice putting them on."

Evie bucked the new trend, preferring her wand mascara. "I hope you have better luck than I do. I always get them lopsided."

Ella blew out her breath in the classic patronizing sigh teenage girls reserve for their mothers. "Bummer."

A rap on the back door followed Bess's voice calling, "We're here!"

"In the kitchen," Evie replied.

At seventeen, Lynn was a few inches taller than Bess, and her dress was a few inches shorter than Ella's. Evie didn't think that possible without risking arrest for indecent exposure.

"I brought eyelashes, gobs of makeup, and the newest *Seventeen* magazine. We'll have a gas," Lynn said.

"We will," Ella replied with a sneaky glint in her eyes.

Lynn grabbed her stuff, and Ella grabbed the snacks. "Later," they said to their mothers in unison as they headed out of the kitchen.

Evie fixed two gimlets, and she and Bess settled side-by-side on the couch.

Bess raised her cocktail glass. "To grand adventures."

The clink of glasses served as an exclamation point to their shared sentiment.

Swathed in contentment, Evie rested her head against her soulmate's shoulder. "The best is yet to be."

***

Thwap. Thwap. Thwap. The back screen door flapped open and shut. Evie dragged her head off the pillow and rubbed her heavy eyelids. Still woozy from gin, she swayed, putting on her slippers. She crept downstairs. As she closed the door, a gust of wind ripped the frame from her fingers and lifted her robe. Light flashed in the sky, followed by a slow rumble. Tying the sash tighter, she snatched the door closed and fastened the hook and eye closure.

She opened and closed her mouth. It was thick and dry like a caterpillar had spun a cocoon in it. She filled a glass with tap water and gulped it down.

"Give me one of those and two aspirin," Bess said, wandering into the kitchen.

Evie grabbed another glass from the cupboard and found a bottle of aspirin in the junk drawer. "Here," she said, handing them to her friend. "Did I wake you?"

"No, the banging door did, but I expected to find Ella down here."

Evie furrowed her brow. "Why's that?"

"I checked in on the girls on my way down. Ella's not in bed."

"She what?" Evie hurried through the downstairs to find Ella. "You check upstairs, and I'll check the store."

Just before Evie opened the back door to the store, lightning zig-zagged its way to their old oak tree with a deafening crack. Evie's hair stood up, and she felt a sizzle of electricity. She darted into the store as a massive branch split from the trunk and crashed to the ground.

"Ella," she yelled into the dark store. "Are you in here?"

No answer. Evie ran back to the house. Lynn had joined Bess in the kitchen.

"Did you find her?" Evie asked, panting.

"Tell her," Bess instructed Lynn.

Dread sluiced down Evie's spine. "Tell me what?"

"Umm. I, uh...I think that, umm, Ella snuck out."

"Where did she go? Who did she sneak out with?" Evie barked.

Lynn pulled a lock of hair to her mouth and chewed on the end.

"Lynn," Bess coaxed, "it's important you tell us. We need to make sure Ella is safe. You don't want to see her hurt."

"She'll hate me for telling," Lynn whined.

"Please," Evie pleaded, growing more worried by the minute.

Lynn nodded. "I, uh, think some boys were meeting her at the pond."

"Thank you, sweetheart." Evie gave Lynn a quick hug, slid into her Keds, pulled on a raincoat, and tied on her rain bonnet.

The wind increased and rain pelted her face as she sprinted the two blocks to the farm with the pond. She climbed the fence into the field. Her shoes sank into the mud, and it spattered her pajama pants as she ran. A flash of lightning lit the pond in an eerie glow. Ella's wet head bobbed up and down, and the wind caught her laugh and carried it to Evie. Evie's gut-wrenching fear turned to white-hot anger with only a momentary stop at relief.

"Ella Fisher Collier," Evie screamed at her daughter.

"Hey, Mom," Ella brazenly responded from the water.

A gangly teenage boy clambered naked from the pond. He lunged for his underwear and scrambled into them and a muddy shirt. As Evie got closer, she recognized him.

"Albert Donovan! Your mother will hear of this!"

"Yes, ma'am," he said, clutching his pants and shoes in his arms. "I'm sorry, ma'am." He hurried across the sodden field towards his home.

The bank of the pond was littered with Ella's dress, bra, underwear, shoes, and an almost-empty bottle of vodka. Evie clenched her fists, face heating with equal parts rage and gratitude.

Ella floated on her back, arms outstretched. "Come in, Mom. The water's fine."

Another crack of lightning hit frighteningly close.

"Get out now!" Evie bellowed.

Ella swam irritatingly slowly to the bank and trudged out of the water. Her naked body shivered in the rain.

"What were you thinking?" Evie yelled.

"Don't flip your wig, Mom."

As Ella tried to pull on her panties, she got her foot caught in the crotch and tumbled to the ground. She burst into laughter and rolled in the mud.

"You're drunk," Evie accused.

"As a skunk," Ella slurred, pushing up to sitting.

Evie stormed to her daughter's side and was tempted to slap the sloppy grin from her face. One, two, three, four…she counted to herself. The day Ella was born, Evie vowed not to repeat history. Unlike her own father, she would never strike her child. Once her anger was in check, she helped Ella slide into her undies. She pulled the dress over her head, not bothering with the bra, and lifted her from the ground. Ella wobbled.

"Can you walk?"

"I can."

After a few unsteady steps, Evie draped her daughter's arm across her shoulder and guided her through the field. Climbing would be unwise in her condition, Evie thought and suggested Ella crawl under the fence. Ella shimmied under the rail on her belly.

By the time they reached home, both were mud-covered and sopping wet. Bess had heated a kettle of water and fixed them hot tea.

When Ella saw Lynn, she exploded in anger. "Traitor! I never want to see you again!"

Tears filled Lynn's eyes. "The weather. They were worried. What could I do?" she pleaded.

Evie and Bess were sure the crack in their daughters' friendship would close.

It never did.

JULY 2000

RUBY

I feel like crap. I'm exhausted and crampy and want to spend the day on the couch, but Roddy solved the puzzle and is picking me up in half an hour to head to Cedar Hills Cemetery. After collecting Gigi from the bread tin, I transfer her from the plastic baggy to the sequin pouch. I tuck her and a copy of Emily Dickinson's *Selected Poems* in my purse. A splash of cold water on my face and a glass of ginger ale liven me up. By the time Roddy pulls up, I'm feeling better (not supercalifragilisticexpialidocious, but better).

I open my front door and a wall of heat hits me. The air is soupy. The heat sucks what little energy I have right out of me. I meet Roddy halfway down my walkway.

"You drive," I say, pointing at Hank.

Knowing how much I hate using his gas guzzler, he raises his eyebrows.

"What? It's only a few miles, and I'm tired."

"Fine by me," he agrees.

We climb into Hank and hit the road.

"So, I called Cedar Hills and gave them Bess's name..."

I snap my fingers, "Oh! As in 'Porgy and Bess.'"

"Are you just getting that now?" Roddy asks.

"Yep, my brain went on strike yesterday, so I'm glad you solved it. When did she die?"

"June 23, 1972. With her name and date of death, the caretaker was able to locate her burial plot. She's in number 125 North, in the far corner of the graveyard, under a dogwood tree."

"Aww, like my dogwood tree, Delilah."

Roddy rolls his eyes as he pulls into a visitor parking spot in the northern quadrant of the cemetery. "Let's not linger. I want to get a jump on a painting job."

"You're working on a Saturday?"

"Why not? What else do I have to do?"

I want to tell him to stop moping over Clara and start making a new life, but I bite my tongue. My unsolicited advice is never appreciated.

"Well, I guess you might as well be productive." I step out of Hank into the oppressive summer heat. "Wow! Feels like I'm breathing gravy."

"Yeah. The humidity is brutal." He wipes his sweaty forehead. "There's the dogwood tree."

My eyes follow his pointing finger. Two women are arranging sunflowers in stone vases attached to the sides of a heart-shaped headstone under the tree.

"Do you think they're here to visit Bess?" I ask.

Roddy shrugs. "We'll see."

We walk through the grass to the corner plot. As we approach the women, I say, "Those are lovely flowers."

Two sets of chocolatey brown eyes framed by thick eyebrows look up. Two bow-shaped sets of lips smile. The older woman looks to be in her fifties, and I'd guess the younger one is late twenties. Mom and daughter? At the very least, related.

"My mother loved them," the older woman says.

I walk to the front of her mother's headstone. Elizabeth Fry Finley was laid to rest beside her beloved husband, George Finley.

"Bess is your mother?" I blurt.

She tilts her head. "You knew my mother?"

"No, but my grandmother did. Evie Collier."

Her voice raises an octave. "Evie was your grandmother?" She throws her hand up to her gaping mouth. "Oh my god, you're the twins?"

"Have we met?" I ask.

"No, but Evie showed me pictures and told me all about you two at my mom's funeral. What a small world." She extends her hand. "I'm Lynn, and this is my niece, Gail."

"Pleasure," I say, shaking Lynn's extended hand.

Gail dips her head in greeting. Her long hair swoops across the right side of her face. She bats full eyelashes at Roddy from under the silky chestnut curtain and extends her hand. (Just what he needs. Another swooning woman.)

Roddy's eyes shine, and his lips curl into a full-out grin as he shakes Gail's hand. "Nice to meet you."

"Likewise," she answers.

They hold hands and gaze at each other for a few beats longer than necessary. What is happening? Where's my indifferent brother?

"I saw your grandmother's obituary," Lynn says, drawing my attention away from the flirtation. "I'm so sorry for your loss. She was an amazing woman."

"Thanks," Roddy and I say in unison.

"That's why we're here," he says. "Gigi—that's what we call—called—our grandmother—"

Lynn interrupts. "Appropriate. She was definitely too hip for Grandma."

"You *did* know Gigi!" I say, laughing. Roddy's gaze has returned to Gail, so I jump in to explain. "Gigi wanted some of her ashes spread on your mother's grave. Is that all right with you?"

"Please," she says, pointing to the headstone. "My mom would be overjoyed to have Evie rest with her. You know they were best friends."

"Soulmates," I say using the word from Gigi's puzzle. "She also wanted us to read a Dickinson poem, 'Unable Are The Loved to Die.' Is that okay?"

"Absolutely. Would you like us to give you some privacy when you spread her ashes?"

I look at Roddy. He's staring at Gail with a dreamy look on his face. I clear my throat to nab his attention.

"Oh, what?" he says.

"Do we want privacy?"

"Um, not necessarily. I mean, you did know our grandmother," he says to Lynn.

"And thought she was amazing. I know it sounds cliché, but she really did light up a room. And she was a blast! She'd plan the most amazing adventures for your mom and me."

I smack my forehead. "Jeez, I didn't even think about that. You knew our mom, too."

Lynn gently strokes her throat and looks off into the distance. She swallows and gives a weak smile.

"I did. I grew up with her, and for a while, we were best friends—just like our mothers."

Her shoulders droop.

"What happened?" I ask.

She presses her lips together and sadness shades her face. "People grow apart. In fact, I even lost touch with your grandmother after I graduated from college. Mom's funeral was the first time I had seen her in years." Tears sneak into the corner of her eyes.

"Well, we know all about Gigi's adventures," I say to lighten the heaviness. "In fact, she even made spreading her ashes into a scavenger hunt of sorts."

"I love it!" Gail chimes in. "So cheeky!"

"And typical Evie," Lynn adds. "What do you have to find?"

I steal a glance at Roddy to see if he's okay with me sharing. He nods slightly, so I give them the (mostly) full story, including the money laundering, but not our suspicions about Hanson's murder.

"So," I wrap up. "We still have one more bag of ashes to spread and more secrets to uncover."

Gail chuckles. "I'm glad to know I'm not the only person with outlaws for relatives."

"We saw Bess and a man, who I'm assuming was your grandfather, in a photo with our grandparents and 'Farmer Boy' Hanson," Roddy says. "Were they involved in money laundering too?"

"No," Lynn pipes up. "But they were involved with Hanson."

"I have an idea," Roddy says. "Let us pick your brain over an early lunch. My treat."

What happened to getting a jump on the painting job?

Gail's eyes light up. "I'm in." She looks at her aunt.

"Why not?" Lynn agrees.

After we spread Gigi's ashes and read poem 809, Gail and Lynn follow us to Sugar & Spice Café on Main Street, across from Roddy's apartment building. Naomi (an old high school chum) renovated the bottom floor and porch of a three-story, brick Queen Anne style building that has served as everything from a classroom, to an electric supply store, to a barbershop. Now it's a darling café offering top-notch bakery items (sugar) and the most creative soups and salads (spice). Usually, I sit at one of the six bistro tables lining the front porch, but today it's too hot. The inside is rustic country chic at its finest. Reclaimed barn wood tops rusty tractor wheels to create one-of-a-kind tables. Long primitive benches serve as seating. Old lanterns hang from metal wall hooks and hold flickering candles, and antique Mason jars filled with wildflower blooms are centerpieces.

"Good choice," Gail says to Roddy. She takes a seat on the bench across from him. "This place is adorable."

"Thanks." He puffs up like a peacock, even though I'm the one who told him where to go.

I stifle an eye roll.

"The signs are too funny," Lynn says, pointing to the walls. "I especially love that one."

Today's Special: Buy 2 Salads & Pay for Both.

Naomi's hand-painted signs showcase her wicked sense of humor.

I twist and point behind me. "My favorite is the parody of Annie Lennox's song. *Sweet Dreams Are Made of Cheese, Who Am I to Dis a Brie?*"

A perky pony-tailed teen pops up at our table. "Hi, folks! My name is Emily, and I'll be your server today." She hands out the menus. "Can I start you off with a fresh-brewed strawberry tea or a watermelon basil lemonade?"

We all order watermelon basil lemonades and peruse the menu. Today's signature salad sounds ah-mazing! Definitely my choice.

Emily returns with our drinks. "Are you ready to order?"

"Citrus salad with pink peppercorns," Lynn says.

"I'll have the avocado, watercress, and caramelized pineapple salad, please," I order.

"Heirloom Tomato Panzanella," Gail says.

"Me too," Roddy orders. "Who doesn't love a bread salad?"

Gail laughs like it was the funniest thing she's ever heard, and Roddy beams. Hope tickles me. I think these two are moonstruck—and if I'm right—Gigi and Bess are smiling from the heavens.

Gail and Roddy start a fervid conversation about their favorite breads. Lynn seems amused by the intensity of their discussion and gives me a knowing look. I nod slightly to acknowledge I see it too, and we both smile at the development. I realize any digging into the past is up to me.

I ask Lynn, "You mentioned your parents were involved with Hanson. In what way?"

"Originally, my dad, George, made booze for Hanson to sell. As my dad put it, Hanson 'took a shine' to him, and he got promoted to his driver and muscle."

"This may be a touchy subject, but I've read that Hanson could be cruel and was responsible for several amputations. Would your dad have been the person to carry out his orders?"

Lynn twists the black bandana napkin in her hands. "He wasn't proud of it, but he admitted to roughing up plenty of men. He said, for a while, he talked himself into believing the accounts of maimings and blindings were just rumors, but when he witnessed Hanson chop off a farmer's fingers, that was it. That's when he drew the line and started making plans to disentangle himself. Lucky for Dad, Hanson died shortly after that event."

Emily brings our meals. "Enjoy!"

Lynn's citrus salad is a sunset on a plate, with fruits in darkening shades of yellow, orange, pink, and red fanning the white dish. Gail and Roddy's panzanella looks fresh and hearty, with crusty bread torn into big craggy pieces mixed amongst red, yellow, and green tomatoes, cucumbers, and white beans. And my salad is glorious. Grilled fresh pineapple smiles up at me from its bed of lacy watercress and avocado chunks. The sweet flavor of the caramelized tropical fruit is heightened by the tangy zing of the house-made cumin and cider vinegar dressing.

Conversations cease as we all enjoy the first bites of our salads.

"Wow!" Lynn says. "It's an explosion of flavors in my mouth. I will definitely come here again!"

"Do you live in Ephrata?" I ask.

She shakes her head, puts a finger to her mouth, and takes a moment to swallow her food. "No, I live about four hours away. In Ithaca, New York. But this food is worth driving for!"

"Do you live near your aunt?" Roddy asks Gail. His voice sounds crestfallen.

"Nope." Her hair shimmers when she shakes her head. "I live in Ephrata, in a townhouse in Lincoln Gardens."

Roddy blurts out, "That's great!" Probably embarrassed by his over-the-top enthusiasm, he backpedals. "I mean, it's great you have a townhouse. Gives you more space than an apartment. And a yard. Yards are nice."

Yards are nice? My poor brother is out of practice. I suppress a giggle.

"Besides," Lynn says, "Most of my family lives around Ephrata, so I visit frequently."

"Never enough," Gail says to her aunt.

Lynn pats Gail's hand. "We do have fun, don't we?"

The green-eyed monster slinks up my spine. I wish Roddy and I had more family. Now that Gigi's gone, it's just us. Roddy notices my wistfulness and leans his shoulder against mine.

"Last night," Gail says to all of us, "Auntie and I went bowling at Dutch Lanes."

"If you can call it bowling." Lynn chuckles.

Gail laughs. "Let's just say we'll be asking for bumpers next time."

"Have you ever tried duckpins? It's a lot easier," Roddy says.

"No, I haven't," Gail answers. "How is it different?"

"Smaller pins. Lighter ball with no finger holes. I know," he says like he just came up with the most brilliant idea. "Why don't we try it some evening this week? Whaddya say?"

I choke on a bite of pineapple. Did I actually hear my brother ask a woman out on a date? Roddy shoots me an annoyed glare but solicitously asks me if I'm okay. I nod and take a sip of my lemonade.

"I'd love to. I'm free Wednesday. Will that work?"

Roddy has a standing pickup game with his buddies on Wednesday nights.

"Perfect. I'll pick you up at six."

So much for basketball. As Roddy and Gail work out the details of their date, I pump Lynn for more information.

"Is it okay if I ask you some more questions about your dad and Hanson?"

Lynn sips her drink. "Shoot."

"Do you know anything about Hanson's death?"

"I know it was murder, but Dad got very uncomfortable when I asked about it. Mom later told me that subject was off-limits."

"What did you make of that?"

"Honestly? I didn't want to think too deeply about it. You might be getting a sense of that yourself as you uncover Evie's secrets."

"Yes, I am," I say, grateful to have someone understand what I'm feeling. "I adored Gigi, and I don't want some awful dead and buried secrets to change that. How do you deal with it?"

"I'm lucky. Dad made amends, as best he could, while he was alive. He founded and funded a drug and alcohol treatment center."

"Because he had been a bootlegger?"

"Well, that and...Oh, I might as well share the rest of the story because I think this may be where my dad's and your grandparents' criminal activity intersected. Hanson, predicting the end of Prohibition, also had his farmers grow marijuana. When he died, my dad took over the sales and distribution of the pot. Dad never said it, but I think Evie and Pete may have laundered his money."

"I haven't found anything showing that, but it makes sense," I reply.

"My dad remained in the marijuana trade for a few years, but apparently, Dad liked his product a little too much, and Mom put an end to it. When Dad died, my brothers and I took over funding the treatment center."

Emily returns to our table. As she clears the plates, I digest what I've learned.

"Do you care for dessert?" Emily asks our group. "Our ice cream of the day is turmeric ginger drizzled with honey."

Sugar & Spice is also known for its wacky, spicy ice cream flavors, churned on site.

Gail raises her eyebrows and shrugs. "I'm game."

"Me too," Roddy agrees.

"I'll have the chili chocolate. It's my favorite," I say.

"Ditto," Lynn says.

"This place is super cool," Gail gushes. "Do you want to eat here before we bowl?" she asks Roddy.

"Perfect," he agrees, and they're back into their own conversation.

"What you shared really focuses on your dad," I say to Lynn. "What about your mom? How does she fit into the story?"

Lynn leans back and crosses her arms. "When they met, Mom was a teller at Ephrata National Bank, and Dad was already working for Hanson, making booze."

"Did your mom know what your dad was doing?"

Lynn nods. "Oh yeah. She knew and condoned it. Supposedly, she never got involved. But this is where it gets fuzzy. Through years of overhearing snippets of hushed conversations, I know she did something major."

"Major good or major bad?" I interject.

She flips her palms open and shrugs. "Like I said before, I was afraid to dig too deep, but I suspect bad since she kept it to herself. I also suspect Evie was involved."

Catching Gigi's name, Roddy directs his attention to Lynn and my conversation.

"Why?" I ask.

"When they got a little tipsy, my mom and Evie would reminisce about their younger days. They'd talk about how smart they were creating the perfect plan and how they had been gutsy enough to grab the life they wanted. They also bragged to each other about never getting caught."

Lynn's words blast me with dread. An unsolved crime—like Hanson's murder.

"I'd bet," she continues, "whatever they did is Evie's last secret."

JULY 1965

EVIE

Evie tried not to stare at the empty patio chair where Ella should have been. She served Bess a slice of strawberry pie and poured Lynn—home on summer break from Ithaca College—another glass of meadow tea. The warm breeze flipped the corner of the green and white checked tablecloth onto the pie.

"Where are you working this summer?" Evie asked Lynn as she wiped whipped cream from the fabric.

"I'm waitressing at Zinn's Diner. How about Ella? Is she working here again?"

When Ella begged to work anywhere but their store, Evie agreed, thinking an unrelated boss may be just what she needed to keep her in line. But unfortunately, her behavior had become more erratic since she started her summer job a month ago.

"No, this year she's working at JCPenney in Ephrata. She's sick of having me as a boss." *And a mom.* Evie slid a glance at her watch. Saturdays were Ella's half days, and she was supposed to have been home from work three hours ago. "I expected her a while ago; I guess she had to work late. I hope you two don't miss each other."

Lynn offered an anemic smile. "Yes, it'd be nice to see her." For their mothers' sake, Ella and Lynn were civil to each other.

"Roddy and his family came to the diner last week. He said they're still dating."

More like Ella stringing him along while she plays the field.

"Mmm," Evie said noncommittally as she freshened her mint julep. "How about you? Any special beaus?"

"Yes! I was telling Mom about him today. He's a year ahead of me and majoring in history. His family is from..."

As Lynn chattered on, Evie's envy grew. She longed for a close relationship with her daughter, but since puberty, Ella rebelled against Evie, wanting as little to do with her as possible. At least she and Bess were still thick as thieves. As if she was reading her mind, Bess patted Evie's hand sympathetically.

The screech of car tires, followed by a blaring horn, startled the women. They jumped from their seats, knocking into the iron table. The pie plate wobbled on the edge before crashing to the ground.

"What the devil was that?" Evie ran to the street in front of the store.

Bess and Lynn followed close behind. A lime-green muscle car was parked haphazardly in front of the store. A sharp-nosed, red-haired man sat in the driver's seat. Ella lounged across him, her head rolling from side to side.

"Okay, blondie," he said to Ella. "Time to get out."

"You get out," she slurred. "Way out. Into the cosmos."

Evie stormed to the driver's side of the car. "Who the hell are you?" From his crow's feet and weathered hands, she could tell he was no twenty-year-old. More like mid-thirties.

"He's Fraser, Momma. Fraser, Waser, Wannamaker," Ella babbled.

"Is she drunk? Did you get my daughter drunk?" Evie barked.

"Not drunk," he said.

"I'm trippin', Momma. Try it; you'll like it," Ella cooed.

"Momma's not happy." The man propped Ella up in the passenger seat.

Ella flopped back against the man, "You're the best boss. I looooooove..." Ella stopped talking and stared at a ladybug on the car's windshield. "I loooove bugs."

"You're her boss?" Evie snapped.

After he propped Ella up again, he got out of the car and extended his hand to Evie.

"Donald Fraser."

Evie smelled the booze on his breath, and his eyes were glassy. She swatted his hand away.

"Donny, Wanny, Weebo. Do you have some more goodies for me to try?" Ella called from the car. "I liked what you gave...no, I loooove...I looove bugs."

Evie turned to her best friend. "Will you and Lynn get her into the house?"

They opened the passenger side door, pulled Ella out, and guided her inside.

"How dare you drive my daughter when you're drunk? And how dare you bring her home in this condition? What the hell did you give her?"

"Look, ma'am. She's old enough to make her own decisions."

"Oh, you think so? You think so?" Evie screamed, verging on hysterics. "She's barely eighteen, and you're damn near middle-aged. You should know better."

He shrugged and opened his car door. Evie kicked it shut, leaving a dent where her foot hit the door panel.

She grabbed him by the shirt and twisted the fabric tight in her hand. "Are you her boss? Are you?"

He ripped her hand away and smoothed his shirt. "I am."

Evie slapped him hard across the face. "Consider that her resignation."

JULY 2000

RUBY

I dash to the back corner of the local Goodwill store. Pawing through a heap of hair, I finally find what I need—a short, brown, curly-haired wig. I throw it into my cart on top of a green plaid men's shirt and white bell-bottom pants. After checking out, I swing by the dollar store and buy a stick-on mustache to fashion into sideburns and a brown eyebrow pencil to bush up Roddy's brow.

I inveigled him (ten points for a favored word use) into helping me at Janet's party. Marty's sister, Becky, was in a car accident late last night on her way home from a business trip, so he had to bail on being my plus-one. Though she'll fully recover, a badly shattered leg will keep her in the hospital for a few days. Bart, her husband, is at her bedside, and Marty's hanging out with Brad.

I pull Sally into my driveway. Roddy's up on a ladder, cleaning out my gutters. I collect Roddy's costume from the passenger seat and step out of Sally.

"You don't have to take care of Pearl. You have enough on your plate with Mirabella's upkeep."

"Just passing the time productively," he says, dropping a pile of rotting leaf goo onto my yard.

Roddy verges on being a workaholic. I think he keeps busy so he doesn't have to think about stuff—like Clara.

I show Roddy my bags. "Come inside. I want you to try on your costume."

He rolls his eyes. "I can't believe I let you talk me into this. Who am I going to be?"

"You'll see. And you agreed because you're a good brother."

"Enough with the brown-nosing," he says, climbing down the ladder. "You've already won."

I take one end of the ladder, and we carry it behind Pearl and slide it into its place in my shed.

"I also made lunch." He wipes his hands on his shorts. "I was inspired by my dinner at Sugar & Spice, so I thought I'd get creative."

I open the back door and we enter Pearl through the laundry. "Oh yeah! How'd your date with Gail go?"

The corners of his eyes crinkle from the width of his grin. "Good."

"Good? That's a more-than-good smile. I'd say phenomenal, or at least great."

"Okay." His cheeks color, and his smile turns shy. "You're right. It was phenomenal."

I grab his upper arms and squeal with delight, "Jeez! I'm so excited! And wouldn't Gigi just love it? You dating her best friend's granddaughter."

"Gotta admit," he says. "I'm kind of excited too. Being around Gail makes me feel lighter than I have in almost a year. I really like her, Ruby."

I point at his enormous grin. "If she can make you smile like that, I really like her too! When's your next date?"

"Tuesday. We're going to the Concert by the Creek at Grater Park."

"Fun! Who's playing?"

He throws open his palms and laughs. "Not a clue."

"Roddy's got a girlfriend. Roddy's got a girlfriend," I tease.

"I just may have," he says, beaming.

I follow him into the kitchen and get a whiff of coconut. Two artistically presented salads are on my kitchen table.

"Ready to eat?" he asks.

My eyes widen with anticipation. "Duh! It looks and smells ah-mazing."

I pour us each a glass of meadow tea and sit down at my kitchen table. A flavor bomb detonates in my mouth with the first bite. Tangy citrus, sweet coconut, and peppery arugula, topped with a touch of jalapeno heat.

"Well?" Roddy asks.

"So good," I mumble through a mouth full of food. "What's in the dressing? It's to die for."

He raises a finger to his lips. "Chef's secret."

"That'd be a great name for your restaurant! Chef's Secret. You really should follow your passion."

Roddy doesn't realize the extent of his culinary talent. Some of the meals he's cooked for me are Michelin star worthy.

His pragmatism flares. "Too risky for me. I'll just keep cooking for fun."

"Well, I'll just keep eating for fun." I take another bite.

Roddy sips his tea. "So, is Marty's sister going to be okay?"

"Yeah, but a long recovery and physical therapy are in her future."

He takes the last few bites of his salad. "Marty seems like a stand-up guy. I'm sure he'll be a big help to her."

Now it's my turn to blush. "He is a good guy."

"Ruby's got a boyfriend! Ruby's got a boyfriend!" he mimics my taunt.

I smile. "Look at us reaching for happiness. Gigi would be proud."

He nods. "She would. And speaking of Gigi..."

I inhale deeply and sigh it out. "I know. We've already put it off for a week."

Neither of us wants the next clue. We're afraid we'll confirm our suspicion that Gigi murdered Hanson.

"Should I bite the bullet and call Mr. Davenport?" Roddy asks.

"I suppose. We have no choice but to see it through." A little spark of hope flickers in my belly. "It is Saturday. He might not answer."

Roddy lifts the phone from the charger in the kitchen and pushes the buttons. I cross my fingers.

A minute later, Roddy says, "Hi, Mr. Davenport. We've spread Gigi's ashes on her friend's grave, and we're ready for the next clue." He pauses to listen. A few seconds later, he says thanks and hangs up the phone. "He's emailing you now. We don't spread any ashes at our next location."

"Hmm," I say. "Wonder why not?"

I open my closet door, pull down my desktop and turn on my computer. As it loads, I make myself a cup of chamomile tea to settle my nerves. Roddy paces. I log into my AOL account and open the email.

PART 1:
Married woman
Pavo cristatus
Between the study and the billiard room
PART 2:
E=N
BCNRWKNLT CXACRUUJ OUJC

"They're not getting any easier," I say, seeing the clue.

Roddy hangs over my shoulder and rubs his eyebrow. "No. They're not. You better print it out. This may take a while."

I hit print on my computer and reread the clues. "Well, number one is Mrs."

"Thanks for claiming the easy one," he grumbles.

I retrieve the printout from the paper tray and we move to the kitchen table.

Roddy points at the word *Cristatus*. "I think this is Latin and means crest."

I spitball a guess. "A toothpaste model who married a rich benefactor and lives in a mansion with a study and billiard room?"

Roddy gives me the hairy eyeball.

"Okay, Einstein," I tease. "What's your guess?"

"Well," he says, pinching his stubbly chin between his thumb and fingers. "Part 2 is a code."

"Really? That helps tremendously!"

He swats my shoulder with the back of his hand in response to my sarcasm. "Don't you have to get dressed?"

I glance up at Mrs. Potts, the teapot-shaped wall clock hanging in my kitchen, and jump up. "Jeez! I didn't realize it was so late. We *do* have to get ready. I've got a ton of things to set up before Janet's party starts. Code-cracking will have to wait."

I throw the recycled grocery bag of clothes to Roddy. "Put these on. I'll fix your hair and makeup after I get ready."

He holds his hands up like stop signs. "Makeup? Whoa there! Nobody said anything about makeup."

"Not makeup makeup. Just eyebrows and sideburns. Besides, it's too late to back out. I won't be long," I say, taking the steps two at a time.

Once in my bedroom, I strip down to bra and undies and slip into a pink and white floral blouse with an oversized bright white collar. I tuck it into a belted lilac mini skirt with a high waist. My red curls are hidden under a sandy blonde, stick-straight wig. The fake hair reaches a few inches below my shoulder. I complete the look with thick-heeled black shoes.

Roddy should be able to guess who I'm dressed as. We binged on hours of reruns when we were in elementary school. My heels click on the wooden steps, and Roddy ambles from the kitchen to the bottom of the staircase. I flick my tresses behind my shoulder.

"Marcia! Marcia! Marcia!" he says in a whiny voice, imitating Jan Brady.

"You figured it out!"

"How could I not know after all the *Brady Bunch* episodes we watched?" He pops the curly brown wig on his head. "I'll play the Greg to your Marcia, as long as I don't have to sing 'Sunshine Day.'"

As I look at my twin brother in the goofy wig, the emptiness I felt at lunch with Lynn and Gail is filled with contentment. I smile at Roddy. I have all the family I need.

JULY 2000

RUBY

The trill of a Jenny wren warbles through my kitchen window screen. My checked curtains twirl in the still-cool morning breeze. I add a smidgen of cream and sugar to my coffee, wrap my summer robe around me, and enjoy the first sip of liquid sunshine. The jarring ring of my phone interrupts the peacefulness.

"Hello."

"Hey, Ruby. It's Marty."

Jitters scamper through my body. Must be the caffeine. (Yeah, right. Who am I kidding?)

"Hi, Marty. How's your sister?"

"Her surgery went well. She's in a middling amount of pain, but that's to be expected."

I twirl a curl around my finger. "And how about Brad?"

"We're having a blast. How did the party go? I feel like a complete heel for letting you down."

"It couldn't be helped, and it went really well, so don't beat yourself up. In fact, one of Janet's friends booked a sweet sixteen party with me."

"Aces!" he says. "So, what's been happening since I last saw you?"

I think back to the last time I saw him. Our kissing pops into my head, and my insides heat up from more than my coffee. I'm sure I'm blushing.

"Well, we met Gigi's best friend's daughter and granddaughter. In fact, Roddy asked the granddaughter, Gail, out on a date."

"Do you think meeting them was part of Gigi's plan?"

Hmm, matchmaking from heaven. I never considered it, but it sounds like Gigi.

"I don't know. Maybe." I take another sip of coffee.

"What else? Any new secrets revealed?"

"No new secrets. Just hints that Bess and Gigi might have done something really bad."

I had mentioned to Marty that I was worried about what we might find out about Gigi.

"Well, no use in worrying. You'll know soon enough. And remember, you can still love the person, even if you hate what they've done."

I shake my head, not ready to travel down that road quite yet. "We did get a new puzzle."

"Oh yeah? Have you solved it?"

"No, that's my plan for the morning. Do you happen to know what Pavo cristatus means?"

"Ah, Latin. You came to the right fellow. I was in Latin Club in college."

I laugh. "They have Latin Clubs?"

"You laugh, but Latin is the root of many languages. Learning it is actually quite practical."

"You're adorably dorky," I say.

He chuckles. "Compliment received. Now let me think."

I can almost hear his brain ticking.

"Cristatus means crested or plumed."

"So Roddy was right. He said it meant crest."

"Well done, Roddy. Now, Pavo. Pavo."

I hear a snap of fingers.

"It's a crested peafowl. Commonly called a peacock."

"A peacock? Are you sure?" I ask.

"I am."

I bet he's puffed up like a peacock right now.

"Mrs. Peacock," I blurt out.

"From the Clue game. You mentioned that was always your grandmother's character."

I jump up, excited. "Yes! The Clue game. What room is between the study and the billiard room on the Clue game board?"

"I don't know," Marty says. "But Brad has the game. Give me a sec."

The phone clatters when he lays it on the table. I hear a door open and shuffling. A few seconds later, Marty's back on the line.

"The library," he says.

"Mrs. Peacock in the library. She must mean our clue will be found in her library."

"A logical deduction. Is there more to the puzzle, or is that it?"

"No. There's more. A code of some sort."

"If you want, you can email it to me. I don't claim to be an expert code breaker, but I can work on it while Brad's playing with his friends."

"I'll send it shortly. Thanks."

Marty hears the loud rap on my door. "Do you need to go?"

"It's Roddy. I forgot to unlock the door for him."

I pad bare-footed to my front door, turn the deadbolt, and open the door.

"Hey, Sis," he booms. "Ready to get to work?"

His eyes are sparkling on his happy face, and his shoulders are relaxed. All remnants of his brooding demeanor are gone. Gail is a miracle worker. I just hope she's as equally enchanted as he is.

I cover the mouthpiece and say to Roddy, "Give me a minute."

He pours himself a cup of coffee and settles in at my kitchen table. I uncover the mouthpiece and continue my conversation with Marty.

"Roddy's here, and we're going to work on the code, so I better go. I'll email it to you. Let me know if you figure it out. Okay?"

"Righto! And Ruby?"

"Yes?"

"I miss you."

My heart does a pirouette. "I miss you, too."

I hang up the phone and let our exchange soak in. I've surprised myself. By now, I would've expected to find some quirk or trait that's a deal breaker, but the more I get to know Marty, the more I like him.

"Sounds like you two are getting cozy," Roddy teases.

I don't bother to suppress my grin. "I think we are."

He walks over to me and hugs me. "Good for you, and lucky him."

I squeeze him tight. I don't know what I would do without my twin brother.

***

Over breakfast, I fill Roddy in on the answers for part one of the puzzle.

"So, if it's in Gigi's library, part two probably refers to a book," Roddy surmises.

I clear our dirty dishes, wipe the crumbs off the table, and lay the printout front and center. I grab two tablets and two pencils and give one of each to Roddy. I write E=N at the top of the yellow lined paper.

"Maybe vowels are represented by consonants?" I suggest.

Roddy studies the puzzle. "Could be. The only vowels in the code are A, U and O. Two Us are side-by-side. There aren't many words that immediately repeat the same vowel."

I tap the pencil against my chin. "I don't know about that. Lots of words have double Os and some with double As, like Aardvark."

"True. Hadn't thought about that."

He writes ??E???E?? ?????OO? ?O?? on his tablet, lays his forehead in his hand, and stares at it.

"Maybe the second word is *Rigadoon*. Celine's novel? Gigi probably has it in her library."

I shake my head. "Can't be. Look." I point to the second "word" of the code, CXACRUUJ. "The first and fourth letter are the same, so it can't be *Rigadoon*."

"Crap." Roddy says.

"E=N is the key," I say. I dredge up a long-buried fact from a Penn State ancient history class. "I think I've got it! E is the fifth letter of the alphabet, and N is the fourteenth. It's a shift cipher."

Roddy's eyebrows draw together. "A what cipher? I don't remember learning about it."

"Because you slept through class."

He shrugs his shoulders. "It was eight A.M. in Schwab Auditorium, and I had you to take excellent notes for me."

I raise my eyebrows. "I'm surprised you passed your major classes without me."

"Don't you mean aced my major classes? After all, my GPA was higher than yours," he razzes.

"By a tenth of a point! All because of one lousy C in gym class," I mutter.

He crosses his arms, leans back in his chair, and lifts his chin. "So we agree? I'm definitely the best...at badminton."

I swat his shoulder and laugh. "I agree to no such thing. I'd gladly challenge you to a match, but we have a cipher to solve."

"Convenient excuse." He laughs too. "Okay, Brains, show me how this code works."

I write out the alphabet. "So, like I said, E is the fifth letter, and N is the fourteenth. That means it's a right shift of nine. Count nine letters to the right of A."

Roddy taps each letter with his pencil point until he hits J. "Okay. So you're saying J=A?"

"Exactly. And K=B, L=C and so on."

Roddy takes my tablet and writes the code letters under the alphabet. Now that we know the cipher, it's an easy solve: Steinbeck *Tortilla Flat*.

"Let's head to Mirabella," I say. "We've got a book to find."

JUNE 1978

EVIE

After dropping the twins at Camp Saginaw for their yearly four-week summer camp, Evie stopped at the liquor store for a bottle of tequila. She and Pete would have margaritas tonight. They started the tradition two years ago, the first summer the twins went to overnight camp. Evie claimed the cocktails were to celebrate a four-week respite from childrearing, but Pete knew the alcohol was to fill her empty nest.

Evie pulled her Mustang into the driveway. After stepping out of the car, she leaned back in to grab the bottle from the passenger seat. A strong hand roughly grabbed her arm.

Fear energized her, and in one smooth move, she tightened her grip on the neck of the bottle, twisted herself back out of the car, and swung. The man ducked and jumped sideways, the bottle missing him by mere inches.

"Donald!" she yelled, recognizing him despite his reflective aviator sunglasses. "What in blue blazes is wrong with you?"

"You almost clocked me!" he snarled.

"You deserve worse." She stepped to the other side of the open car door to keep it between them. Even though they were nearly six feet apart, she could smell the booze on his breath. "Get off of my property and stay away!" she said through gritted teeth.

He smoothed his red hair and took off his glasses, tucking them into the pocket of his shirt. His eyes were glassy and bloodshot.

Staring straight at her, he calmly said, "I told you at the school: I want a new deal."

Anger flashed through Evie's body. "You're not extorting any more money out of me. I've paid you more than enough."

He closed the car door and stepped close to her, their noses less than a foot apart. "I don't want money," he said in an unsettlingly quiet tone.

Evie's palms sweated, and nausea swirled in her stomach. Her inclination was to take a few steps back, but she held her ground. "Then what do you want?"

"Evelyn," he said almost as a reprimand. "You know."

She *did* know, and if she gave it to him, the wonderful life she built with Pete and the twins was over.

JULY 2000

RUBY

Without the bustle of an occupant, Mirabella is starting to smell musty. I open the front windows and the back patio door to let the azalea-scented air flow through.

Roddy adds a few envelopes to the toppling stack of mail on the dining room table and says, "Either Mr. Davenport or I am going to have to deal with this soon."

I nod in agreement, and we head into Gigi's library. A thin layer of dust covers the edges of the bookshelves. Gigi would be appalled. The rest of the house could be a bit untidy, but the library was always spotless.

"Be right back." I leave the library to grab a dust rag from the utility closet. "Okay," I say when I return. "Want to work from top to bottom?"

Evie had no rhyme or reason for how she shelved her books. Luckily, the top two shelves only have a few novels tucked between the encyclopedias and dictionaries, and the bottom two shelves are stuffed full of photo albums, ledgers, and the like. We should be able to make quick work of them. The middle shelves will take longer. Roddy and I methodically scan each title. I find Steinbeck's *Cannery Row* and *East of Eden*, but no *Tortilla Flat*.

"Let's look again," I say. "It's got to be here."

After two more passes, we decide the book is not on the shelves.

"You search the desk, and I'll look in the credenza," I suggest, moving to the back wall of the room.

I pull the hand-forged black iron handle on Gigi's prized antique oak credenza. The door creaks as it opens. Inside are two shelves. Hanging file racks span the space and are tightly packed with files. There's not much space between the top of the file and the bottom of the shelf, and when I try to wiggle out the first folder, the whole rack comes crashing down. Papers slide out of the folders into a jumbled mess.

"What a disaster!"

"It *is* that." Roddy holds back his smile.

"What should I do with it? Do you think we'll need these files?"

"Don't know. Until we know our inheritance, we can't be sure. Just put all the loose pages in a pile. We can refile them later if we need to."

As I'm shuffling the papers into a stack, I come across our childhood immunization records.

"Check it out, Roddy. Measles, mumps, polio. This shows all of our vaccines."

Roddy barely looks up. "Cool. No doubt we'll find all kinds of stuff when we clean out the house."

I don't want to think about that. It's too...permanent. I stack more papers: insurance policies for cars and the house, a contract with Pest Control Services, a jury duty summons, and old dental receipts. Wait. What's this? Donald's name catches my attention. It's a copy of a peace bond sworn out in 1978.

Donald R. Fraser, you are hereby placed under a peace bond by Judge Carl A. Shea for a period of six months. You are ordered not to contact the following victim(s) personally, by phone or mail. You are further ordered not to go within two (2) square blocks of the residence or household of the said victim(s).

The victims listed are Evelyn Fisher Collier, Ruby Ella Finch, and Roderick Alistair Finch Jr. Jeez! This looks bad. Very bad. Maybe Roddy and Marty were right about Donald.

"Roddy, I found a—" I cut myself off when an image of Donald's kind eyes pops into my head.

"You found what?" he asks, looking around the desk from his perch on the floor.

Crap. I think Donald deserves a chance to explain, and if Roddy sees this, Donald won't get one for sure.

"Umm, dental records from when I had braces."

"Okay?" he says, annoyed. "Let me know when you find the book."

When Roddy's head is back behind the desk, I fold the peace bond and slip it into the pocket of my shorts.

"Got it!" Roddy exclaims. "Tucked way in the back of the bottom drawer under a cigar box full of pennies."

I scramble over to the desk just as Roddy opens the hardcover of *Tortilla Flat*. About thirty pages in, the book is hollowed out. A small red envelope rests in the niche.

Roddy pulls it out and reads what it says. "Keep one safe deposit box key in this envelope. Loss of key will cause you considerable expense."

Handwritten under the printed words is #346. He unsnaps the envelope and slides the key out. It's silver and unmarked.

"Which bank is it from?" I ask.

He shakes his head. "Doesn't say. I know Gigi had accounts at Fulton, Orrstown, and Ephrata National."

"Ephrata National. Didn't Lynn say Bess worked there?"

Roddy blushes. "Honestly, I didn't hear much of what Lynn said."

"Oh yeah, right. You were making goo-goo eyes with Gail."

He ignores my teasing. "I do remember Ephrata National was the bank where Gigi made the deposits to launder Hanson's money."

"That's right! Let's start there."

Roddy wags his finger at me. "Not so fast. Opening Gigi's safe deposit box won't be that easy," he says, using his best accounting teacher voice. "As executor of the will, Mr. Davenport will have to accompany us, and unless he's filed an inventory form with the State Department of Revenue, even he won't be able to open it."

"Jeez! Why do they make it so hard to access? Gigi gave us the key."

"Inheritance tax. They don't want us getting a boatload of cash or expensive jewelry without claiming it."

My eyes widen. "Do you think there's a boatload of cash?"

"I suppose it's possible, but since safe deposit boxes can be seized if there's suspicion of criminal activity, I doubt it."

Criminal activity. My loving, fun, intelligent, whimsical Gigi was a criminal. I think about Donald and the peace bond in my pocket. Is no one as they seem?

JULY 2000

RUBY

Yesterday afternoon, Mr. Davenport faxed the necessary paperwork to Dustin Gotlieb, the Ephrata National Bank manager, arranging for Roddy and me to access Gigi's safe deposit box. We're all set for today's visit. I pull Sally into a space in front of the impressive stone building. Four stone columns shoot two stories skyward and are topped with a massive entablature carved with the bank's name.

Roddy drops a quarter into the parking meter, and we enter the building through the double glass doors. I get in line behind a Mennonite woman. Her blonde hair is pulled back in a bun, covered with a pinned-on white lace square, and she's wearing a mid-shin length jean skirt and super cool cowboy boots. Something in her stance is familiar. When she turns her head to look at the wall clock, I see it's Naomi, the owner of Sugar & Spice.

"Naomi! Hey! It's nice to see you."

When she smiles, dimples appear in her cheeks. "Hi, Ruby. And Roddy. Oh my word, it's been years since I've seen you."

"Hi, Naomi," he says. "We ate lunch at your place a week ago, and it was so phenomenal I had to go back for dinner."

Naomi's apple cheeks pinken, and she clasps her hands in front of her heart. "That is so kind of you. The Lord has blessed me with such loyal, wonderful customers."

"And mad cooking skills," I add.

Her cheeks deepen to red. "You're making me blush."

"I'm serious. The combinations you come up with are ah-mazing."

"Next!" one of the tellers calls from behind the long service desk.

"That's me," Naomi says. "Next time you come into the café, say hi."

"Will do," Roddy and I say in unison as Naomi steps in front of the teller on the left.

"Next!"

Roddy and I step up to the middle teller.

"Hi," I say. "I'm Ruby Finch. My lawyer spoke to Mr. Gotlieb. We'd like to access my grandmother's safe deposit box."

"Yes," she says. "We were expecting you. Let me escort you into the vault." We follow her quick steps through the large vault into a room with rows and rows of metal boxes. A plain wooden table sits in the middle of the room. "Please let me know if you need further assistance." She shuts the door when she leaves.

We search the rows until I find box #346. Sliding the box out, I set it on the table and take a deep breath. "This is it."

Roddy inserts the key and turns. We hear a click. Roddy lifts the lid. Save for two index cards the box is empty.

"No boatload of cash," I joke before I pick up the top card.

L 23 4x, R 44 3x, L 16 2x

"Is this a lock combination?" I say, showing it to Roddy.

"That'd be my guess. What's on the other card?"

My eyebrows furrow as I look at the writing. "Hmm. I'm not sure."

"Maybe it's Arabic?" Roddy suggests.

"No. Arabic has more dots and loops. Cyrillic? Hebrew?"

He flips his palms up and shrugs. "Could be. We need to do some research."

"Can we take the cards?"

Roddy snickers. "Mr. Davenport said the contents of the box are ours."

"He's got a dry sense of humor, doesn't he?"

I slip the two cards into my macramé purse while Roddy replaces the safe deposit box. We exit the vault, but as we're leaving the bank, we notice a bank history exhibit to the right of the main doors.

"Let's take a look. Never know what we might uncover," Roddy says, pulling me into the room.

Old coins, canvas bank bags, handwritten money wrappers, and canceled checks from as far back as 1881 are encased in glass displays. There are black-and-white photos of mustached tellers standing behind iron bars and female customers in long dresses and hats. As the photos progress through time, I come upon a Polaroid shot dated 1968. It's of the first single woman to be allowed to open her own bank account at Ephrata National Bank.

"Can you believe women weren't allowed to have their own bank accounts until the '60s?" I grumble.

"Ridiculous." He's perusing a wall of framed newspaper articles. "Oh, crap!"

"What?"

He points to one of the frames. "Read this."

ROBBERS RING IN 1932!

A bold bank robbery was perpetrated New Year's Day, in broad daylight, at Ephrata National Bank in Lancaster County. The three-foot-thick steel vault door was easily breached with an acetylene cutting torch, and $198,000 was stolen.

At this time, the authorities have no suspects and no witnesses. Homes, hotels, and rooming houses in Ephrata and surrounding towns are being subject to visitations of detectives. All roads leading out of the county are being watched. If you have any information regarding this crime, contact your local authorities immediately.

The blood drains from my face, and my shoulders slump. Were my grandparents the Pennsylvania version of Bonnie and Clyde?

"Are you thinking what I'm thinking?" I ask, looking around to make sure no one can overhear us.

"Pop learned to weld, and he and Gigi said it changed their life."

I bite my lip. "Mmm hmm. And Bess was a bank teller for ENB."

Roddy runs his fingers through his hair. "A sudden influx of cash would be a good reason to buy a store and start laundering money."

"And George was a driver for Hanson. Perfect man to drive the getaway car."

Roddy blows out a forceful sigh. "Seems like it all adds up to a New Year's Day heist."

I rub my face with my hands as the certainty sinks in. All the clues point to this conclusion. Gigi's involvement in this robbery is likely. Wait! A spark of hope flares in my belly.

"You know, if you think about it, this might not be too bad."

"How is learning your grandparents are thieves not bad?" he says with raised eyebrows.

"It's not murder."

"True."

"I mean, that's what we thought was coming, right? We were pretty sure Gigi poisoned Hanson. Robbery's not great, but I can live with it."

"What makes you so sure murder's off the table?"

"Gigi's clues don't lead us there."

"Not yet. Don't forget we have another clue to solve and another bag of ashes. Gigi's funerary adventure is not over."

"Do you always have to pop my balloon?" I snap, frustrated at his pessimism.

He gives me a tolerant smile and chucks me under the chin. "You're right. No need to think the worst. We'll know the truth soon enough."

I know he's patronizing me, but it's okay. I can feel it in my bones: I'm right.

JANUARY 1932

EVIE

"Five, four, three, two, one, HAPPY NEW YEAR!" the foursome shouted over the cheers of the raucous crowd.

From the back corner of Green Dragon, Evie, Pete, Bess, and George welcomed 1932 with an RC Cola toast. This year, hooch was verboten. They had to be sharp for today's caper.

Desperate for money, Evie had been planning the heist since the day she heard about the Farmers National Bank robbery on the radio. Her cohorts were easy to convince. Pete's failing marks in watchmaking convinced him his fortunes lay elsewhere. George, having already strayed into unlawful activities, was ready to get out from under Hanson's thumb and score some real dough. And Bess was sick to death of fending off her lecherous boss; though to allay suspicion, she grudgingly agreed to continue working at the bank for six months after the robbery.

The couples stood and sang along with the band's rendition of "Auld Lang Syne," swaying to the nostalgic melody. At the end of the song, they settled back into their seats.

Rattled with pre-performance jitters, Evie asked, "Shall we go over the plan one more time?"

Pete leaned in and pecked her cheek. "No, we should get some sleep. Dawn will be here in no time."

Evie was spending the night with Bess in her room at the boarding house. George had "borrowed" Hanson's Roadster pickup, and he and Pete planned to collect the girls at six sharp. Hopefully, if any witnesses spotted the vehicle, the robbery would be blamed on Hanson. Evie chose early morning New Year's Day, expecting most folks would still be in their beds sleeping off hangovers.

"He's right, Evie," Bess said, patting her friend's arm. "We're ready."

Evie tamped down her nerves, but she knew she would never forgive herself if her friends ended up in the can. "Okay, then, let's hit the hay."

Pete helped Evie into her navy blue, fur-trimmed coat—a welcome hand-me-down from Mrs. Caldwell. Once bundled against the biting winter air, they left the drum. Evie and Bess waved to the fellas as they drove off into the night. The girls linked arms and walked the mile to Hutchinson's Boarding House.

"Oh, I can't wait to be done with my lunkhead boss," Bess said as they snuggled in her twin bed to warm up.

"At least his penchant for getting too close made it easy for you to swipe the key."

Bess yawned and rubbed her eyes. "Like taking candy from a baby."

Once Bess had grabbed the key, she handed it off to Evie on a coffee break. Not wanting to risk a worker at the local hardware store connecting the dots, Evie took the trolley into the city to have it copied. Bess had it back in her boss's pocket before the close of business.

As Bess drifted off to sleep, doubts plagued Evie's mind. She clenched her teeth, took a deep breath, and willed them away. After all, she was no shrinking violet. *Look what doing it the "right" way has gotten me.* She rubbed her chapped hands and shifted to ease her aching back. *I work till I drop and am getting nowhere.* The painful rasp of her mother's wheezing echoed in her head. *If I don't do this. If I can't get her help, she will die.* She crept out of bed, careful not to disturb a softly snoring Bess. She sat on the edge of the deep windowsill and stared out the window into the inky blackness. When the sky lightened to a soft gray, she knew it was time.

The last vestiges of her girlish innocence were shed with her nightdress. She slid into a daring pair of wool trousers and faced the dawn unafraid.

***

At six on the dot, Evie and Bess climbed into the Roadster. At 6:15, they cruised through lifeless streets past the darkened bank. At 6:20, they pulled into an empty alley behind the stone building. Pete grabbed the bag of tools he borrowed from school, and he, Evie, and Bess climbed out of Hanson's truck.

George cocked his bowler and winked. "Abyssinia!" He was the lookout and getaway driver.

The threesome slid on their gloves and hurried to the back door. Bess inserted the key into the lock and opened the door. As Bess led Pete to the vault, Evie took watch at the front entrance to the bank. The street was clear. Not a soul was out. A few minutes later, she heard sizzles and pops. She ran to the vault to take a gander. The cutting torch sliced through the thick steel doors like butter. It wouldn't take long.

Evie returned to her post at the front door. A man was crossing the street, heading straight for the bank. Her heart thumped in her chest, and beads of sweat popped out on her upper lip.

"Hurry up!" she yelled to Bess and Pete.

As the man got closer, Evie noticed him rubbing his bare hands together. His pants were torn, exposing patches of pale white skin. His coat wasn't much more than tatters, and he was shivering. Her heartbeat normalized. He was simply a hobo looking for an alcove to shield himself from the wind. She ducked out of sight as he climbed the three steps to enter the bank and huddled against the stone columns.

"He's in!" Bess shouted when Pete entered the bank.

Evie dared a peek at the hobo. He had folded himself into a ball, with his head tucked between his knees. His presence would actually serve as a diversion if anyone came along. Hugging the wall, Evie made her way to the vault and helped Bess and Pete gather the cash and coins into the feed sacks they'd brought along.

Pete whistled and shook his head appreciatively. "This trip was not for biscuits."

Evie dragged three stuffed bags towards the back door as Bess and Pete continued filling them. Two more bags later, the vault was empty.

"Let's make tracks," Bess said.

Pete flung two of the heavy bags over his shoulder, and together the women pulled the remaining three out the back door of the bank. After Pete hoisted their haul into the truck bed, they all hopped in. Pete, Evie, and Bess panted from the exertion and adrenaline coursing through their bodies.

George motored through the back alley and onto Main Street before he asked, "How'd we do?"

Giddy with success, the threesome howled with laughter. Bess and Evie held hands and bounced on the seat.

"We're rich! We're rich!" Bess chanted.

Pete shook his head with disbelief. "I think it's close to two hundred large."

Stunned, George's mouth fell open, and his eyes widened to saucers. He grabbed a deck of Lucky Strikes from his coat pocket and lit up a butt. Sucking in the acrid smoke, he blew it out in a forceful puff. "That's nuts!"

The buildings of Ephrata faded behind them, and the paved road gave way to dirt lanes. Acres of farmland, dotted with clapboard farmhouses, stretched as far as the eye could see. As the enormity of what they had done sunk in, they fell silent.

Assuming they got away clean, Evie could procure the very best medical care for her mother. Tears of gratitude welled in her eyes.

The truck bounced over the rutted dirt. George brought it to a stop in front of a charming farmhouse. The two-story homestead had a fresh coat of white paint. Green shutters framed the windows. Three brand-new porch rockers graced the front porch. Evie was impressed to see George had spent his money on more substantial things than Mary Pickfords at the drum. He'd make a good match for her best friend.

The men each grabbed two money bags. Bess and Evie carried the remaining one as George led the trio into his house. They dropped the bags of loot on the wooden kitchen floor.

"The cans are on the bottom shelves of the larder," George said.

"Hurry back," Bess said.

"Come here, dollface." He scooped Bess into his arms, dipped her and planted a dramatic kiss on her rosy lips. "I'll be as quick as I can."

He would return the truck while Evie, Pete, and Bess transferred the money into the dozens of coffee tins they had saved. Evie and Bess lined the empty tins up in a long row spanning the farm table. Pete plopped the first bag onto the tabletop, and they started stuffing bills and coins into the cans.

A mix of nervousness, excitement, worry, and relief flooded Evie. "Except for a poor homeless sap, no one was on the streets."

"Once we hide the cash, melt the key, and return the torch, we're in the clear," Pete assured them.

Bess's shoulders crept up to her ears with tension. "They're going to figure out I had a key."

"How?" Evie said. "Robbers who get away with this amount of spinach don't keep working. You're going to go to work, be properly horrified at the theft, and put up with your boss's groping. No one will think twice about you. If they suspect anyone, it will be your boss."

Bess shook her head, unconvinced. "I sure hope you're right."

"I am," Evie said with confidence.

"She is," Pete said. He picked Evie up and swung her around. "And we're getting hitched, my clever moll."

Three days earlier, Pete had asked Evie to marry him if they pulled off the heist, and Evie had eagerly agreed.

Evie's laugh was contagious, and soon Bess was smiling too.

"Okay, dolls. You finish this up," he said, pointing to the last bag of money. "Time for me to melt down the key and return the tools. I'm sorry to leave you with the dirty work."

Evie and Bess shrugged it off. As women, they were more than accustomed to cleaning up messes.

"Be careful!" Evie warned. "Make sure you're not seen."

"Don't worry. The school and shop are empty on holidays. Be back in two shakes of a lamb's tail."

Pete headed out the door, and Evie and Bess finished moving the money. As agreed upon from the get-go, Evie pulled out enough cash to send her mother to a sanitarium. Other than that, no one would touch the cash until they had figured out a way to launder it.

Once the lids were tightly secured on all the cans, Bess rummaged through George's closet to find dungarees and warm work shirts. The women changed into the oversized garments, gathered the tins into a wheelbarrow, and wheeled the money into the barn.

A horse whinnied in its stall. Three cows munched on feed, ignoring the women. Bits of straw floated in the icy breeze. The smell of animal hair and manure was pungent. Evie grabbed a shovel from the wall and slid it into the pile of dung, clearing a spot to stash the coffee cans full of money.

Bess crinkled her nose. "Coppers won't look here."

"That's for sure," Evie agreed.

Shovelful by shovelful, they scooped the heavy manure until they had enough space cleared for all the cans. Once all the coffee tins were stacked in the middle, they covered them in dung.

Leaning on the spade's handle to catch her breath, Evie said, "You know what I was just thinking?"

Bess wiped her forehead, which was sweaty despite the January air. "What?"

"Our lives have just changed forever."

JULY 2000

RUBY

Roddy and I are back at Mirabella's library. After comparing the strange writing to several other alphabets, we realized it was not a different language. It's a mirror image. When we held the card up to a mirror, it was easy to read.

Through The Looking Glass and What Alice Found There~ Lewis Carroll

Once again, Roddy's on the rolling library ladder, searching for a title.

"The book's not here," he says. "I guess we'll have to buy a copy or go to the library."

"Maybe we don't need the book. The clue could be more literal, like Gigi's *Tell-Tale Heart* clue."

"You mean we should go through the looking glass?" he asks, stepping down the ladder.

"Exactly!" I call over my shoulder as I dash out of the library and bound up the stairs.

Roddy's right behind me. This time, when we enter Gigi's bedroom, the lingering scent of Shalimar is a comfort. I make a beeline for the full-length mirror mounted on the wall beside her walk-in closet and run my fingers along the sides of the gilt frame, looking for a latch.

"Bingo!" I say and push a button that's embedded in the frame.

We hear a click, and I swing the mirror open, revealing a heavy metal safe door a few inches taller than Roddy and as wide as my outstretched arms.

"Do you have the combination?" I ask.

Roddy slides the index card out of his pocket and hands it to me. "Call out the numbers to me," he says.

"Left 23," I say.

He moves the lock. "Next?"

"After the 23 it says 4x. I think that means turn it left to 23 four times."

"Okay. We'll give it a shot."

After the fourth time, I say, "Right 44, three times."

"Next?" he asks after he completes that instruction.

"Left 16, two times."

When he finishes the two turns, we hear a click. Roddy twists the safe's handle, and the door opens.

"It's a walk-in safe."

"Yeah," Roddy says, stepping inside.

The safe runs six feet back. Shelves line each wall of the interior, with a narrow walkway in the center. A row of leather-bound ledgers spans the right bottom shelf.

"These look like the store ledgers in the library," I say, pulling one dated 1934 from the shelf. I flip through the pages. "Roddy, this is a second set of books for the store. The *real* records." I study a few of the pages. "Wow, by the amounts, it's clear she was laundering more than just Hanson's money."

Roddy rubs his chin. "More evidence they were responsible for the bank robbery." He roots around the back corner of the safe's interior. When he opens a cigar box, he recoils and knocks into me. "Damn!"

I lean my head around his body to see what he found. Cash. Lots of it. Across the inside flap of the box, scrawled in Gigi's handwriting, are the words *Petty Cash*. (Apparently, Gigi's and my definition of petty is quite different.)

"How much is in there?" I ask.

Roddy does a quick count. "Around twenty thousand."

"Jeez! What else is back there?"

"A signed copy of Betty Friedan's *The Feminine Mystique*, Gigi's passport, and a manila envelope with birth certificates."

"Whose?"

Roddy pulls a stack of notarized papers out of the envelope and flips through them. "Ours, Gigi's, Pop's, and our mother's. And there's a locked firebox."

"Look around for a key," I suggest. "And I'll check out the file cabinet."

I open the top drawer of a metal file cabinet on the bottom left shelf. It's stuffed full of hanging files with alphabetized tabbed labels: deeds, investments, life insurance policies, retirement accounts, tax returns, and the like. I pull out the first file. As expected, I find the deed to Mirabella, but there's another deed for a house at 342 Wissler Road, Vogansville.

"Roddy, look at this." I show him the second deed. "Three names are listed as owners, Gigi, Pop, and Gladys Buch. Why would they own a house with Mrs. Buch?"

He tilts his head and furrows his brows. "I don't know. Maybe an investment property. The date of purchase is March 4, 1934."

"That doesn't make sense. If it was an investment, why did Mrs. Buch live there?"

"I can't answer that. We should check Pop and Gigi's tax returns. If they're collecting rent, it will be listed as income."

I pull out Gigi's tax return from 1999 and hand it to Roddy. "Decipher."

He flips through the pages, rubs his chin, and flips through again. "Well, it's odd."

"When it comes to Gigi, what isn't?" I quip.

"She pays real estate tax on the property, but she isn't claiming depreciation."

"So?"

"So, if it's a rental property, depreciation is a write-off. Also, she isn't listing any income from the property."

"So not an investment property."

"Doesn't appear to be," Roddy says, sliding the return back into the hanging file.

"Since we're guessing Gladys Buch is dead, who owns the house now?"

"Well," Roddy says, reading over the deed. "Pop, Gigi, and Mrs. Buch were joint tenants with right of survivorship, so when Mrs. Buch died, her ownership passed to Pop and Gigi. When Pop died, it all went to Gigi. And now that Gigi is gone, whoever is named in her will owns it." Roddy scans the other file tabs in the top drawer of the cabinet. "Until Gigi's will is read, I don't think we should bother mucking through these files, but I do think a visit to 342 Wissler Road is in order."

I nod. "Agreed." I open the second drawer of the file cabinet. It contains only one file. The color drains from my face. "Jeez, Roddy. Look."

The plastic tab sticks above a black hanging file, and written with blood-red marker are the words, *I'm dead.*

"Gigi always did have a flair for the dramatic," Roddy says.

I swallow and lift the file from the drawer and open it. A creamy piece of parchment paper is covered with Gigi's cursive writing.

> My dearest loveys,
> Thank you for indulging me in my valedictory adventure. I am confirming your suspicion. Your grandfather and I, along with Bess and George, stole $198,000 from the Ephrata National Bank—

an exorbitant sum in the thirties. The purchase and establishment of the Vogansville General Store allowed us to launder our purloined funds.

Ruby, I see you grasping for a justification—a way to keep your sunny worldview. It's true. My intentions were admirable—at least at the beginning. My mother was dying from tuberculosis. Her only hope was a sanitarium that cost more than I could ever earn. I convinced myself it was a valid and noble reason to commit theft.

And Roddy, I see your cynicism flaring, and you're also correct. Like the bedraggled saying goes, "the road to hell is paved with good intentions." Yes, I was able to save my mother, but stealing significantly more than I needed, laundering Mr. Hanson's money, and selling marijuana from the store were for my self-interest. And still, the choice is one I'd make again.

I know I preached honor and integrity, and you may abhor me for my hypocrisy. Judge me as you will.

All that I owned is yours. Do with it what you choose.

I wish I could tell you all my secrets have been laid bare, but unfortunately, one remains. One that is decidedly worse. The last puzzle will lead you to the truth. I hope you can find it in your heart to forgive me.

My eternal love,
Gigi

My hands are trembling, and tears spill onto my cheeks. "She killed him. Didn't she? She killed Hanson."

I sink down to the floor of the safe. I pull my knees against my chest and rest my head on them. My shoulders bob up and down with my sobs.

Roddy gently rubs the back of my head. "It's okay, Ruby. It's okay."

I raise my tear-streaked face and meet Roddy's eyes. "Is it?" I growl. "Is it? You were right. Gigi was a murderer." I burrow my head between my knees and mutter to myself, "I was so naïve to believe the robbery was her deep, dark secret."

Roddy sits down on the floor and wraps his arm around me. "It could be something else. We don't know for sure."

"'Decidedly worse' than bank robbery. A secret that will be hard for us to forgive. What else could it be?"

"Well," he says, standing. "We won't know until we solve her last puzzle. I'd bet it will lead us to the key to the firebox."

He pulls a white sheet of paper from the *I'm dead* file and waves it at me. I wipe the tears with the back of my hand and push myself up.

"How about I make you a cup of tea, and then we'll take a look at the puzzle?" Roddy suggests.

I sniffle and nod my head. Roddy and I step out of the safe, closing it behind us. The scent of Shalimar has changed from comforting to cloying. I hurry out of Gigi's bedroom and down the stairs into the giant kitchen.

Roddy leans against the counter as the tea kettle heats. "Do you want to go to the Wissler Road house this afternoon? I'm really curious about that deed."

"Delaying the big reveal. Sounds good to me." I offer a weak smile. "Does the last puzzle look difficult?"

He hands me the page.

Logic puzzles are my favorite, but after what we just discovered, I'm too wrung out to figure it out.

"I'll take it home with me and solve it later."

LOGIC PUZZLE

Deduce the name of the mother, what she drinks, and where she lives to find the key.

1. Hope is six-years-old.
2. Joy only likes hot drinks.
3. The mother has never been south of Virginia.
4. Joy has no siblings.
5. Hope is allergic to citrus fruits.
6. The aunt and mother have never been west of Ohio.
7. The person who lives in San Francisco only drinks tea.
8. Joy lives on the East Coast.
9. Patience has never seen the Liberty Bell.

	Mother	Sister	Aunt	Patience	Joy	Hope	Lemonade	Tea	Coffee
Philadelphia									
Miami									
San Francisco									
Tea									
Lemonade									
Coffee									
Patience									
Joy									
Hope									

He pours the hot water over a lavender chamomile tea bag and hands me the cup. As it steeps, I hold the warm cup between my hands and breathe in the soothing scent. Being in Mirabella used to feel like a nurturing hug, but now it's tainted. I know I could've come to terms with theft, especially since Gigi was desperate to help her mother. But mur— No! I can't even think the word. Roddy notices me struggling to hold back tears.

"Sis," he says, soothingly rubbing my back. "No matter what Gigi did, it doesn't invalidate her love for us and our love for her."

My trembling lip changes to silent sobs. Roddy leans down in front of me and holds my hands while I cry.

"I can't...I can't love a killer," I wail.

Roddy stands and puts his hands on his hips. "Ruby Ella Finch, Gigi was not a killer!"

"The...last...secret," I stutter out between sobs.

Roddy puts his hand out like a stop sign. "No!" he barks. "If that truly is her last secret—and I'm not prepared to make that assumption—Gigi was not a killer. She was a strong woman who did whatever was necessary to protect her family. One act does not define a person's life. We can loathe what she did without hating her."

I want to buy into what he's saying. I want to find the light. But, the darkness is oppressive, and shards of rose-colored glass are scattered over Mirabella's tiled floor.

MARCH 1934

EVIE

The bells jingled on the store's door. A blast of arctic air came in with Mary Buch. Her teeth were chattering, and her body was racked with shivers. The lightweight coat and holey shoes offered little protection against the winter cold. Mary's bare hands and cheeks were bright red, and her greasy hair was pasted to her head.

"Your lips are blue," Evie said to the lanky teen. "Sit on the bench and let me get you a hot cup of tea."

Evie hurried to her kitchen to heat the water and grab the young girl one of her winter coats. When she returned to the store, tea in hand, she saw Mary stuffing food into her coat pocket. Evie cleared her throat and pretended not to have noticed.

"Here you go. Warm up with this." Evie wrapped the coat around her and then handed her the warm cup.

"Thank you, ma'am." Mary said, not making eye contact.

Evie sat down behind the store counter. "How's your mother handling everything? I've been meaning to get out to your farm for a visit."

"We don't live there no more," Mary said quietly.

Evie wrinkled her forehead and furrowed her brow. "Since when?"

"Since the sheriff kicked us out. Momma don't have the money to pay the mortgage or the taxes, so they made us leave."

"Well, where are you living?" Evie asked.

Mary hung her head until her chin almost touched her chest and shrugged her drooping shoulders.

"Mary," Evie said gently. "Look at me, child."

Mary barely lifted her head but raised her eyes. "Yes, ma'am?"

"Where are you living?"

"Here and there. We stayed in the church one or two nights."

Outrage fueled Evie. Even after his death, Hanson's depraved actions were still wreaking damage on this poor family. "I won't have it! Where are the boys and your mother?"

"Momma's nursing old Mr. Samuels in exchange for him letting us sleep in his outbuilding, and the boys went out to see if they could find any paying farm work."

Evie wrapped her arm around the scrawny girl, "Come in the house. I'll draw you a warm bath, and you can soak while I find your mom and the boys. You're all coming to live here till we figure this out."

Mary burst into tears. "Oh, Mrs. Collier, thank you so much. It's been so hard, and Momma's sickly herself. I was so scared she'd die, and they'd put me and my brothers in the orphanage."

Evie bent her head and stared Mary straight in the eye. "Mary, listen to me. I swear on my life your family will never be without a home again. Do you understand?"

Mary sniffled and nodded her head. "I have to tell you something, and you might change your mind."

"What's that, Mary?"

Mary stuffed her hands in the pocket of her coat and pulled out some cheese and a few turnips. "I stole these from the store." Her chin dropped back to her chest. "I'm sorry."

Evie lifted Mary's chin with her finger and smiled at her tear-streaked face. "I appreciate your honesty, but don't be sorry. You did what was necessary to protect your family. I would've done the same thing."

I have done the same thing.

JULY 2000

RUBY

I drag myself out of bed and shuffle downstairs. I'm trying to rally, but the thought of having a murderer for a grandmother is onerous. Roddy's picking me up in fifteen minutes. We're going to pop in on the resident of 342 Wissler Road.

My coffee is tasteless, but I drink it anyway. My body hurts as if my dread has morphed into physical pain, and I feel sick. It's too much to climb back up the stairs, so I pull a T-shirt and shorts from the dirty laundry and slide into them. I finger-comb my hair into a messy ponytail, grab a loose piece of minty gum from the bottom of my purse and chew it to cover the smell of my unbrushed teeth.

Roddy's bringing a picnic lunch to eat under the mulberry tree on the wide wall of the cemetery. Maybe if I wallow in some happy memories, I'll be able to pull myself out of this funk. I flop on the couch to wait, and my phone rings. It's Donald.

I think of the peace bond, and a prickle of apprehension raises goosebumps. I shove the concern away. After what I found out about Gigi, how bad can the truth be?

"Hello," I say.

"Ruby, it's Donald. I was hoping we could get together soon."

Pumping fake enthusiasm into my voice, I dive right in. "How about tomorrow? Lunch?"

"Yes, yes. That's perfect."

"Meet me at Sugar & Spice at noon."

"See you then," he says and hangs up.

Hank beeps from my driveway. I trudge out and climb in. "Hey."

"Look what the cat dragged in," Roddy says.

I flick the back of my hand at him. "Yeah, yeah. Just drive."

"I made us fluffernutters," he says, trying to coax a smile.

They were my childhood favorite. I muster up a feeble grin. "Thanks."

Roddy looks at Hank's clock. "Since it's almost noon, do you want to eat before or after our visit to the house?"

I haven't eaten more than a few bites since we found Gigi's letter. "I'm not that hungry. How about after?"

"Suits me," he agrees. He drums his fingers on the steering wheel, fiddles with the radio, then switches it off. "Gail and I had another date last night." He sneaks a quick look to gauge my reaction.

I'm too disheartened to bite. "Mmm."

"She's really smart and funny. She was telling me..."

I zone out, and his chattering becomes white noise. Next thing I know, Roddy's parking on the street in front of 342 Wissler Road. A rusted-out Suburban sits in the driveway. We step up onto the porch where we had many glasses of meadow tea and knock.

Seconds later, a scruffy-faced old man with a beer belly opens the door. "Yeah?"

"I'm Roddy Finch, and this is my sister Ruby. Evie and Pete Collier were our grandparents. We are—"

He interrupts Roddy. "When I read Mrs. Collier's obituary, I figured it wouldn't be long till you were on my doorstep. Come on in."

Roddy shoots me a questioning look, and we follow the man inside. The house was the same as I remembered, only faded. He gestures to two worn upholstered chairs facing the couch. Roddy and I take a seat.

"Can I get you some water? Lemonade?"

"Lemonade, please," I say.

"Me too," Roddy says.

The man sets the glasses of lemonade on coasters on the wooden coffee table and situates himself on the couch. "So, how long do I have?"

"Pardon me?" Roddy asks.

"How long until I have to leave?"

"Sir, I uh..."

"The name's Earl. It's okay, son. Just spit it out."

Roddy looks at me and then looks back at Earl completely flustered. I rescue Roddy. "Do you mean to leave your home?"

He sucks in a big breath and sighs. "Yep. Ain't that why you're here? To give me notice, now that you own the house."

My eyebrows furrow, and I cock my head. "How do you know we own the house?"

"Your grandmother told me after Mr. Collier died."

"Told you what exactly?" I ask.

"That when she died, you two would own the house, and I may have to pay rent or move out. I just figured you'd want to sell the place."

"So, help me out," Roddy interjects. "You live here but don't pay rent?"

"Right." He pulls at a loose thread on the armrest of the couch. "The Colliers never asked for one red cent from my mother, Gladys, or from me after she died."

"Gladys? Gladys Buch? Was that your mom?" I ask.

"Sure was. Did you know her?"

"We did. She used to give us the best meadow tea when we were little. I don't think we ever met you, though."

"Probably not. I woulda been in Nam when you were kids."

"Thanks for your service," Roddy says.

"Don't thank me," he growls. "I was drafted, and I cussed every stinkin' minute of it." His face scrunched into a scowl, and he crossed his arms tight in front of him.

I can tell war talk is making Earl uncomfortable, so I guide us back on track. "We also saw her name on the deed to this house."

"Yesiree. Even after my mother fessed up to what she did, Mrs. Collier insisted my mother's name be put on the deed. And on top of that, she let us run an account at the store. Charge as much as we liked and only pay when we could. Your grandmother was a kind woman."

A tiny frizzle of happiness wends its way into my psyche.

"What did your mother admit to?" Roddy asks.

He wiggles back into the couch cushions and props his feet on the table. "Now, that's a long story. You got the time?"

"We do." I nod.

"My old man worked every day of his life since he was nine years old. He met my mother when he was seventeen, and—his words, not mine—it was love at first sight."

I smile. "How sweet."

"He was a proud young man, and he wouldn't ask her to marry him until he had a down payment on a farm."

Earl stands up, walks to his front window, and motions us over. "Look past the cemetery to the white farmhouse in the distance. Do you see it?"

"Yep," Roddy says.

"That was our family farm, and it would still be if 'Farmer Boy' Hanson hadn't fleeced my old man."

"Hanson?" I gasp.

Earl's jaw clenches and his face reddens. "Yep. That son-of-a-bitch deserved exactly what he got."

Earl takes a deep breath and runs his hand through his thinning gray hair. "Ain't good for me to get mad." He taps his chest. "Bad ticker. Let me fill up your lemonades."

As Earl is refilling our glasses, I whisper to Roddy, "I've got a good feeling about where this story is going."

Roddy crosses his fingers and nods his head. Earl returns with our drinks and settles back into the couch.

"Where was I?"

"Hanson deserved what he got," I cue him.

"Damn right he did! But I'm gettin' ahead of myself. Once my old man purchased the farm, he and my mom got married. My oldest brother, Aaron Junior, popped out a year later. By the time the Depression hit, Pop had five kids and a wife to feed."

"All boys?" I asked.

"Four boys. I'm the youngest. One girl, my sister Mary. Out of the five of us, I'm the only one still livin'."

"Oh, I'm sorry to hear that," I say.

He brushes it off and continues his story. "The Depression hit us hard. Pop was struggling to feed us, let alone pay the mortgage. Bank threatened to foreclose, but Pop was bound and determined to save the farm."

I take a sip of my drink and lean forward. "I'm guessing this is where Hanson comes in?"

"Yesiree. Hanson talked my old man into setting up a still in the barn to supply him with booze. The money started rolling in, and all was going good until Hanson went bonkers. Accused my old man of selling some of the hooch himself and keeping the money." Earl raises his hand skyward. "I know, I know. My pop was a moonshiner, but he was honest. He would've never cheated Hanson."

I realize I'm holding my breath, so I exhale. "What did Hanson do?"

"Took an ax and chopped off Pop's fingers. Right in front of all us kids, and my mother, too."

I pull back in my seat, and sour bile rises in my throat. "Oh, my God!"

"Yeah." Earl shakes his head and stares past us. "He was a ruthless son-of-a-bitch."

"I'm so sorry," I say, swallowing the bile. "How awful."

"It was. But that ain't the worst of it. About a month after it happened, my pop died. Blood poisoning from the wound."

"Man, you've been through a lot," Roddy says.

"It was tough times when Pop died. Mom became a shell of herself and vowed revenge. Got it too."

"How? How did she get revenge?" Roddy asks.

"She killed the bastard."

"Hanson?" I ask and hold my breath for his answer.

"None other. Mom poisoned him a month after Pop died. She crushed up thousands of apple seeds and spiked his personal stash of moonshine."

Relief floods my body, but it's short-lived. Stabbing pain jabs my stomach. If Gigi didn't murder Hanson, what is her "decidedly worse" secret?

"The guilt ate Mom up," Earl says. "She was a mess. Us kids tried to do what we could to earn money, but it was no use. We lost the farm at the end of February, and Mrs. Collier swooped in to save us in March. Not only did she give us a house and food, she got my mom back to living."

I take a sip of my lemonade. "How?"

He leans back and props his feet up again.

"Visited her every day. Told her over and over that Hanson deserved what he got. Told her she saved a bunch of other people from his torture. Eventually, it sunk in and, other than missing Pop desperately, she got back to normal."

"Wow! That's quite a story."

"Ain't it, though? If not for your grandmother..." He trails off.

Roddy and I drink our lemonade and let what we just learned sink in.

Earl leans forward, props his elbows on his knees, and rests his chin on his hands. "So, back to why you showed up on my doorstep. When do I need to be out?"

I look at Roddy with raised eyebrows. Our twin connection kicks in, and I can see we're thinking exactly the same thing. He gives me a nod.

"Earl, we don't want to kick you out. Live here as long as you like," I say.

"What's my rent gonna be? I'm on a fixed budget."

"No rent. Just pay the property taxes," Roddy says. "Your family was important to our grandmother, so you're important to us. Besides, drafted or not, you fought for our country. This is the least we can do to say thanks."

Earl picks imaginary lint from the couch and clears his throat a few times. "You Colliers are a good bunch."

When Roddy and I stand to leave, Earl does, too.

"Earl," I say. "Thanks so much for sharing your story. You can't imagine how much it means to us." I pull a business card from my purse and hand it to him. "Any problems with the house, just give me a call."

Roddy extends his hand. "Good to meet you."

Earl shakes Roddy's hands and then mine. "Thank you both." He shows us to the door, and Roddy and I step out onto the porch. "You know," Earl says from his front doorway. "Mom gave me her meadow tea recipe. Mine's almost as good as hers. Stop in for a taste next time you're in Vogansville."

I smile. "Thanks, Earl. We will."

We wave as he shuts his door. Roddy grabs our brown-bagged lunches from Hank, and we walk across the street to Village Chapel. A wide stone wall separates a pasture from the cemetery. Roddy and I climb onto the chest-high wall and walk to the far back corner, under the swooping branches of a mulberry tree. A muscular chestnut horse with a white blaze wanders over to us and bumps Roddy with its nose. Roddy scratches between its ears, and it moseys away.

"Remember Cloud?" Roddy asks.

Cloud was an all-white pony that used to graze in this field. We'd bring him carrots and apples, and he'd come running whenever he saw us.

"I do." I lie back on the wall and drink in the warmth of the summer sun and the pleasant memories.

Roddy unpacks our food. "Lunch is served."

I sit up and dig into a peanut butter and marshmallow sandwich. The sticky goo coats my mouth—the joy of childhood on a plate. "So good," I mumble.

"I think anything would taste good after Earl's story. Thank God it wasn't Gigi."

I suck in a deep breath and exhale. "Right? I feel a hundred pounds lighter." I take another bite of the sandwich. "Do you think Earl finds it hard to live with what his mom did?"

Roddy shakes his head. "No way. After what he witnessed Hanson do to his dad? He probably would've killed him if his mom hadn't."

I finish my sandwich and lick the traces of peanut butter off my fingertips. "So, the question remains. What is Gigi's dark secret?"

JULY 2000

RUBY

My mood is cheery, but my body is cranky. I spent the morning pulling weeds and tidying up my yard. Now, my low back aches. After I freshen up and slip on a cute floral sundress, I pop two Tylenol and sit on the couch with a heating pad tucked behind my back. I'm meeting Donald at Sugar & Spice in an hour.

While the heat soothes my pain, I take a look at the logic puzzle. If Hope is six years old, she can't be a mother. I mark an X in the correct box. Joy only likes hot drinks, so lemonade is out. As I'm making another X, a sharp pain zings from my back to my abdomen and I wince. Jeez, that hurt. Maybe if I walk, it'll ease up. I check the time. 11:30. Plenty of time to walk the mile and a half to the café. I unplug the heating pad and grab my purse, tucking the peace bond inside.

The air is sticky, and there's no breeze. I pull my hair up into a ponytail. Tendrils at the back of my neck frizz in the humidity. When I'm at the bottom of the hill and turning onto State Street, a wave of nausea hits me. I sit down on the curb until it passes. Maybe walking wasn't such a great idea. As I'm standing up, my neighbor, Carol, pulls up to the stop sign and opens the passenger side window of her burgundy CRV.

"You okay?" she asks.

"I think I'm overheated," I answer.

Her blue eyes cloud with concern. "Want me to drive you home?"

"No thanks. I'm meeting a friend at Sugar & Spice."

"Hop in. I'll take you there."

An air-conditioned car ride sounds divine. I climb into her Honda, and she heads to the café.

"I bumped into Roddy and his new girlfriend, Gail, the other day at Oriental Kitchen," Carol says. "I haven't seen him smile like that in ages. He so deserves to be happy."

Carol is married to Charlie, one of Roddy's basketball buddies. When Roddy and Clara were married, they hung out as a foursome. Luckily, Carol and Charlie's friendship was one thing Roddy got to keep after the divorce.

"Girlfriend?" I say.

"Uh-oh! Did I spill the beans?"

"No, no," I assure her. "I know he's dating Gail. I just didn't know he considered her his girlfriend."

Carol's cheeks round with her wide smile. "That's how he introduced her. I was tickled pink."

"Me too, and Gail seems really nice."

"Well, here we are," Carol says, pulling into a parking space along State Street. "Feel better?"

"Yeah, thanks. I guess I just needed to cool off." I step out of her car and wave as she turns onto Main Street. The nausea is gone, and the pain in my back has dimmed to a dull ache.

I walk a hundred yards or so up State Street to the center of town and up the steps of Sugar & Spice's porch. Donald's waiting for me.

His smile widens. "Hi, Ruby. I'm so glad to see you."

I shy away when he leans in for a friendly hug. He notices my hesitancy, and his smile dims. I don't want to hurt his feelings, but until I know more about the peace bond in my purse, I need to use caution.

"Mind if we eat inside?" I ask.

"Not at all." He opens the door for me, and I claim a table in the back corner.

He scans the crowded café. "Nice place."

"A friend from high school owns it. She creates amazing things with spices."

"Clever signs. I especially love the *Sweet Dreams* parody."

"That's my favorite, too," I say.

Emily pops over to our table. Today her hair is in one long braid down her back. "Hi, folks! Welcome to Sugar & Spice. Our newest drink is the Waikiki. It's half pineapple juice, half sparkling water, and fresh muddled cilantro."

Normally I'm game for anything new, but my stomach's still feeling unsettled. "Water for me, please."

"I'll try the Waikiki," Donald orders.

"Great! Here are your menus. I'll be back in a minute with your drinks."

"She's perky," Donald says.

"Always."

The back pain intensifies, and I shift around to find a comfortable position on the backless bench.

"You okay?"

I grimace. "Think I might have strained a muscle pulling weeds this morning."

"Let me grab you a cushion."

He swipes a throw pillow from a nearby bench and I tuck it behind my back.

"Any better?"

Now fingers of dull pain reach around my waist and settle in my stomach. "A little," I say, willing it to go away.

Emily returns with our drinks, and we both order today's special: Sprout Salad with shredded Brussels sprouts, parmesan cheese, pine nuts, cranberries, and topped with a lemon dressing.

"So," Donald says when Emily's left our table. "How's Evelyn's puzzle coming?"

He's given me the perfect opening. "Actually, as Roddy and I were solving a clue, I came across something concerning."

He leans his elbows on the top of the farm table. "Oh? What's that?"

I pull the peace bond from my purse and hand it to him. His jaw tightens and his eyebrows furrow as he reads the paper. He hands it back to me.

"Well?" I ask, ignoring a sharp pain that shoots into my belly.

He crosses his arms in front of him. His nostrils flare, and he presses his lips together. After a deep breath, he says, "I think it's time I explain."

"Yes, I think—"

A searing pain cuts off my words. I double over and groan. Donald leaps to his feet and slides in beside me on the bench.

Wrapping his arm around me, he asks, "Ruby, what's happening? Are you okay?"

Another wave of pain grips me, and I croak out, "No. It hurts."

"Where?"

"It was in my back, but now it's around my belly button and the low right side of my stomach," I grit out through clenched teeth. Another sharp pain stabs me. I've never felt pain like this. "I think I need to go to the hospital."

Donald springs into action.

"Emily," he yells to our server. "Ruby needs to go to the hospital. Help her to the door while I get my car."

He dashes outside, and Emily and another server help me off of the bench and guide me to the door. The pain is severe, and I'm hugging my belly. Walking makes it worse, and I get cold and clammy from nausea.

"Hurry, please," I say.

As the servers help me down the stairs, I vomit into the planter of red geraniums.

"I'm so sorry," I say.

"Don't give it a second thought," Emily says.

Donald rushes from his truck and picks me up. "Open the passenger door," he barks at Emily. He gently slides me into his pickup and straps me into my seatbelt. "Ephrata Hospital, okay? It's closest."

"Yes," I say through gritted teeth.

Minutes later, Donald pulls into the bay of the Emergency Room. He grabs a wheelchair, lifts me into it, and wheels me into the triage area.

"She needs help!" Donald yells to anyone who will listen.

I moan with pain.

A nurse hurries from the triage area, grabs the handles of the chair, and starts wheeling me back. "Are you her father?" she calls over her shoulder to Donald.

Though I'm in a pain-induced fog, I hear his answer clear as a bell. "Yes."

"Stop! Wait!" I plead with the nurse. "Turn me around, please, please. For just a second."

She obliges.

I lock eyes with Donald. "What? I, I don't understand."

He rushes to the chair and bends down. Taking my hands into his, he says, "I am your father, and I'll be waiting right here to give you all the answers. Now please, Ruby, let them take care of you."

I'm too stunned to speak, so I simply nod, and the nurse hurries me through the double doors into an ER room.

AUGUST 1978

EVIE

Evie checked on the twins in their makeshift tent in the backyard. Tuckered out from their "camping" adventure, they were sound asleep.

Earlier in the day, Evie helped them hang an old sheet over the wash line and stake the corners into the ground. They spent the day searching for bugs, tracking bears, and blazing trails through the shrubbery. Pete was in charge of dinner: grilled hotdogs and s'mores.

At twilight, Evie gave them two jelly jars with air holes punched into the top. The twins collected fireflies to serve as their nightlight. Now that their soft snores filled the tent, she joined Pete on the front porch to enjoy the warm summer evening.

"Snug as two bugs in a rug," she said, relaxing back into her rocker with her Tom Collins.

Citronella candles lining the porch danced hypnotically, casting flickering shadows across the bricks. Crickets chirped as darkness settled in.

"We've been lucky to raise them," Pete said.

"We certainly have," Evie agreed.

The rattle of a beat-up truck intruded on the tranquility. Headlights flashed across the porch as the truck turned into their driveway.

"It's nearly nine. Who in the devil would be visiting?" Pete grouched.

A cold pit lodged in her stomach. Evie was afraid she knew.

"Oh! I know who it is. I talked to an arborist about having the trees pruned. It must be him."

"He's coming when it's dark? That doesn't make any sense."

"Oh, that was the only time he could meet me. Don't worry yourself. I'll run out and talk to him. Just enjoy your cocktail."

Evie hurried out to the driveway. "Donald," she hissed once she was close enough. "You absolutely cannot be here. You know Pete knows nothing about you."

"Nor do my children," Donald growled.

"They're not your children. You gave up fatherhood when you took my twenty thousand."

"Not legally, and you know it. All I need is a paternity test."

"Fine!" she snarled between clenched teeth. "I'll pay you more money. How much?"

"Evelyn, you're not listening." He takes hold of her arm and stares into her eyes. "I don't want more money. I want to know my kids."

"Everything all right?" Pete yelled from the porch.

"Yep. Just hashing out the price," Evie answered. She turned back to Donald. "You're a drunk and always have been. If you really care about the twins, you'll leave well enough alone."

"I'm going to get sober."

"Right. I could get drunk smelling you."

"I need them," he whined. "I need something to stay sober for."

"What about their needs?" she pleaded. "Have some compassion. Haven't the twins suffered enough? Let them keep their memory of a war hero father instead of a worthless boozehound who seduced a woman who was barely more than a child and then claimed she was loose when she told you she was pregnant."

Donald deflated in front of her eyes. His shoulders, arms, and head folded into his chest.

"You're right. I am a worthless drunk, but I won't always be. I promise you: I'm going to get sober. I'll start AA tonight."

She shook her head. "I hope you do, but that won't change things."

"Evelyn, please. Please tell me once I have a year-sober chip you'll reconsider? Isn't a man who made mistakes a better dad than a dead soldier?"

Though she had no intention of ever letting the children know about Donald, Evie kicked the can down the road, "If you stay sober for a year and swear to never, ever show up here or anywhere the kids are without my express permission, I will consider letting you back into their lives."

"Agreed. I swear," he said earnestly. "You'll see, the next time we talk, I'll be a changed man."

Evie was taking no chances. She swore out a peace bond on Donald, legally requiring him to steer clear of them the very next day.

JULY 2000

RUBY

I crack my eyelids. Swirls of light make me feel woozy, and I shut them. I smell a mix of alcohol and bleach.

"You're in the recovery room," a low-pitched voice says. "The surgery went well."

My head rolls in slow motion.

"Your dad is right here."

If my dad is here, does that mean I'm dead? I turn my head towards the speaker and open my eyes. The bright lights blot out the details, but I can tell the voice belongs to a man.

"Am I dead?"

He chuckles, "No, no. You're quite alive, just groggy from the anesthesia. I'm Brian, your nurse."

Nurse? Surgery? I can't quite fit the pieces together. "What happened?" I ask.

A white-haired old man steps into my line of vision. "Ruby," he says. "You had appendicitis."

Donald! Father! my brain screams. I struggle to sit up, but my limbs are leaden. The monitor beeps.

"Sir," Brian says to Donald. "I'm going to have you wait outside while we get her stabilized."

"Is she okay?" Donald asks.

"Don't worry. She'll be fine. Some folks take a little longer to settle back to normal after anesthesia."

Once Donald has left my curtained area, Brian rests his hand on my shoulder, "Just relax. Breathe deeply. In, one, two, three, four. Out, one, two, three, four."

I comply.

After a few rounds of deep breaths, Brian says, "Good. Much better. Would you like to sit up?"

"Yes." My throat is raw, and my voice sounds hoarse.

He pushes a button and raises the upper part of my hospital bed.

"Could I have water?"

He fills a pink plastic cup from a pink plastic pitcher and hands it to me. "It's normal for your throat to be sore. How's your pain?"

"No pain. Just heavy, numb."

"Good," Brian says. "You're doing great. I need to check on another patient. Would you like me to ask your dad to come back in?"

My dad. Donald's my dad. The revelation is too much for my brain to process.

"No. Can you call my twin brother to come for me, please?"

Brian wrinkles his eyebrows questioningly, but he doesn't ask. "Sure," he says. "What's his name and phone number?"

After I give it to him and he goes to make the call, I must have dozed off. A persistent beeping rouses me. When I open my eyes, Roddy's sitting on a hard mustard-yellow chair beside my bed.

"Hey, Sis," he says, smiling down at me. "How you feeling?"

"What's that noise?" I croak out.

Roddy shrugs. "Some kind of monitor in the next room."

My head feels less fuzzy. I grab the bed rails and wiggle myself up. A sharp pain shoots through my stomach, and I groan.

"Is the pain bad?" Roddy asks.

"Kind of," I say.

"Completely normal," Brian says, whisking through the curtains. "Expect moderate pain for today and tomorrow. The doctor has prescribed two days' worth of Percocet. After that, use Tylenol and Motrin. I have your first dose of Percocet for you now."

I swallow the pill Brian gives me. He checks my monitor and then looks at his watch. "Hang tight for another thirty minutes. If your heart rate remains normal, we'll let you get dressed and get out of here."

"Thanks," I say.

"Sure thing." Brian squeezes my toes and hurries to another patient.

I flop my head back on the pillow, close my eyes, and sigh.

"You've had quite the day," Roddy says.

"More than you know," I reply without opening my eyes.

I hear his chair scrape against the linoleum floor as he pushes it back and stands. "Ruby, what do you mean? Was it just appendicitis? Is there something else wrong that you're not telling me?"

I lift my head and open my eyes. "I know what Gigi's big secret is."

Roddy swipes his hand across his hair. "For God's sake, don't scare me like that. I thought they found cancer or something." He pulls the chair up and sits back down. "Ruby, now is not the time to worry about Gigi's puzzle. It'll keep. Right now, you need to focus on healing."

I shake my head. "It won't keep."

"Why's that?" Roddy asks.

"Because it's in the waiting room."

"What? Wait. Are you sure you're thinking clearly? You know anesthesia can last for twenty-four hours?"

"I'm washed-out but clear. Gigi's last secret brought me to the ER and is sitting in the waiting room right now. It's Donald."

"The white-haired guy who was following us around?"

"Yes."

"How? I mean, why was he the one to bring you to the ER?"

"We were having lunch."

"Ruby, I warned you about that—"

I hold up my hand to cut off his lecture. "He's not a threat. He's our father. That's Gigi's secret."

Roddy's mouth falls open. He shakes his head forcefully. "No. No. Not possible." He paces around my hospital bed. "I'm named after our father, Roderick Alistair Finch. He died in the war. No, Donald is not our father."

"I think he is," I say quietly.

"Exactly!" Roddy raises his voice. "You think! You don't know! He could be a con artist trying to score some of Gigi's inheritance. Or a...a stark raving lunatic. How can you believe him? How can you think Gigi would hide something like that from us?"

"Well," I say. "I don't have all the answers yet. He was getting ready to explain everything when the pain doubled me over."

Roddy sits on the chair, puts his elbows on his knees, and holds his head in his hand.

"You've always been gullible," he growls without lifting his head.

My temper flares. "Call him in here and ask him yourself."

Roddy jumps up and kicks the chair back. "NO!"

Brian pops his head through the curtains. "Everything okay in here?"

I nod. "Yep. All good."

"Okay, five more minutes, and you can get dressed." He pops back out.

"I do not want to see the liar," Roddy says through gritted teeth.

I'm too wrung out to argue. "Fine. We'll solve Gigi's last puzzle first."

I text Donald a message. *Thanks for getting me to the hospital. I need some time to digest what you told me and to heal. I'll call you soon.*

Less than a minute later, Donald replies. *I understand. Take as much time as you need.*

I can feel it in my bones. Donald is telling the truth.

AUGUST 2000

RUBY

The doorbell chimes. As I push up from the couch, I get a brief flash of pain. Five days post-surgery, and the tenderness is considerably better. I gingerly walk to the front door and open it. I'm greeted by a gargantuan edible fruit arrangement.

Marty's bright eyes peek over a flower made from pineapple and cherry. "Hi."

"Wow!" I say. "It's huge."

"A fruit palooza. If an apple a day keeps the doctor away..."

"I should be good for the year." I laugh. "Come in."

His flip-flops smack against my wood floor as he walks to my kitchen. After setting the get-well gift on my counter, he asks, "Shall I make room for it in the fridge?"

"After you fix me a plate with a flower or two."

"Righto!"

"Plates are to the right of the sink. Second shelf."

I settle myself back onto the couch, and Marty fixes me a snack.

"How's your sister?" I ask.

"Everything's on track, but I'm still helping out with Brad. Give her less to worry about. How about you? How's the pain?" he asks as he pulls fruit flowers from a watermelon bowl.

"The pain's bearable."

"Did you go to the hospital by ambulance?"

"No, by Donald."

His eyes widen, and his eyebrows inch up. "Donald?" Marty sets the plate of fruit on the coffee table and sits in the chair across from me. He rests his right ankle on his left knee. "Sounds like a story. Fill me in."

Roddy has absolutely refused to discuss Donald, so it's wonderful to have someone to talk to about my discovery.

"It's big news." I twist the chenille throw between my fingers.

Marty notices my hesitance. He uncrosses his legs and scoots forward in his chair, sitting on the edge. "Do you want to tell me? It's okay if you don't."

"I, uh..." Saying the words out loud almost feels like a betrayal to my, my...oh, Jeez, to whatever Roderick Finch is to me. I swallow and blurt it out. "I'm about ninety percent sure Donald is Roddy's and my father."

His mouth falls open. "Really? Why is that?"

"Donald told me he is."

Marty crosses his arms and leans back in his chair. "Okay. You think he's credible?"

My body tenses, preparing to defend my belief. "I do." I tap my heart. "I feel it."

Marty rubs his chin. "I put a lot of stock into gut feelings. Assuming he is your father, how do you feel about it?"

My shoulders relax. Finally, someone is really hearing me.

"A million different things. Loss is the biggie." There's a catch in my voice.

Marty gets up and moves to sit on the floor beside the couch. "Loss? How so?"

"Loss of my dad. I mean, the man I thought was my dad for all of these years. Loss of the opportunity to grow up having my real dad in my life. Loss of, of..." Tears roll down my cheeks, and my lips tremble as I try not to cry. "Loss of respect for Gigi. And anger." I give in to the sobs, and Marty holds my hands. "Why? Why did she keep this from us?"

He strokes my hand and arm and lets me cry. When I'm cried out, he wets a paper towel and gently wipes my tear-stained face.

"Sorry," I whisper, embarrassed by my outburst.

"Don't be sorry. You're grieving. Not only your grandmother's actual passing but the person you thought she was. And you're grieving both fathers. Crying is healthy. It's a release."

I rub my face. "Between the fruit palooza and my copious tears, I'll never have to see a doctor again."

He smiles at my lame attempt at humor.

"You know, he was a drunk," I blurt out.

"Who? Donald?"

"Yeah. He told me he's been sober for nineteen years. Do you think that's why Gigi kept him from us?"

"That's a question for Donald," he suggests.

Forgetting about my stomach, I swing my legs off the couch cushions to sit up and wince in pain.

"Careful. Take it slow," Marty says.

I nod and take deep breaths until the hurt subsides. "Roddy doesn't want to talk to Donald until we solve Gigi's last puzzle."

"Are you close to solving it?"

"We have only one left, and I'm certain it will confirm Donald is our father."

"Maybe it will provide insight into why your grandmother chose to keep you apart?"

I cross my fingers. "Here's hoping."

He pats the empty couch beside me. "Mind if I sit here?"

"Please," I say, pulling the throw blanket out of his way.

He sits sideways on the couch so he can look at me. "What did you discover from the puzzles you've already solved?" He notices my grimace. "No worries if it's too personal to share," he says quickly.

"No, no. It's fine." I take a deep breath. "We found out that Gigi and our grandfather robbed a bank in the '30s."

His eyebrows lift. "Really? Holy Toledo, you've had lots of surprises."

I nod. "Yeah. Too many. For a while, Roddy and I were convinced she was a murderer. Thank God we learned that wasn't the case."

He wrinkles his forehead. "I would say so."

"But then there's the robbery. Gigi has left us everything. Do I take stolen money?"

Marty scratches his bald head. "What else would you do with it?"

"I don't know. Give it back to the bank. Donate it to charity."

"Viable options," he says.

"No advice?" I ask.

"Ruby, I would never presume to tell you what to do. Sit with it. Let it germinate. Wait until the answer is here," he says, pointing to my stomach. "And then know, whatever you choose is right."

I can do that. I can wait. I can let it unfold as it will.

AUGUST 2000

RUBY

I put a pillow between my stomach and the seat belt. It's my first time out of the house since surgery.

"Are you sure you're up for this?" Roddy asks.

"Yes! Yes! Yes! One-hundred percent yes! I'm so stir-crazy."

Roddy would probably prefer to avoid the inevitable, but I solved the final puzzle days ago: Joy is the mother from Philadelphia and likes coffee. I've been badgering him to help me decipher it.

Minutes later, we pull into Mirabella's driveway. Roddy helps me out of the car and we enter the house we now own. That's another thing Roddy has refused to discuss: what he plans to do with his half of the inheritance.

We head into the kitchen. The coffee part of the solution leads Roddy in this direction.

"There it is." He points to the collection of coffee tins on the top of the cabinets. "The lime green and white one."

"I'll get the step ladder," I say.

"Absolutely not. You just had surgery. You'll sit." He pulls out one of the kitchen island stools for me, then grabs the ladder from the utility closet. After retrieving the Mother's Joy Coffee tin from the high shelf, he reads the can. "Made in Philadelphia. This is it." He sets it on the island. "You do the honors."

I wedge my fingernails between the lid and side and pry off the top. There's a square of jewelry box cotton in the bottom. I lift it out and find a key tucked into the middle.

"Another safe deposit box?" I ask, holding the key up.

Roddy shakes his head. "No. Doesn't look the same." He snaps his fingers. "The firebox in the safe. I bet it's for that."

"I bet you're right," I say, moving as fast as my post-surgery gut will allow to Gigi's bedroom. "Do you remember the combination?"

"No, but I put the index card in Gigi's desk. Be right back."

He dashes down the stairs, and I sit on the edge of Gigi's bed. I lay my hand on her pillow and whisper, "I miss you, and I love you, but I'm really mad at you."

Coldness enters her room and suddenly I'm enveloped in the scent of Shalimar. I don't hear the words, but I feel them, "I'm mad at me, too."

"Got it!" Roddy says, stepping into the room.

The smell and chill disappear.

"You okay? Are you sick?" He rushes to the bed. "I told you it was too soon for you to be out of the house."

I give the pillow a little squeeze before standing up. "I'm fine. Let's open it up."

Roddy makes quick work of the safe. He picks up the firebox. "Where do you want to do this?"

"Here," I say, pointing to the floor in the middle of her room

"Damn! This is heavy."

Grunting, he carries it out of the safe and puts it on the floor. He inserts the key and turns.

"Ready?" he asks.

I nod and he lifts the lid. The box is stuffed with envelopes. I randomly pull out a green envelope. It's postmarked March 28, 1979. The return address says *Donald Fraser, 139 Buchanan Avenue, Ephrata.* A card is tucked inside. As I slide it out, two ten-dollar bills fall from it to the floor. The front of the card says

You're Officially a Teenager! I open it. Under the printed Happy 13ᵗʰ Birthday is a handwritten note.

> Dear Roddy and Ruby,
> Though I can't be with you, please know I think about you every moment of every day.
> I love you,
> Dad

I hand the card to Roddy and pull out the next envelope. This one says Happy Easter and has two five-dollar bills and another handwritten note.

> Dear Ruby and Roddy,
> I'm so sorry we're spending another holiday apart. Know that I love you with all my heart.
> Dad

Card after card contains money and handwritten declarations of love from Donald, our dad. Every birthday, every holiday, and some just because, from our thirteenth birthday on. Once dozens of cards are scattered around us on the floor, I pull out a large manila envelope full of photos with notes from Donald written on the back of each one. A candid shot of Roddy winning a track-and-field ribbon. The note said, *Way to go, son!* A picture of Roddy and me being inducted into the National Honor Society. *I'm so proud!* A close-up of me going to the senior prom. *You're beautiful.* Our high school graduation. *You did it!* Shot after shot capturing the important moments in our lives.

Roddy lets the photos fall from his hand. Silent tears stream down his face.

"He was there," Roddy stammers. "The whole time he was there, cheering from the sidelines."

I scoot closer and wrap my arms around him. We cling to each other and cry. Gigi stole more than money. She stole our father.

Tears spent, we gather the photos back into the envelope. Before I tuck it back into the firebox, I notice a parchment envelope taped to the bottom of the box. I pull it out and open it. This time the letter is from Gigi. I read it aloud.

My dearest loveys,

Now you know my most terrible secret, I kept you from knowing your father. I kept you from a relationship you deserved to have. All these years, I convinced myself it was the right thing to do. I had to keep the secret to keep you safe. But now, in the last days of my life, I realize that I kept this secret to benefit me—regrettably, to the detriment of you.

From the cards and photos, you will have realized once you were teens, Donald wanted to be a part of your life. It wasn't always the case.

When your mother found out she was pregnant, Donald claimed no responsibility. In fact, he quit his job and skipped town. I know it may be hard for you to understand, but in the sixties, unwed mothers were ostracized, hidden away for being a scourge upon society. I couldn't let that happen to my Ella. I did the only thing I could do. I forced her to marry Roderick Finch. He adored your mother and he would've been a good husband and father.

Your grandfather had no part in this. Ella's mistake would've broken his heart, so we kept it from him. When Roderick died, Pop sprang into action, converting a spare bedroom into a nursery. Of course, we'd help our widowed daughter raise her child. When we learned there were two of you, we were thrilled, but your mother's pregnancy was difficult.

When Ella died, the only thing—the absolutely only thing—that saved me from the abyss was you two. The four of us settled into our life, and your grandfather and I were able to rediscover happiness through raising you. You were our world, and then Donald showed up.

Right after your fifth birthday, Donald reappeared—drunk and belligerent. He demanded twenty thousand dollars or he'd sue me for custody. I paid without hesitation. No way would I allow an alcohol-addled man to destroy our lives. He swore I'd never see him again.

For a time, he kept his word. But in '78, he darkened my doorstep once again—drunk as usual. He wanted to change the terms of our agreement. He wanted you to know he was your father. You two were already rife with teenage angst; I couldn't risk it. Your mother dabbled with booze and drugs and ended up pregnant. I wasn't about to allow a drunk into your lives, so I swore out a peace bond.

It worked for nine months, but then the cards started arriving. I'd catch glimpses of him at school events. He mailed me his one-year-sober chip, and I wavered, but ultimately, I couldn't chance it. What if I told you and you hated me? What if you cut me out of your life? I would not survive.

Fear won, and I'm so sorry. I'm so sorry that I kept you from your father, and I'm so sorry I wasn't courageous enough to tell you while I still had breath.

I don't deserve forgiveness. I know that, but I beg you not to let your anger consume you. Find a way to let it go.

You have one bag of ashes left. Decide what you want to do with them, even if that is flushing them down the toilet.

You have my eternal love,

Gigi

I sit unmoving, too stunned to speak.

Roddy pounds his fists on the floor and screams to the heavens, "DAMN YOU, GIGI!" He throws a stack of cards across the room. "Why are you just sitting there?" he yells at me.

I shake my head to snap out of the fog and feel the hot lava of anger rising in my gut. I assumed Gigi had made the decision to keep us in the dark to protect us from a drunk father who wasn't able to care for us. I don't know what is more devastating: finding out Donald basically sold us to Gigi or finding out Gigi blocked him from being a part of our life for the last twenty-two years. I stand up, letting Gigi's letter fall to the floor.

"I've got to get out of here. Out of her room. Out of her house."

Ignoring the searing pain in my stomach, I run down the stairs and out into the front yard. My chest is heavy and I can't catch my breath. I sink down on the grass. Roddy barrels out of the house a minute later and sits down beside me. I pull my legs into my chest, wrap my arms around my knees, and rock frontwards and backwards. My fragility douses his anger.

Roddy rests his hand on my shoulder. "I haven't seen you rock since we were kids. It's going to be okay."

I keep rocking. "I'm trying. I'm really trying, but where do I go with all this pain?"

Roddy moves beside me, wraps his arm around my shoulder, and we rock in tandem.

He leans his head against mine. "We'll work through it together."

AUGUST 2000

RUBY

Roddy finishes washing our breakfast dishes and returns them to my cabinets. It's been over a week since we found the cards and photos. He's brought me supper every night, but we shared nothing more than small talk. I'm still shell-shocked, and I think he is too.

Roddy looks at his watch. "He should be here any minute."

"Yeah." My stomach roils with too many emotions.

We hear the pickup truck rumble into the driveway. A second later, the truck's door slams.

Roddy grabs my hands in his and gives them a reassuring squeeze. "Together."

I open the door before Donald knocks. "Come in." I extend my arm towards the living room.

His shirt is rumpled like he dug it out of the bottom of a laundry basket. He sinks down into one of my comfy aqua chairs, and Roddy and I sit side by side on the couch.

Donald wrings his hands and stares at his feet. Roddy and I stay silent. He scratches the back of his neck. We remain still. Donald clears his throat.

"Do you think I could have a glass of water?" he asks without looking up.

I go to the kitchen, fill a glass from the sink and hand it to him. After a few swallows, he sets it on my coffee table.

With eyes still glued to the top of his shoes, he says, "I've been waiting for this chance for decades. I rehearsed what I would say, and now that I have it, I...my mind is blank, and I don't know where to begin."

Neither Roddy nor I offer encouragement. Let him squirm.

He gulps down the rest of his water, stands up, and walks behind the chair. Resting his hand on the chair's back, he takes a deep breath. "Here goes nothing. From the first sip of booze at age twenty, I was hooked. After a few shots, I was king of the world. Alcohol gave me a confidence I never had and helped me fit in—or so I thought. I started out slow, having a few drinks after work. After-work drinks increased to a lunchtime shot and eventually to a morning tipple to start the day. By the time I met your mother fifteen years later, I was deep into my addiction, and it wasn't just booze. I gave your mom her first quaalude."

"Something to be proud of," Roddy sneers.

Donald rakes his fingers through his hair. "It was contemptible. I own that and much more."

"Hmph," Roddy grunts.

I touch his leg and say to Donald, "Continue."

"I knew I was too old for her; thirty-five to her eighteen. And too embittered. My childhood was, was..." He pauses and squeezes his temples. "Let's just say I craved her carefree exuberance." He picks up his empty glass. "More water?" he asks.

I nod.

Donald plods to my kitchen. As he fills his glass, Roddy mumbles under his breath, "Maybe Gigi was right to keep him out of our life."

"Let's just hear him out," I whisper.

Donald returns and sits back in the chair. "The summer with your mom was the best I ever had until it became the worst. When she told me she was pregnant, I panicked. I knew I was a drunk who was barely able to take care of himself. What would I do with a kid?"

Anger bubbles up, and the words I've been biting back spew out of my mouth. "Lots of people have issues with alcohol and don't sell their children."

Donald recoils into the chair as if kicked. "I didn't...it wasn't... Dear God! Is that what you think? That I sold you?"

"Didn't you?" Roddy demands. "Gigi gave you twenty-thousand dollars to keep custody of us. What else would you call it?"

Donald's shoulders sag, and his face falls. He shakes his head dejectedly, "I guess you're right. I never thought of it that way." He sits in his shame for a minute before continuing. "I was desperate. I needed booze, and I needed drugs, and I was dead broke. I had already sold my car and all but the clothes on my back and was living on the street. Evelyn was the only option my addicted brain could come up with." He leans towards us, rests his elbows on his knees, and clasps his hands. "I'm sorry. Deep-from-the-depths-of-my-soul sorry." Tears well in his eyes, and he blinks them away. "What I did was horrible. To you, to your mother, and to your grandmother. I was lost in my disease. That's not an excuse or justification, only an explanation. All I can do is continue to make amends."

He looks at us with an older version of Roddy's eyes, awaiting our verdict. The heat of my anger is morphing to the warmth of empathy. My mother died from eclampsia, abandoning us, yet I don't blame her for her condition. How is the disease of alcoholism any different? Once sober, Donald changed. The cards and the photos (that are now tucked in my makeshift office) are evidence of his efforts. Even though Gigi kept Roddy and me in the dark, Donald has been trying to reconnect—to be our father—for twenty-two years.

I turn and embrace Roddy, whispering in his ear. "I love you, and whatever you decide for you, I support you, but I have to do this for me." I move from the couch and sit on the coffee table directly in front of Donald. Our knees are mere inches apart. "I once told you everyone deserves a second chance. Do you remember?"

He nods and raises his eyebrows, waiting for me to continue. "I meant it."

The tears he was holding back spill from his eyes. He reaches out with a tentative hand, and I take it in mine.

"Thank you, Ruby. My beautiful, kind daughter. Thank you."

At the word daughter, I lose it. To suddenly have a father...it's, it's ineffable. My shoulders bob with soft sobs.

I hear a sniffle from the couch and turn. Roddy's lips are quivering. After roughly wiping his eyes with the back of his hand, he stands up from the couch and kneels between Donald and me. "Okay, I'm in. Let's give this family thing a whirl."

***

Hours later, after we pored over the snapshots Donald took throughout our childhood, we take a break from reminiscing. As Roddy whips up a light supper of tilapia and roasted squash, Donald and I set the table.

"I love these plates," he says, looking at the name Fiesta on the bottom of the plate. "I'm surprised you actually use them. Aren't they extremely collectible?"

"Yes. They were Gigi's. She always said they were meant to be used, not collect dust." My fond memory quickly turns to anger at her betrayal. "I might as well sell them. The less reminders of her, the better."

At my harsh tone, Roddy looks up from the pan. "You okay?"

"Fine," I snap. "Just ready to get rid of her ashes and be done with the whole stinking mess."

Concern darkens Roddy's face, but he doesn't reply.

Donald, however, pipes up. "Where's all this anger coming from?"

"You, of all people, should know the answer to that. She kept us from you. She didn't let us have a dad."

Donald gently grips each of my upper arms and bends his head to look me straight in the eyes. "She protected you. She raised you. Yes, I disagree with her choice to keep us apart, but I understand it." He pulls one of my lilac chairs out and gestures to it. "Sit. Please."

I comply, and he takes the chair across from me. "Roddy," he says. "We haven't discussed how you're feeling about your grandmother, but I'd like you to listen to what I have to say, too."

"Okay," Roddy agrees and flips the fish filets.

"When you were young, I wasn't worthy enough to be allowed in your life. And when you were older, Evelyn didn't trust my sobriety. Hell, to be quite frank, I could slip any day. It happens all the time, so her fears weren't farfetched."

"No one is perfect," I say. "She should have given you a chance. She didn't have the right to make that decision."

"As your guardian, she did have the right to decide and the responsibility to keep you safe. She did what she thought was best."

"She was wrong," I growl.

Donald smiles patiently. "Ruby, as you said seconds ago, no one is perfect. The most you can ask of a person is for them to give you their best. She did that."

"Donald?" Roddy asks. "How are you not angry with her?"

"She cherished, loved, and nurtured the two people who are most precious to me. She helped you become smart, self-sufficient, loving, and kind human beings. She instilled wonderment and joy into your lives. I could never have given you that. Am I angry at her? Far from it. I am grateful, and I hope you can find it in your hearts to be grateful, too."

AUGUST 2000

RUBY

As the sky blushes a rosy pink, Roddy lights the tiki torches in the backyard of his new home—Mirabella. I was delighted when he told me he would move in. He insisted on putting the deed in both our names, but I consider it solely his. As for the rest of the sizeable inheritance (nearly five million smackeroos), we haven't decided what to do with it. Even though we filled Donald in on how Gigi and Pop came to have such a substantial sum, he's been encouraging us to accept it. We'll see. For the time being, Mr. Davenport will manage the funds.

I tuck my bare feet under a chenille throw and snuggle into the chaise lounge. A soft wind flutters the tree leaves, and the sweet scent of poet's jasmine twirls through the air.

"It's a perfect night," Donald says from his perch on the cushioned glider.

He looks quite debonair in his tan linen suit and crisp white shirt.

Roddy joins us on the brick patio. "It is." He adjusts his sage green tie between the collar points of his dark gray shirt.

When Donald and Roddy are side by side, their resemblance is obvious.

Roddy points to the blooming sunset. "I think it's time."

I stand up, straighten my floral party dress, and slip on my sandals. We gather around the table. Roddy hands us each a delicate, gold-rimmed flute and opens the sparkling white grape juice.

The fizzy beverage foams over the edge of the bottle when Roddy opens it, and I clap.

Roddy fills our glasses, and we toast. "To Gigi!"

I grab the sequined pouch from my purse, and we all move to the hole Roddy's dug in a quiet corner of the backyard. I unzip the pouch, and together, Roddy and I kneel and pour out the last of Gigi. Donald comforts us with a hand on each of our shoulders as our salty tears mingle with the rich soil. When the vibrant streaks in the sky change to a dull purple, we stand. Roddy lifts the dogwood sapling into the hole and fills the space with earth. When Roddy finishes planting the tree, I move the stone marker with the bronze plaque in place in front of it.

The three of us stand at our memorial. Roddy and I, side by side, and Donald behind us. As I recite Emily Dickinson's 'Unable Are The Loved To Die,' Roddy takes my hand. My voice catches, and Roddy leans his head to touch mine. Donald wraps his arms around both of us. I can feel pure love emanating from his touch. Roddy relaxes and leans back into his embrace. I do the same.

As the last vestiges of sunlight fade into the darkness, so do the words on the plaque: *Gigi—Beloved & Forgiven.*

Next Book in the Series:
Banking on the Truth

ACKNOWLEDGMENTS:

A huge thank you to the members of the Pennwriters Area 5 Critique Group. Your insightful comments pushed me to create a better story.

To Cathy Teets and the crack team at Headline Books, I appreciate all of your efforts in bringing LAST WILL & PUZZLEMENT to fruition.

And, I am deeply grateful to my family for their unwavering support.